FLIRTING
WITH
CHAOS

KENYA WRIGHT

OMNIFIC PUBLISHING
LOS ANGELES

Omnific Publishing
1901 Avenue of the Stars, 2nd floor
Los Angeles, CA 90067
www.omnificpublishing.com

First Omnific eBook edition, November 2013
First Omnific trade paperback edition, November 2013

The characters and events in this book are fictitious.
Any similarity to real persons, living or dead,
is coincidental and not intended by the author.

Library of Congress Cataloguing-in-Publication Data

Wright, Kenya.
    Flirting with Chaos / Kenya Wright – 1st ed.
    ISBN: 978-1-623420-60-4
    1. Interracial Romance — Fiction. 2. Mental Illness — Fiction.
    3. Addiction — Fiction. 4. Artist — Fiction. I. Title

10 9 8 7 6 5 4 3 2 1

Cover Design by Micha Stone and Amy Brokaw
Interior Book Design by Coreen Montagna

Printed in the United States of America

To Miami,
My city of bright-colored night life,
drugged dreams,
tantalizing bodies,
and everything else in between.

PROLOGUE

"**S**ometimes it's okay to kill, if you're saving someone else in the process, Rainbow." Dad wiped my tears from my face with bloody hands. "Go ahead, sweetheart. Do it for Daddy. Pull the trigger."

And I did.

CHAPTER 1

Eve and the Apple

Five years later

I'd been washing blood off of my hands for five years. It was time to stop slogging through guilt and make a go at being normal.

Tonight, I would lose my virginity to my best friend, Jude. He didn't know and it didn't matter. He was a sex fiend wrapped in tanned muscles, with blue eyes that made the Caribbean ocean in spring feel jealous. Even worse, he knew it. Once I'd joked that more women walked into his bedroom and spread their legs than at a women's health center. He'd winked and proudly agreed.

Jude will say yes. Stop worrying.

The difficulty rested on me and whether I could lock my heart and emotions away into a steel cage where nothing could slip in or seep out while we shared the most significant moment of my life.

I can do that. No big deal, right?

Once summer was over, I would return to art school and he would go into the studio to produce his first album. Our lives would return to normal, and neither of us would regret tonight. Our friendship would remain intact.

"Don't overthink this." I crossed my fingers on both hands for added luck.

My driver, Thompson, drove the town car along the path between lush hedges manicured in the shape of musical notes and stopped the vehicle in front of Jude and his dad's gray stone mansion. I did a quick check in my compact mirror and realized my blue contacts still covered my eyes. "Shit."

Jude hated the contacts as much as I did. Mom never demanded that I wear them, but I knew she thought I looked better with blue eyes instead of hazel, that they complimented my caramel complexion—which seemed to be the only thing about me that pleased her. Her skin was dark like chocolate, but I believed she didn't see the beauty in her skin like I could. Regardless, I did whatever she preferred since she paid the bills. I wore the blue contacts and straightened my naturally curly hair whenever I dealt with her. We were supposed to meet for lunch before she headed to the airport—hence, why those horrid blue things covered my eyes now—but, of course, she'd backed out at the last minute.

"One must maintain one's appearance at all times, darling," Mom had admonished when I'd spoken to her. "Phones and cameras are everywhere, recording and judging. We don't need any extra attention."

Thompson turned off the car, got out, and headed to my door. I sighed as those blue contacts sparkled back at me in the mirror. "Well, I can't take them out now." My hands weren't clean enough to start messing around with my eyes. Plus, I didn't have my contact case or solution.

Thompson opened the door. Tossing my mirror into my purse, I took his hand and climbed out. If I didn't get this moment over with, I was going to explode into a frenzy of anxious bursts. My nerves were on edge as I picked up the gift bag. A print of colorful apples covered it.

I hope Jude laughs when he sees the apples.

"Let me get that bag for you, Miss Rain." Thompson reached for it.

"I'm fine." I held up my hands to stop him. "Thanks, Thompson. By the way, take the night off. Mom's out of town. She won't find out about you getting some free time to yourself. You definitely deserve it."

He flinched at the mention of Mom. "Miss Rain, I do not like this game. I told you before, I won't be a part of this."

I tapped my foot on the ground in annoyance. "Okay. I'm sorry. I won't talk about her with you anymore."

"Thank you. And I don't like the idea of leaving you alone this weekend. Are you sure?" He glanced at the mansion's front door. The song lyrics to "After the Storm" were engraved into the white wood and painted in black. "I'd feel more comfortable with being the one to drive you and Mr. Jude around."

"Thank you for the offer, but that won't be necessary. I'm a big girl, Thompson." I formed my lips into a wide smile. "Please. If something happens, and trust me it won't, but if it does, I'll make sure to call you immediately."

He rubbed his bald head and dropped his shoulders in defeat. "Please call me if you need me, and check in every day."

"Of course."

"What day and time should I pick you up?"

"There's no need. Like I said before, Jude will take me home later. We're hanging out the whole weekend so I don't need you to come by Saturday or Sunday. I'll see you on Monday."

"Well, then — " he did another quick glance at the house " — since I won't see you on Sunday, happy birthday, Miss Rain."

"Thanks so much. And you have a good night."

"I'll keep my phone next to me just in case your plans change." He headed back to the driver's side of the town car.

"Bye." I continued to the mansion's entrance. Worry pulsed in my veins, but I did my best to ignore it.

Hi, Jude. Yes. I know I'm here early, but there's something important I want to talk about. Remember when we joked last year on my birthday about you taking away my V-card if I was still with it at twenty-one? Ha ha. Yes. That was so funny, but do you remember your promise?

I wobbled in my heels as I approached his door and almost dropped the small gift bag. My hands shook. My teeth chattered against themselves as my heart boomed at a staccato pace. Dampness appeared under my arms and probably soaked into the red, sleeveless dress I wore.

I should have put on the black one. Why did I wear red?

I stank of peach lotion and rose perfume. I'd slathered so much lotion on my legs that they shined and gave off a glossy look. Next, I'd spilled a whole bottle of perfume in my lap.

Sweat, peaches, and roses. Jude will vomit before I even get to ask him.

I combed my fingers through my curls. I usually straightened them with a flat iron until they were a long mass of brown and blond streaked strands that hung past my waist. But Jude loved my hair natural. I didn't care what my mother thought, since Jude loved it this way. He said it added to my exotic look, made me look Brazilian or a mixture of many different races instead of a look that helped me fit in. Being half Jamaican and half white guaranteed I didn't fit in with the African Americans at my college or identify with any of the Caucasian preppy kids from my high school years. I was an anomaly to all except Jude, who took me for what I was and never expected anything more or less.

I look fine. It's just Jude. Everything will be okay. He'll so understand.

I knocked on the door with shivering fingers. The gift bag swung back and forth in my other hand. Footsteps sounded on the other side of the door. I figured it was Douglas, his butler.

"Jude, are you expecting anybody?" That deep voice flowed from the other side and froze me. I recognized that voice. Kaden. Jude's father.

I spun around to leave, but the heels slowed my pace. My town car had already left. *Damn it.* Right as I slipped my phone out of my purse, the door squeaked open.

"Hello?" Kaden asked behind me.

Think. How do I get out of this? Maybe I just won't let him see my face.

"Um…never mind." I kept my back to him and turned my phone on. "I left something in my car…I'll be right back and then —"

"Rainbow? Is that you?"

My shoulders tensed. He remained behind me, and I refused to turn. "Yes. I'll be right back."

Kaden stepped around and faced me. "Dear God, you're beautiful! You've grown so big."

"Thanks."

Now what do I do?

His blue-eyed gaze greeted me. He had a gorgeous face outlined in ruffled brown waves. He embraced me, encasing my body in hard, muscular arms and the scent of designer cologne. When I was a little girl, he'd towered over me. Now he was still taller, but my head at least reached his shoulders. Not sure of what else to do, I hugged him back and readied my lies. He'd have questions, ones that I'd rather not answer and things that I avoided thinking about.

"Where have you been?" He leaned away from me and looked just like Jude, just older with less of a tan.

He wore no shirt. Sleek layers of muscle wrapped around his waist and shoulders. An intricate pattern of colorful tattoos decorated both of his arms. It was a mural of his life—stars intertwined with musical notes; guitars interlocked with microphones; nude, big-breasted angels riding bulky demons. Those arms and that face had adorned the covers of magazines for years. Now he was a legend of rock history. To obtain his interview would mean lots of money and required skilled maneuvering through his agent, publicist, bodyguards, entourage, and any of the other people that walled him away from society. Just driving onto his property had required Thompson's and my name to be checked against a long list of approved guests at the front security gate.

"Where have you been all these years?" Kaden asked.

Here we go.

"I was in Miami, and now I'm up in Sarasota at Ringling College of Art and Design." I edged away from him.

"Well, I know that, but why haven't you returned my calls, emails, or any of the messages I sent through Jude? I travel the world with my tours and movies; it's hard enough to keep in contact with Jude, but with you it's been impossible." Hurt glazed those blue eyes.

My stomach clenched into guilty knots. "I thought it would be best if I kept minimum contact with Dad's friends."

He crossed his arms over his chest. "Why?"

"To ease the mourning process." I stared down at the ground. "I'm sorry."

"No. That's fine." He placed his fingers on my chin and lifted my face. "I don't want you to feel bad or anything. I just really wanted to be in your life. You're Jack's girl, for God's sake. You're Rainbow."

I cringed at the nickname. "No one calls me that anymore. I only go by Rain."

"You're Rainbow to me." His gaze traveled down my body. He instantly looked away, cursed under his breath, and moved around me to the door. "You've grown a lot since I last saw you."

I followed him into the house. "Well, I was sixteen."

"Well, you're damn sure not still sixteen. You're bloody captivating." He captured my hand and guided me through the solid white entryway toward the kitchen as the door slammed closed behind us. A huge staircase rested on our right. On our left were sitting and entertainment rooms full of awards for the band Depraved Minds. In a smaller room, where not many people ventured, stood my father's prized piano and so many memories of him that it suffocated me to even think of stepping inside. My stomach twisted into gloomy knots as we passed its doorway.

An abstract expressionist painting done by Jackson Pollock hung on the center wall above the hallway to the kitchen. One of the best things about Kaden was his incredible eye for art. The painting exemplified the artist's great drip-painting method. I'd read in several of Pollock's interviews that many times he had simply set a canvas on the floor and then poured and dripped paint on it until he believed it was done. It was similar to Kaden and Dad's songwriting process. I had witnessed them creating song after song on the *After the Storm* album. They would lay blank sheets of music on the floor right next to their instruments and spill out pictures of themes and symbols that inspired them. For hours, they fondled piano keys and caressed guitar strings, searching for the song they yearned to sing.

"Did you ever do beauty pageants like your mom? If you did, I bet you won tons of them."

Has he forgotten what I looked like as a teen?

"No way. Mom tried." It was one of the few things I'd put my foot down on when it had come to my overbearing mother. No freaking beauty pageants. "I couldn't do it. Being Miss Jamaica's daughter and then entering a pageant would pretty much send a whole lot of unwanted expectations and criticism my way."

"I forgot she won. When Jack met her, she was dreaming about being Miss Jamaica. It was all she talked about. So many years have passed by."

"Yeah."

"Can I get that for you?" He gestured to the gift bag.

"No." I put it behind my back. "I've got it."

Why didn't Jude tell me his father was in town? I'm going to kill him.

"It's been five years."

"Yeah."

"That's too long, Rainbow." He got in front of me before I could walk into the kitchen. "No more avoiding me. I know the whole band could've done more for you after your dad…did what he did. I think we were just all taken aback by that tragedy. But you're a woman now. I'm here for you if you ever need me. Call me any time."

"I'll try."

He shook his head. "Do more than try."

"Dad! You have any condoms?" Jude rushed down the staircase with only his boxers on, and what a glorious sight that was.

Nervousness from earlier surged back into me. *Goodness.* He was honey poured over an athletic body. Short, sandy-blond curls outlined his face, which boasted full lips, high cheek bones, and long lashes that any woman would envy. Even with those soft features, his face appeared hard and sculpted by an artist. "I need a few condoms. I ran out."

It's early in the evening and he's already having sex with some female. This night gets better and better.

It was then that Jude noticed me standing there.

"Fuck! Rain, what are you doing here so early?" He glanced at his watch. "I thought I was supposed to pick you up in three hours."

"I wanted to talk to you about something."

"What?" He skipped over to me and pulled me into a hug. "You better not be canceling out on me. Damn, I love this dress, and your hair is so sexy. What's this bag about right here?"

"Nothing." I tried to move the bag out of his reach, but he yanked it out of my hands.

Everything fell out. The packet of condoms, warming strawberry lubrication, furry glow-in-the-dark handcuffs, my iPod full of the unique playlist for tonight, and the hotel key card all dropped to the floor in front of him. The urge to escape bounced around in my body. Silence met my ears. No one moved for a few seconds, and when they did, it was in a rush to sling everything back into the bag.

I covered my face. "This is so embarrassing."

A smirk plastered on Jude's face. "Dad, could you give us a minute?"

"Sure." The handcuffs dangled in Kaden's fingers as he studied them.

Just awesome. They were meant to be a joke to lighten the mood, but now Kaden probably thought I was a horndog.

"Dad, could you go ahead and give us some time?" Jude cleared his throat. "Now, please."

"Oh, yeah. My bad." Kaden avoided looking my way. "Rain, don't leave this house without finishing our conversation."

"Okay," I mumbled.

Once he disappeared into the kitchen with my handcuffs tucked in his back pocket, I scurried toward the door. "Okay. Pretend you didn't see that. I'll see you tomorrow. I'm actually feeling a bit sick now."

Jude seized my waist from behind and towed me back to him. "Stop, Rain."

I leaned back into him, not wanting to show him my blushing face. "I'm not playing. Pretend that didn't just happen."

Laughter bubbled out from his chest. "Lube, really? Who's that going in, me or you?"

I spun around and hit his chest. "Not funny. And you didn't see that or anything else. We won't talk about this."

"We're definitely talking about this." He covered his mouth, but a chuckle burst from between his fingers. "Holy shit. Did you see my dad's face?"

"Hello. It didn't happen." I waved my hands. "Nothing occurred."

He studied the apples on the front. "I give you an A for symbolism."

Years ago, he'd proclaimed in a drunken stupor that the act of a woman giving her virginity to a man was like Eve handing over the apple to Adam.

"The world would change for everyone involved," he had slurred. "She'd see things clearer and so would he. No more Garden of Eden for her. She'd be cast out into deserted territory, Rain. Save your apple! For all of the world's sake, save your apple!"

I had called him a moron, and he'd passed out on my bed.

"Jude! What's taking so long?" a female yelled from upstairs.

"Just a minute!" he called back.

"Who's that?" I leaned to the side.

"Vicky."

"One of your dad's groupies?"

"Of course."

Of course.

I sighed.

"Well, there are your condoms. Feel free to use them on your dad's groupie." I gestured to the bag and simply accepted that I'd made a bad decision in choosing him. "Tonight's a bust anyway. Let's just hang out tomorrow."

"What the fuck?" He dropped the bag and caught me before I could turn around again. "Now you're mad? That's not fair. I didn't even know you would be here or that you would...you know...want me to...deflower you."

"Deflower?" I buried my face into my hands. "Just kill me now."

"That *is* what you wanted, right?" He moved my hands away from my face. "You were going to ask me to take your virginity, or am I to assume that you intended on taking mine?"

"You're so not a virgin."

He fluttered his long eyelashes. "I could be."

"I thought I told you to forget about it."

"No way. We're discussing this."

"Jude! Can you bring up some wine too?" Vicky, the groupie, called out.

"You better get her that wine." I rolled my eyes. "See you tomorrow."

"Hell no." He brought me back. And just like that, his face shifted from fun-loving to pissed. He pressed his lips into a straight line, and his blue eyes glittered with an edge of annoyance. "I planned all types of shit for us tonight. In fact, I've been putting it all together for months."

"I didn't know —"

"Of course you didn't. It's a surprise."

"None of it can wait until I'm less embarrassed?"

His right cheek twitched as if he was holding in laughter. "Rain, you'll be embarrassed for years after this. I'm going to make sure I remind you about that moment for a long, long time. You might as well stop pouting like a baby."

"I'm not pouting."

He poked my bottom lip. "Yes, you are."

"Fine. Just a little." I tucked some of my curls behind my ear. "Do we really have to hang out tonight?"

"Hell yes. You just got back yesterday, and I don't get to see you much anymore. You're always up there painting with geeky guys that aren't as awesome as me. You barely come home. You said your summer was mine this year."

"It is."

He raised his hands in the air. "And this is your birth weekend!"

"Oh God."

"I have twenty-two surprises for you."

"I'm turning twenty-one, not twenty-two."

"Doesn't matter." He shrugged. "I had an extra surprise pop up this time, so we're starting a new tradition. For each of our birthdays, we add an extra surprise for luck."

"I'm scared."

"You should be." He winked. "Are you pissed at me?"

"No."

"Let me go tell Vicky that plans have changed." He motioned his head toward upstairs. "I'll tell her never mind on the sex. I'll just jump in the shower and get ready to go."

"You might as well have sex with her." I bent over, picked up the bag, and tossed it to him.

He caught it with ease. "No way I'm hooking up with someone else while you're here. I've been waiting forever to see you and—" he dangled the apple bag "—how can I even think about another woman with this shoved into my head?"

"No." I envisioned him messing with his dad's groupie and cringed. "I'm taking back the crazy thought that you should be my first."

"It doesn't matter. It's too late. You can't take it back."

"Actually, I can."

He held his hands against his chest. A mock hurt expression spread across his face. "You hurt me bad, Rain. You hurt me bad."

"Just go upstairs and have fun with Vicky. Eww, by the way."

"My dad's teaching me the most important lesson in life."

I shook my head. "What's that?"

"Sharing."

"I think I just vomited in my mouth."

"Oh, no. Don't throw up now. Save all of that for later. So, change of plans. I'll be down after I shower and dress. Don't leave." He twirled the bag and stared at it for a second.

"I'm not staying here with your dad," I whispered.

"Oh, yeah. Well, then I'll pick you up in less than an hour. And about your virginity—"

"Not talking about this with you."

"We are."

"Not now." I rushed off to the front door and dug my hand into my purse to get my phone.

"Fine. You won't be able to escape this conversation later." He raced up the stairs with my bag in hand. "I'll pick you up soon. Please keep that sexy dress on."

"Oh, be quiet." I opened the door. "You're not special anymore. I'm wearing sneakers and jeans."

Kaden stood outside on the porch and wagged his finger at me. "Where are you going?"

I glanced over my shoulder and then back at him. "Umm…didn't you go into the kitchen?"

"You're avoiding me again. I figured you would sneak out without finishing our discussion."

He's just as insane as his son.

"I forgot."

He tossed me a skeptical look.

"I did."

Kind of.

"Well, then I'm glad I came around the house and got to the front door to remind you." He wiped the sweat off of his forehead. "Which now seems pretty odd as I stand here."

"Don't worry. This night just seems to get weirder and weirder."

"Hungry?"

"No."

"Good. Let's eat. I'm cooking."

He hooked his arm around mine and tugged me back in.

"But—"

"Just dinner."

Best. Evening. Ever. I groaned and went back into the house.

CHAPTER 2

Uncle Hottie

Kaden chopped mushrooms. "Pour me a glass of wine, please."

I walked over to the cabinets, pulled out two solid black wine glasses, and filled them with Pinot Noir. The whole time, Kaden watched me with his eyebrows raised.

"What?" I asked.

"I was going to tell you where everything was, but you already know." He tossed the mushrooms into the hot pan. "Are you over here a lot?"

"I used to be when Jude and I were in high school." I handed him his glass. "Now it's only during the holidays, but not every holiday."

"You mean, not the ones when I'm here."

Exactly.

"No. Things just come up." I displayed my most innocent smile.

"Did your grandma know you hung out here?"

"No." And she still didn't know I planned to be with Jude all summer. It wasn't that grandma didn't like Jude; she just didn't like him hanging around me. He reminded her too much of my dad, the one who'd taken her little girl away. I'd planned on going to see her in Jamaica at the end of the summer.

"So, you were okay sneaking over here to see Jude but not your uncle?"

"My uncle?" I sipped some wine to hide my smirk.

An image of Kaden snorting coke on one of my Barbie tea set plates came to my mind. I'd been six and had begged him to come upstairs to my tea party. He'd obliged and, after a few lines of coke, had given me the coolest tea party of my young life. He'd mimicked my stuffed animals in various foreign accents, did back flips off of my bed's headboard, and set a bonfire in my sink to teach me why playing with fire was bad. Mom had caught us right as we were trying to put it out. That was back when Jude still lived with his mother and Kaden hung around our house all the time. By the time I was a preteen, I unfortunately had a crush on Kaden. Thankfully, Jude's mom dumped him with his dad. Because of that, Jude came around more, smashed away my unhealthy crush for Kaden, and shifted my infatuation to him.

"Uncle Kaden. I kind of like that," he said.

I shook my head and laughed at him. "Uncle?"

"What? Uncle sounds weird?"

"Definitely. You never acted like an uncle should act."

He stirred some more. "Well, the shitty thing about having a baby at twenty is that you grow up with your kid. Jack and I were never ready for children. Shoot, we weren't ready for our band doing so well at such a young age. If my dad hadn't already been a famous jazz musician, we would have never gotten that record deal so quick and with such a huge budget. Not to say our music didn't break down barriers and rock the world, but fame and money rushed to us with just our first song. A month later, we're on tour. When the girls starting coming around, we never considered using protection. Just having fun."

"And having kids." I sighed. Both Jude's and my parents had had us in their early twenties. Their parenting skills provided the perfect example of why people should never have unprotected sex.

"If I could do it all over again, I would've waited until I was well into my thirties." Kaden took a sip of his wine. "I made a lot of mistakes. At least I won't be making any more."

"You won't?"

"Well, I'm done with…half of the things I used to do back then. Now I should look like a proper uncle to you."

I snorted.

As he sautéed the mushrooms, he looked like many things, standing there with bare feet and wearing only tight jeans. He was a rock fan's dream and the vision women focused on when they touched themselves between their thighs. In my darkest moments, even I had tipped over to the kinky corners of my heart and slipped my fingers inside of me while I thought of Kaden's bare-chested movements as he strummed his guitar. It had been so wrong on so many levels. Afterward, I'd promised myself not to do it again, but I had done it a few more times before shifting my naughty thoughts to Jude.

"No disrespect, but I don't really consider you my uncle." I placed the glass on the table, sat on the barstool near him, and kicked off my heels. "How old are you now, forty-two?"

"I'll be forty-two in a few months." His gaze strayed to my legs as I crossed them. Again, he looked away and cursed under his breath. "So, you don't think of me as your uncle. What do you consider me then, Rainbow?"

"I prefer Rain."

"I prefer Rainbow."

I sucked my teeth. "I think of you as my dad's friend and Jude's father, so you're pretty much a friend of the family to me. Do you need any help? I'm a decent cook. I don't burn things like Jude does."

"Nope. Once the mushrooms are how I like them, then I'll drop in the steaks." He wiped his hands on a towel hanging over the oven's handle. "I thought I remembered Jude mentioning once that you were a vegetarian?"

"When I was around my mom, I was." I grinned. "Now, I'm a card-carrying carnivore."

To Mom's dismay.

"Love it." He raised his wine in the air. "A toast to a long-awaited reunion and a budding new friendship."

Our glasses clinked together.

"So, what's up with this groupie, Vicky?" I asked.

"I met her at a concert. She interviewed me for her local newspaper and offered me a blow job afterward."

"Wow. Does that happen a lot?"

"Enough to make me a happy man." He set his glass back down. "She did a good job too. Real good. I asked her to come along with me. It's no big deal. Every now and then, I ask a woman to spend a few days or weeks with me, and it's no problem."

"They just drop what they're doing and follow you around from city to city?"

"Of course. Wouldn't you for someone you idolized?"

"No."

"That's only because you've been around enough stars in your day to realize they're just messed up people that happened to get lucky."

"Not all of them are messed up." I took another sip.

"So, you're still a virgin?"

I choked on some of my wine.

Kaden rushed over, hitting my back until I calmed down.

"I'm okay." I cleared my throat.

"Maybe I should have asked that after you'd finished drinking."

"Maybe you shouldn't have asked me that at all."

"Well, you said I'm not your uncle. Cool friends of your dad can ask things like that, right?"

"Nope." I scrunched my face up. "I think your friend's daughter's virginity tends to be off the table for discussion."

"Really?" He quirked his eyebrows. "Well, I'll have to give Jack my apologies next time I see him."

My body stiffened. I gulped some wine.

"That's why I came back, you know." He leaned on the counter. "I always check on him when I'm in town. Make sure there are fresh flowers out there, and Ned the groundskeeper is maintaining the space around his gravesite."

"Ned told me." I stirred in my seat.

"I never miss his birthday. It was so important to him." His eyes brightened as he stared off in the distance. "You wouldn't believe all of the crazy times we had on his birthdays. I mean, the man knew how to party, but the best birthday had to be the one we spent in the hospital."

I tapped my toes on the floor.

"Only Jack, who loved birthdays so much, would be gifted with his precious little girl on his birthday."

I slid off of the stool. "I'll be right back. I have to go to the bathroom."

"Okay."

I escaped from the kitchen with my glass still in my hand. The downstairs bathroom flanked the right side of the kitchen's entrance. I got in and shut the door. I knew Kaden would do this — bring up memories, go on and on about Dad, trudge through the past like it was a necessary journey to take. Kaden might've loved Dad more than any person walking this earth. Even me.

If he knew the last days of my dad's life and the part I played in them, would he still want to get to know me?

I finished the wine. In the mirror, my reflection stared back at me. Water glazed my guilty eyes. My curls flailed out like a lion's mane of blond streaks and brown strands.

Had Kaden seen my guilt? Did he realize I was nervous?

Those fake blue eyes stared back, mocking me. At least the tears didn't show. *Thank God.* Instead, they ducked back into my eyelids as I tucked my sadness back into my core. Some things needed to be ignored and not dwelled on. The more my mind flew off in one direction, the more my sanity shattered into pieces that no one could sweep up and glue back together.

Someone started knocking at the door.

"Are you okay, Rainbow?" Kaden asked on the other side.

Dear God, I wish he would stop calling me that.

"I'm okay." I stepped out of the bathroom, closed the door behind me, and gave him the glass. "I'm not really hungry."

As he did when I was a kid, he put himself in my way, forcing me to duck under him if I wanted to escape. I leaned back on the door. He stepped closer. Too close. "Talk to me."

"About?" I scowled at him.

"Why are you upset?"

"I'm not."

"You are."

"I'm fine."

"If you keep lying to me, I may have to do something about that."

I laughed. "Like what, bend me over your knee and whip me?"

He leaned in closer, beyond the proper distance he should. Dad wouldn't have liked it. Jude probably wouldn't either. But the Kaden

I remembered always skirted the line and tended to push the limits when he longed to make a point. His breath brushed over my skin. My body shuddered in response, and it wasn't due to fear or nervousness.

Why am I so wrong?

Kaden moved in further as if not even noticing the effect he had on me. "You're actually seconds from me bending you over and whipping you right here."

"What?" I flushed with heat.

"Oh, wait." He backed up a little but not enough for me to flee. "I guess in this context, with you now being…full grown—"

"Full grown?"

"Propped and stuff."

I twisted my lips in confusion. "Propped?"

"You know what I mean. Breasts and other things."

"Other things like what?" I giggled.

He stepped back once more. At this rate, I'd have him out of my way in no time. He ran his fingers through his hair. "What I'm trying to say is the whipping threat isn't the same when you're not a bony little knucklehead with braces and acne. Now that you're…curvy."

"Curvy?" I battled to hold in my laugh.

"Stop it and give me a break here." A smile spread across his face as he held out his hands to his sides. "This is awkward enough with you in that tiny, little dress."

"Fine, but you have to ease up on me too."

"I'm not pressuring you."

"You're literally cornering me." I did dramatic gestures to show his guarding of the hallway exit. "And besides, I was never bony."

"You were a walking mold of sticks with a huge mop of hair. Either way, back to what I was saying. You should talk to me whenever you need to."

I banged the back of my head against the door. "You and Jude are two of the most aggravating men I've ever known."

"I'll take that as a compliment."

"You shouldn't." I shoved past him. "I'm fine, Kaden."

"Are you sure?"

"Dad killed himself five years ago. I've moved on."

He nodded. "Okay."

"I'm at peace."

"Sure." He dug his hands into his jeans.

"I barely even go to his grave."

"Interesting."

"What?"

"When was the last time you went to his grave?" he asked.

"It's been years."

He gave me another skeptical look. "Then who leaves the slices of birthday cake?"

"Beats me." I averted my eyes.

"And the 'Happy Birthday, Daddy' card?"

I tapped my foot. "I may have done that once or twice."

"You never miss a birthday."

I left him there in the hallway. "Okay. You've got me. I visit his grave several times during the year. It's no big deal."

"He hates chocolate, by the way," Kaden called back.

"Liar. He loves chocolate."

"He hated it and only ate it because it's your favorite. Your only saving grace for subjecting his grave to chocolate is that the cake always tastes so goddamn good."

I rolled my eyes. "Are you eating his slices?"

"Just a few bites."

"Disgusting and wrong in so many ways."

What type of person eats food off of a grave?

"You have good taste in desserts, and I'm sitting there on the ground for a while talking to him. I tend to get a little hungry with it sitting there and taunting me." He followed me back into the kitchen and poured me another glass of wine.

"On Sunday, I'll leave two slices."

"So, then you'll be there?"

"Of course. It's our birthday. I always celebrate with him, as you've rudely pointed out."

"And does your grandma know?"

I leaned my head to the side. "Does it matter? She lives out of the country."

"Just a question. I'm wondering if she's finally forgiven your dad."

"No, she doesn't know, and I doubt she'll ever forgive him." I seized my second glass of much-needed wine and drank it until it was half gone. Grandma never said I couldn't go to Dad's grave, but she never motivated me to do it either. I couldn't speak his name around her. She hadn't even buried his body anywhere near the rest of the family.

You don't like that, do you, Mom.

"Why do you think Jack did it?" Kaden interrupted my thoughts.

Only Kaden would ask me that. No one else would dare. Others had too much tact and discretion.

"I don't know why." My voice sounded low.

"That week we'd been hanging out, and I never got the impression he would go crazy like that. I just never...It just blows my mind, man."

I clamped up inside and gulped more wine. I barely drank alcohol and hadn't eaten anything since breakfast this morning. Already, I felt a little light-headed.

"You don't want to talk about this?" he asked.

"No. It's still fresh in my mind after all these years." I finished the glass. "I'd rather not."

"I'm sorry, then." He slapped his forehead. "Of course you wouldn't. Forget I even brought it all up."

"I will."

He watched me set the empty glass on the table. "You're drinking that Pinot pretty fast."

"I like wine, Uncle Kaden." I gave him an air kiss and hopped back on the stool. My breasts jiggled in my top. The bottom of my dress rose on my thighs. I yanked it back down.

"Hmm." He let his gaze travel over me. "You're right. I'm not your uncle."

"Oh, you just realized that?" I stuck my tongue out. "And what made you decide?"

"Uncles don't have the thoughts I just had." He put his back to me. Some mumbled words left his mouth as he stirred the mushrooms and lowered the heat. "Are those your girly things in the guest room next to Jude's bedroom?"

"Girly things?" I asked.

"Fruity lotion, brushes, buckets of gel."

Buckets? He's such an exaggerator.

"Yes. That stuff is mine."

"You keep some extra clothes in there?"

Where's this going?

"Yes."

"Please, for God's sake, put something else on."

"Change my clothes? Seriously?" I placed my hand on my hips.

"Yes. It would make things easier for me. I am a dirty old man, after all."

I laughed and jumped off of the stool. "I did read your biography, so I won't argue with the dirty part, but I definitely don't think you're an old man. I don't think forty-one is old."

"Compliments like that are only going to get you everywhere."

"I'm serious. You're still hot."

He peeked at me as I walked by him. "Me being hot is an off limits topic for you, Rainbow."

"Okay, Old Uncle Kaden." I saluted him.

He swatted my behind. It stung and delivered pleasurable shivers all at the same time. *Wow. I wasn't expecting that.* I rubbed the area. He watched my hand as it moved up and down and around the curve of my behind.

He licked his lips.

Warmth rose within me.

Our eyes met. An uncomfortable silence bridged between us as his face transformed from lust to shock within seconds.

He went back to the stove. "Go change."

I knew I should have fled right there and hurried upstairs. Maybe it was the wine or the horniness that had been bubbling in me all day as I'd considered Jude taking my virginity. Perhaps it was the instances of what I had imagined Kaden doing to me as I'd masturbated. Possibly it was all those things mixed with the fire in his eyes when he stared at me with such desire. Or in the end, maybe I just liked to do bad things sometimes.

Either way, I stayed right there. "Any requests?"

"What?" He averted his eyes when he faced me.

"What do you want me to wear?"

"Clothes."

"Do bikinis count?" I flirted.

He shook his head and disappeared to the fridge. "Jeans and a shirt, Rainbow."

"Bra or no bra?"

He groaned and stuck his head into the freezer as if to cool him off. "You come down here without a bra, and you won't be a virgin any longer. Meanwhile, Jack will turn in his grave and return to the world to haunt me. You know, when Jack married your mom, he got real involved in Jamaican culture. He used to call ghosts duppies. Said it was what Jamaicans called it. Would you like your dad to come back as a duppy?"

"No." I gritted my teeth at the mention of Dad and duppies. My legs wobbled a little as if I was going to pass out.

"Are you a duppy, Rainbow?" Dad woke me up with a gun pointed to my head.

"No, Daddy."

"Rainbow, are you okay?" Kaden appeared in front of me and tapped my shoulder. "You look scared."

I backed away from his touch. My stomach tightened into painful knots. "I'm fine."

"Go put on something big, baggy, and preferably unattractive looking."

I twisted around and did my best to get ahold of myself. "Yes, Uncle Kaden."

"You're killing me, Rainbow."

CHAPTER 3

Friendly Touching

"**M**uch better outfit." Kaden set the plate full of food in front of me as I sat down, wearing blue jeans and an Oscar the Grouch T-shirt. "Now I'm not forced to not stare at all of the things I should not be staring at."

"Awkward."

"Exactly." He sat down in front of me with his own plate. "So, back to your virginity."

"Are you insane?" I sliced a piece of steak off. "I thought we agreed my virginity existed in the realm of things we shouldn't discuss."

"I just want to stress that my son may not be the person you should choose to lose your virginity to."

"Oh." I chewed on the steak and savored the sauce Kaden must have slathered on while he'd cooked it. "Do you have someone else in mind?"

"What? No. I'm just thinking that your first time should be with someone you love."

"I love Jude."

"Not the way you should when you're giving away something so precious. Jude loves you, but not the way a man loves a woman, or am I wrong about this?"

"You're not."

"So, why would you give it to him?"

Heat flushed on my cheeks. I was sure my face held a red tint. This was not the topic I wanted to talk to anyone about, but especially not Kaden, my dad's best friend and my virginity-taker-to-be's father. Plus, the whole talking of sex thing filled the air with that odd energy between us. He still wore no shirt and continued to drip with gorgeousness. Each time I took a tiny peek at his smooth skin, caught a bit of that exotic tattoo art on his arms, or spied the lush curve of his full lips, I experienced a thrill between my thighs and disgust within my mind.

What's wrong with me?

"Just wait for the right guy," Kaden said.

"Okay."

"You're not going to wait, are you?"

"No."

"Rainbow, you're sweet and innocent."

Laughter burst from my mouth. "Kaden, there is nothing sweet or innocent about me. I hang with Jude, for God's sake. I'm not Snow Fucking White. Just because I'm a virgin doesn't mean I'm some prissy little innocent girl."

Before Dad had died, I'd done other things with many guys—kissing, touching, sucking, fingering, blow jobs—everything but actual penetration. Once Dad died, things changed. When I kissed or made out with a guy, sometimes I vomited afterward and sometimes I didn't. I never figured out why certain guys triggered my body into sickness, while others only made my stomach rumble. Either way, it hadn't taken long for news to spread around school that weirdo Rain tended to barf on guys' shoes after making out. My list of suitors had transformed from full to nonexistent in one week. The only reason people continued to say hi to me was because Jude hung around me, and everyone hoped to be in his favor.

"Well, you must've had a reason to save your virginity," Kaden offered. "Why give it up now? You might as well wait for the right guy."

I stuck my fork into another piece of steak and swirled it around the plate, making circles and zigzag lines. "I just don't feel like waiting anymore. I understand what you're saying, but I'm freaking almost twenty-one and curious."

"Of course you're curious."

And horny.

He cut into his own steak. "I guess what I'm trying to say is don't rush into it."

"Again, I'm twenty-one in two days. Clearly, I don't rush into things."

"Yet you're acting desperate. You came here with lube and condoms."

"Ouch. You're saying I'm desperate." I accidentally dropped my fork on the table. It hit the wood with a bang. "Thanks a lot. Wouldn't desperate be standing on the corner with a huge sign, yelling out to anybody that walks by, 'I'll give you a hundred dollars if you destroy my hymen'?"

Kaden hadn't seen me in five years and already thought he understood me in an hour or so of actions and conversation. *Ridiculous.* I huffed, got my fork, and punctured the meat in front of me hard.

He raised his hands in surrender. "Okay. You don't rush."

Stomping sounded from outside. I figured it was Jude running down the stairs. He never could stroll or tiptoe. Every step he made pounded or slammed against a surface, as if he craved to imprint himself into the earth for people thousands of years in the future to see.

"Dad, we should probably call the venue and make sure everything is going good for tonight." Jude skipped in there without looking our way and headed straight to the stove to dip his finger in the pan, putting his back to us. A massive tattoo decorated his entire back. A huge red and orange dragon hissed fire at a knight wielding a long sword. The tip of the weapon was barely an inch from the dragon's neck, telling the viewer that the dragon would be slain in no time.

"This is delicious," Jude said. "The steaks are done already? Where's mine?"

"I gave it to Rainbow."

Jude turned our way. "Rain? You're still here."

"Your dad forced me to stay."

"I wouldn't say forced." Kaden took a sip of wine.

I waved him away. "He ran around the house and guarded the front door so when I walked outside to leave, he was right there to shove me back in."

"Really?" Jude licked his fingers as he journeyed over to me. His jeans hung low, revealing chiseled cuts of muscle. He didn't possess the thick muscular body his father boasted, but women swooned around him just the same. He tapped my shoulder. "Up, please. I never gave you a proper homecoming welcome."

"No biting." I rose.

"Where's the fun in that?" He embraced me, pressing his body against mine and kissing my right cheek, my left, forehead, chin, and finally stopped with a peck on my lips. "I missed you."

"Sure you did." I smirked.

"Trust me. It's been six weeks, three days, four and half hours, one minute, and ten seconds. No, eleven. Twelve, thirteen, fourteen, fifteen, sixteen —"

"Stop it." I groaned.

"Six weeks?" Kaden raised his eyebrows at us. "When was the last time you saw each other?"

Jude collapsed into my seat like he'd been running all day. "I flew to Sarasota to see her during spring break. She refused to come down to Miami because of some geek stuff. And to tell you the truth, that trip didn't count. We sat in a dusty studio all week, getting food delivered to us. It was uneventful."

"Uneventful? You slept with a pizza girl and one of the visiting art professors at my school."

"Only because I was bored out of my mind."

I lowered onto his lap. "I had to finish that sculpture. It had to be perfect. Let's not forget that I warned you many times before you flew up that I was obsessed with that project."

"Regardless, the whole time was geek shit." He grabbed my fork and started eating. "This is good, Dad."

"You're just going to eat my food?" I snatched my fork back.

"Technically, it's *my* food. Dad planned to cook this for me, but I'll let you finish the rest." He placed his hands on my waist, slid them under my shirt, and massaged circles into my skin. The movement soothed away tension that I hadn't realized was there. He dramatically whimpered. "I'll just sit here without anything to eat and spoil you with my fingers as I die of hunger. Beautiful Rain, I suffer for you and ask for nothing in return."

"Isabelle left trays of food for us in the fridge," Kaden offered.

"I don't want what the maid left. I'm hungry for what's on Rain's plate." Jude kneaded his fingers into my flesh.

I purred and leaned back into him as he continued to massage me some more. "Fine. I'll share."

"You're so kind." He moved his hands down to my hips where he kneaded his fingers with more pressure. I fed him a piece of steak and then tossed one in my mouth.

The whole time, Kaden sat back in his chair. An odd expression expanded over his face.

"What?" Jude mumbled in between bites.

"You both are pretty comfortable with each other," Kaden said. "I had no idea."

"Rain is my homie." Jude chuckled. "My home slice. My deuce dog. Down shorty."

"Please stop." I scooped up a couple of mushrooms.

"My partner in crime. Rider for life. Sister from another mister. Dog pound mate from the kennel in the sky."

"Oh God." I rolled my eyes. "He's determined to bring back old slang."

"And is he just going to go on and on like this?" Kaden finished his steak.

"Pretty much." I smirked. "He'll do it as long as it annoys me. I haven't mastered the technique of ignoring him yet. It's pretty hard."

"Especially with his hands all over you." He watched Jude caress me some more.

I didn't respond to Kaden's comment. Jude's touching me was never a big deal. We touched each other with the familiarity of people who'd known each other for all of their lives, because frankly we had. I couldn't think of a moment in my life where Jude didn't exist. Every significant situation I'd experienced, Jude had stood there by my side to support or comfort me, enjoy it or suffer through it with me.

He'd taught me how to ride my bike; he had learned years before me. He'd encouraged me to paint, and when I had done oil scenes or watercolors, he'd lied and said it didn't suck. Even when my period had first come, he'd ridden with me to the store to buy bags of sanitary napkins and tampons. I'd been too uncomfortable to ask Mom or Dad about what to do. They had remained busy arguing, having make-up sex, and arguing again. Instead, Jude had gone online and yelled out instructions from outside the bathroom as I'd stood inside putting tampons in the wrong place and leaving the plastic on. It must've been an hour before we'd gotten it right.

"You both are pretty touchy." Kaden poured himself a glass of wine.

Jude sighed. "Here we go."

"What?" I finished the rest of the food on the plate. Jude had only left a couple of mushrooms.

"Every now and again when Dad is sober, he gets in the mood to father me," Jude whispered in my ear. "Don't worry, by the end of the night, he'll be back to the Kaden Everett we all know and detest."

I laughed.

"I heard that." Kaden displayed his middle finger at Jude.

"That explains why he was doing the whole concerned father act before you walked in. He just called me desperate." I mock pouted. "Do you think I'm desperate for wanting you to take my virginity?"

"Hell no. I feel honored." Jude placed his hand over his heart. "And if I'm awarded the duty, I shall serve you and my country to my last living breath."

I laid my head on the table. "Maybe I am desperate."

"I told you," Kaden said. "And I'm serious. You both look like a little couple over there."

"It's just friendly touching, Dad. Don't rush out to call a wedding planner." Jude patted my leg. I rose and he left his seat. "And why does Rain have to be desperate if she wants me to make love to her? You of all people know how much I care about her."

"Yeah, but you can't be the man she deserves."

Jude's face creased in annoyance.

Kaden leaned back in his chair, as if daring Jude to say anything else. The kitchen turned quiet for a few awkward seconds.

"So, Kaden, you're really a great cook," I said, trying to break away the silence.

"I'm not the man she deserves?" Jude took my glass of wine.

"Maybe I should reword that." He brushed his fingers through his hair.

"Maybe you should," Jude countered.

"You both need some sort of clear line." He pointed at Jude and then me. "You told me you were just friends. Next thing I see is condoms and fondling."

"Stop it. Let's not do the daddy thing tonight. The whole 'I'm your buddy one hour and I'm your dad the next' spins me around in circles and gives me a headache." Jude scratched his head.

"I'm always your dad—"

Jude interrupted him, "You've barely been in town for eight hours, and you're already causing a commotion."

Kaden jumped up from the table. "How am I—"

"Okay. Let's stop." I held up my hands in the "time-out" sign. "And for the record, the apple bag and condom situation didn't happen, so there's no reason for us to discuss this. That was a momentary instance of insanity. I no longer think Jude taking my virginity is a good idea."

"Why not?" Jude held his hands out. "Because of Dad?"

A redhead sashayed into the kitchen, dressed in my high school chess club T-shirt.

I glared at Jude. "No, not because of your dad." I gestured to the redhead. "More because of things like that, and is that my shirt?"

The woman giggled. If I were a bolder person, I would have snatched it off of her.

"You both wear the same size, and she didn't bring any other clothes when Dad and her flew in." He shrugged. "I didn't think you would mind."

"This is exactly why I'm saying no. You're a bit insensitive, and you don't know the concept of boundaries and respect."

"Whatever." He rolled his eyes. "Vicky, this is my best friend, Rain, and you already know the cock-blocker over there."

"Hello, Rain." Vicky yawned and swayed her hips as she pulled out the chair next to Kaden and plopped down. "What's the plan for the night?"

Jude stared at me for a few seconds. A neutral mask covered his face.

I wondered what he could be thinking as he bit his lip. I mouthed the words "be nice."

He winked at me in response, his expression changing from unclear to reasonably-not-pissed. Maybe it was because Kaden rose and left the room. I wasn't sure if his dad had been annoyed or in a rush to get some fresh air, but I was glad things returned to normal.

They'd been living together off and on for years. The only thing that made the situation work was the fact that Kaden constantly toured during the year. If he wasn't traveling the country doing promotion for a new solo album, then he starred in small parts for action movies, did a few commercials, or flooded the music gossip waves with a scandal—sleeping with an A-list actor's wife, getting caught picking up a hooker, or being arrested for a brawl in a night club. Due to Kaden's behavior, Jude pretty much ignored any parental advice his father had to offer, which pissed Kaden off to no end.

"So, are we staying in for the evening, or what?" Vicky scratched under her arm.

"We're going to party like rock stars!" Jude rubbed his hands together.

I raised my eyebrows. "We are? And by the way, do you ever get tired of saying that line?"

"Rock stars never get tired of saying that line."

"You're not a rock star yet, son," Kaden called out from another room. "What was that you wanted to talk about with the venue?"

"Oh, yeah." Jude dipped his finger in a jar of peanut butter and left the kitchen with it. "I'll be right back."

And just like that, all had been forgiven between Jude and his dad. Meanwhile, I stayed in the kitchen with the groupie. I almost screamed, "No! Don't leave me in here with Vicky."

She grinned at me and scratched around her neck. Icky. *That's what I should call her—Icky Vicky.* Yet Jude and Kaden had both slept with her, or at least Jude was going to before I'd arrived. Being in college away from Jude had provided me with the opportunity to forget who my friend truly was: a guy who stuck his penis in anything that breathed. Now that I had stepped back into his world, I remembered why I'd never considered Jude as the right person to take my virginity.

Vicky dabbed at the leftover juice on Kaden's plate and sucked her finger. "Are they sharing you too?"

I battled with not scrunching my face. "No. I'm just a friend of the family."

"Hmm. But not a close friend?"

"I'd say we're pretty close." *Closer than you.* "But no sex. Have you already had sex with Jude?" I'd thought he said he wouldn't.

"When we first landed here, he picked us up. I gave him a blow job in the back of his car. Have you seen it? It's spectacular."

Jude owned many cars. I just nodded my head and smiled at Vicky.

"I don't see how you can be around them and not try them both out. Kaden and his son really are a feisty pair. I bet they're both tigers in bed and different in their own ways." She picked up the wine bottle next to us and chugged it. "Jude's dick is almost as long and thick as this bottle."

"I'm sure that's an exaggeration."

"He's pretty close, and Kaden's tongue, for fuck's sake, is blessed from Buddha. It's like those blades on top of a helicopter. It just spins and spins and never stops until I'm riding high and squirting all over his face."

Eww. Bile rose in my throat. My stomach rumbled. I jumped up and rushed out of the room right before the vomit burst out of my mouth.

CHAPTER 4

Butt Tickle

We rode in Jude's car, Kaden and Vicky tagging along. Darkness served as my view because a blindfold covered my eyes. *I hate not being able to see.* The sound of an electric guitar flowed in my ears and was accompanied by the deep banging of bass drums. Wind blew through my hair and cooled my skin, since Jude had the top down on his car.

"Are you cold?" he yelled over the music.

"No. I love the breeze, but how long do I have to keep this on?" It must've been fifteen minutes by now, which was a long time to sit in a car with a blindfold.

"Be patient, Rainy. We're here."

I felt the car stop as the song turned off. A car door creaked open. People cheered around me. Women screamed Jude's name. Others begged for his autograph. Clicking and snapping of cameras sounded on my right.

I hope no one takes my picture.

I heard Jude's voice to my left as he ordered somebody to push on forward.

"Where are we?" I asked when he grabbed my hand and helped me out of the car.

"You'll see when we get there. Just let me guide you."

"I'm close to taking this blindfold off."

He tapped my behind. "Behave."

"What's up with you Everett men slapping my bottom tonight?"

"Excuse me? What the fuck?" Jude's voice had a hard edge to it. "My dad's hand was on your ass?"

"Not the way you're saying it."

A Duran Duran song played. At least, I assumed it was them. I had no freaking idea where we were. After another minute of walking, Jude undid my blindfold, took it off, and pierced me with his gaze. "What do you mean 'not the way I'm saying it'? Dad was rubbing up against you?"

"No." I scanned the area in pure amazement.

Jude's body guard, T-Bone, got in front of us, wearing a white pair of sunglasses with rainbows on top of them. He donned a different pair each week. Shades were just his thing. He loved collecting them. The man was a mountain of muscle under dark black skin. His typical stare could cut through the thickest concrete block. His punch knocked many men out in seconds. I'd witnessed him take guys down several times when Jude ran his mouth or got himself into trouble. However, the best parts of T-Bone had to be his smile, when he chose to bless me with it, and his outstanding sense of humor.

"When did you get here?" I hugged his huge body.

"I've been here waiting for hours for you and Jude to show up. I had a doctor's appointment, and since Jude was going to be home most of the day, I took the time to get that and some other things done."

"Are you okay? You didn't go to the doctor for anything important, right?"

"I'm fine. I just got a little high blood pressure. My doctor thinks I need to change my diet." He held his hand up. "Don't start with that tofu crap, Rain."

"Fine. I'm just saying. You should try it."

"Moving on." He lifted my hand, opened my fingers, and placed a small box wrapped in violet, flowered paper on my hand. "Happy birthday, Rain. Additionally, when are you going to stop hanging around with this treacherous white boy?"

"I can hear you." Jude smirked.

"Good." T-Bone tapped the present he had given me. "Open that when I'm not around. I don't want to have to wipe your tears away when you start getting all flushed with my romantic genius."

I gave him another quick hug, knowing T-Bone liked to keep a hard persona out in public. "I'll be sure to open it when Jude isn't around too. You know how he envies our undying love."

"It's shades. You've been getting her a pair every birthday. You give everyone a pair for Christmas and their birthdays." Jude pointed to the box. "I don't even know why you wrapped it."

"Because I'm a gentleman." T-Bone smoothed the collar on his shirt. "And you're a barbarian."

"Do you think you'd like to guard something now?"

He saluted Jude and got in front of us. "Happy birthday, Rain."

"Thanks." I grinned.

Crowds of excited people surrounded me as we headed into the night club. I had no idea who all of these people were. "Happy Birthday, Rain" banners hung from the ceiling. The whole place was dark except for the tiny dots of blue light that sprinkled down from the ceiling as if it were a light storm. The sweet scent of chocolate lingered in the air. I sniffed and twisted in the direction it was coming from. A massive fountain lay behind me with three crystal dolphins in various leaping poses. Different colors of chocolate spouted out of the dolphins' mouths — dark, light brown, and white. At least, I hoped it was chocolate. I planned on dipping my entire body in there and remain floating in it the whole night.

"So, what was that statement about with my dad?" Jude asked. "The whole 'him slapping your ass' thing."

"This party is amazing. I can't believe you did this for me."

"Rain, answer me."

People were dressed in the craziest outfits. Most of the women wore fluorescent colored tutus with socks up to their knees and holes scattered in their stockings. Pigtails dotted the sides of their heads. They tied various rock band shirts in knots on the sides of their hips. Guys had chains hanging from their belts. Most had their hair moussed up in spikes. Makeup painted almost everybody's faces in different symbols in black, white, or any color one could imagine. Thick, gold chains linked around their necks. Iconic eighties images like Pac-Man adorned their cut-up shirts. *He must have themed the party.* Jude loved parties with themes or costume requirements. Besides his birthday, Halloween served as his top holiday. Perhaps because his birthday was the day before Halloween.

"Holy shit. You did this all for me?" I hugged him.

"Hell yeah. Now stop avoiding my question."

I leaned away. "What question?"

"Did my dad try to mess with you?"

"Oh, God, no." I rocked with the music. "He just hit my butt."

The muscle in Jude's jaw twitched. "Excuse me?"

"It sounds wrong, but it wasn't at all what you're thinking."

"No?"

"It was playful."

"How is a slap playful?"

"Like a really short butt tickle."

He scowled at me. "So he was tickling your ass?"

"Oh, goodness. No. It was a quick smack. I was just trying to explain it that way to show you how someone can touch a person's behind and it wouldn't be sexual."

"There's no such moment. If an adult man is touching an adult woman's ass and they're not related, it's not a butt tickle. It's him trying to have sex with her."

"He's your dad, Jude."

"That's why I asked. I know him very well. I wouldn't put it past him to try and fuck you."

Shock splashed over my face like cold water. Somehow, him mentioning *fuck* and *his dad* in the same sentence ruined the moment for me. "I'm going to ignore that and pretend like you didn't say it so I can return to this excellent party."

People bumped into my side. I didn't care. I looked off to see where everyone was in a rush to get to and spotted all of the members of Depraved Minds on the stage. Well, not all of the members. Dad wasn't there, but his replacement, Tech T, did a few tests of the microphone as Kaden tuned his guitar.

I covered my mouth. "How the hell did you get all of them together tonight?"

After my dad died, his band had separated. They'd never played another song together again. It'd hit Kaden the hardest, Grandma had said. She'd claimed my dad and the band were the only things Kaden truly cared about. Thank goodness she hadn't said that in front of Jude.

"I asked Dad to play for you for your birthday this year, and he got all crazy excited. The next thing I know he's calling up his publicist and convincing the band members to do a onetime gig on South Beach in honor of you."

"Where are we on South Beach?"

"The Circus! And your name is all over the beach, baby. Signs everywhere say '80s Birthday Bash for Jack Kenner's Rainbow.'"

"Oh God." I hid my face. *Mom is going to kill me.*

"What?"

"Nothing. I was just thinking Mom might find out."

He sighed loudly. "I thought you said you stopped doing that?"

"What?"

"Is that why you're wearing those ridiculous blue contacts?"

"She likes them on me."

He looked away for a minute. "Please stop that."

I pretended to be confused. "Stop what?"

"You know what. I don't like that shit, Rainy. You know that."

He hated talking about Mom with me, but tough. "I'm the birthday girl. You have to do it with me." I stuck my tongue out.

"It's fucking bizarre. Crazy stuff like that is going to make you lose it."

"It's called a coping mechanism."

He studied me for a minute. His eyes moved from side to side as if a true answer swirled around my head. When it came to my sanity, he believed he was the maintenance man. "Just one more time. I'll do it with you tonight, but don't do it around me anymore."

"Fine."

"Okay." He muttered some curse under his breath. "How is old mom doing these days?"

"She's in Paris filming her new show. It's a worldwide success now."

"Worldwide success?" He quirked his eyebrows.

"She's bigger than Oprah."

"Well, of course she is. How can Oprah compete against your mom?"

I scowled at him.

He raised his hands in the air. "Fine. Fine. So, you think your mom will be worried about you partying tonight? Don't stress about it. Just let her know that you're a woman now."

"It's not that easy." My mom was holding my trust fund over my head. I wouldn't get it until I turned twenty-five. How she'd managed that requirement, I didn't know. She had feared I'd be as wild as my dad, but instead I'd proved her wrong. Well, kind of. I snuck a few joints every now and then. Plus, hanging with Jude caused me to get involved with things that she surely wouldn't like.

"Yes, it is easy." He hooked his finger in my jeans' belt loop and tugged me to the staircase farther away. "She can't control you all of your life."

"I wouldn't bet on that. Hold up." I tapped his back. "We're going away from the chocolate. The birthday girl does not want distance between her and the chocolate fountain."

"You're just going to speak in third person now?"

"Yes. The birthday girl will be doing that all night."

"I'll have one of the guys make you a plate." He towed me on, darting through shocked faces as they realized he was coming their way. "We need to get to VIP before we get rushed by crazy people."

"You mean *you* get rushed. No one's coming after me."

"Men would if I wasn't around."

And if I wasn't loony.

"Well, then I should stop coming around you, right?" I nudged him with my elbow. "Maybe tonight will be the night when I give some hot guy my apple."

"If you don't vomit all over him first."

"Low blow, Jude." I made my lips form a fake frown. "Low blow. One day I'll find a guy that won't mind being vomited on while he takes my apple, and then you'll feel stupid for all the times you picked on me."

"Well, that guy will have to pry that lush apple from my cold, dead hands."

I burst out laughing. "That statement really doesn't work in this context."

"It's the truth though. You handed me the opportunity to take your apple. I'm not giving it back."

He better be joking.

"I took it back," I pointed out.

"You can't take that back."

"I really can."

He's no longer taking my V-card. He must be playing with me.

He laughed.

I took that as a good sign. There was no way he was serious about still being my first. You don't have a girl ask you to take her virginity and then run upstairs and shower like it's no big deal. In fact, I'd taken his action as *"Hey, Rain, we're just friends. I'll do it if you want to. If not, no big deal."* Granted, I didn't know what I'd expected him to do. Maybe I was being a bit ridiculous. Or, perhaps Vicky telling me about how she had given him a blow job earlier set my desire for him back a bit.

We approached the entrance to the VIP area. Two big guys stepped to the side as we entered and headed up the stairs. Jude crashed onto the closest couch. I continued standing as I drank in all of the excitement around me. Black leather chairs and glass tables littered VIP. I spotted a pop star here and there. Other media-noteworthy loitered about—kids of famous parents mainly, a D-list actress, a couple of comedians, and a group of old guys that I think were popular musicians around my dad's day. Bodyguards and security drifted among the stars. Marijuana smoke lingered in the air. Our space hovered over all of the people down below as the club became packed and the music soared to a higher level.

"Hey, Rico." Jude motioned for a waiter with a blond mohawk and polka dot suspenders to come over. "Get Rain a tray with some cups of chocolate, cakes, and anything else down there."

"Jude meant *please* get it," I corrected.

"Thanks." Rico smiled and ran off to do Jude's bidding.

"You shouldn't boss people around, not even the staff." I wagged my finger at him.

"Why not?" He gently pulled me down next to him. "People do what I say because of who I am."

"And who are you?" I gave him a skeptical look.

"The god of heavy metal rock Kaden Everett's son, and jazz legend Tommy Boy Everett's grandson. Music runs through my blood, woman. They think I'll be some big name in the music industry one day."

"You will."

"If Dad lets me."

"Huh?"

"Dad's trying to produce the whole damn album and thinks it'll be a great bonding experience for us." He laid his head back and closed his eyes. "He's already called writers and all these people I never heard of."

Not good. Jude wrote all of his music himself. Everything inspired him. Once, I'd witnessed him staring at the sky for an hour, humming a tune in his head. By the end of the day, he'd written a song with a sad melody. The next night, I'd sat in his studio as he produced the song himself, all with electronic instruments. Days later, we'd taken on the project of making a video for his song. It was just supposed to be something fun to pass the time. I'd painted a huge mural of a dark sky with many of his song's elements floating between bright stars, and then videotaped him singing half-naked in front of it while I flicked various colors of paint onto his bare chest, making sure to capture his essence on film. For a good laugh, we'd uploaded it to YouTube and tweeted the link to his friends. By the end of the day, it had received over a thousand views. By the end of the week, views had reached into the hundreds of thousands. Phone calls from record labels had come at the end of the month with offers of representation and money advances to rival the monthly allowance his dad gave him.

"Is he at least interested in going in the musical direction you want to?" I asked.

"No. He's still in the past, and I'm trying to do something that's never been heard before. He doesn't get it."

I kissed his cheek and squeezed his hand. "Sorry."

"No big deal. I'll deal with it eventually." He grabbed me before I could move away from him and then landed kisses on my cheek and closer to my lips than his usual pecking. "Let's talk about your apple."

"You better be joking. I said no."

"Hmm. We'll talk about it later then." He sat up. "You like your two surprises so far?"

"Two?" I gestured to the whole party. "This is way more than two. I figured this was all twenty-two. Seriously, if you have any more surprises, I don't need them."

"Too bad. You're getting them all. One surprise was the party. The other was that Depraved Minds would sing for you. We have twenty more to go." He formed his lips into a frown. "So, why did my dad hit your butt again? Is that why you're saying no, because of the butt tickle?"

"Are you really still thinking about the butt thing? It was a quick hit. That's it, and it has nothing to do with why I don't want you to take my virginity." I shook my head. "I can't even remember why he did it. I made some smart remark. He hit me on my butt. The whole thing was playful and fun."

"Okay." He bobbed his head but didn't seem relieved. "Either way, tell me if he gets out of line."

"He won't. I have been around him before, you know."

"That was years ago. You're a woman now." His gaze strayed to my breasts.

"New topic."

"Cool." He rubbed his hands together. "Are you ready for surprises three, four, and five?"

"Yes."

"Ted, get your ass over here!" Jude glanced my way and rolled his eyes. "I mean, *please* get your ass over here."

"Thanks. I hate being around you when you're a pretentious asshole."

"Luckily, there are only rare moments when I'm like that."

"Bullshit," I muttered under my breath.

A tall blond guy carried over a big box with no top on it. Paint brushes stuck out of it. Excitement exploded in my chest. I jumped up to see what else was in there as he set it down. Jude pointed into the box. "These are just some of the supplies I'm putting in your creative cottage."

"Creative cottage?" I asked.

"That big-ass mansion is ridiculously chaotic when Dad is there. I need you in there with me this summer, painting, keeping me from killing him, and inspiring my music. You're my muse."

"I'm your muse." I twisted my lips to the side. "How many times have you said that to a woman this week?"

"Zero. And I'll pretend like you didn't accuse me of being deceitful where you and my music are concerned." He pushed the box away from me. "These supplies are just a symbol of your creative cottage. I had Isabelle clean out the office next to my music studio. I'm making it your place to paint and do your art."

I lifted the different tubes of paint, dragged my fingers along the white, threaded surface of canvas, and studied the different sizes of brushes. "Oh my God, this is your best present yet. You're spoiling me."

"So, are you going to come paint, sculpt, and do artsy shit every week?"

"You know I will, and I'll probably paint and draw you most of the time." I stared longingly into his eyes and tried not to laugh. "You know, Jude, you are *my* muse."

"Ha ha. You're so funny. I was actually being serious when I said it to you." He tapped his chest. "Anyway, I just want you to promise me that all the things you paint, I get to keep."

"Sure. I'd like to get one of you and your father."

"Maybe."

"Please?"

"Fine. You can paint us together." He grimaced.

"You rock." I groped a few of the different paint brushes with lust then forced myself to back away from the box and direct my attention back to Jude. "You're pretty much my only fan."

"Because you hide your art from everybody. Your mom would love it if you showed her." He winked at me.

Would Mom like my art? I doubt it.

Not the stuff I painted. Especially my darker ones. I loved to paint with blood—animal blood mainly. The ones I did of my mom and dad always tended to be drenched in it. Many of those pieces were abstract in some ways, but there were enough things in there to recognize what I was painting—broken pieces of guns scattered across a field of evil spirits, dripping in crimson liquid; real acid strips plastered on canvas with eyes surrounding them; bloodied guitars; and Jude's favorite: a shattered rainbow done in dyed cocaine powder. I imagined Mom stepping into my studio and journeying to the far back where my collection hung in a darkened room. She would probably be enraged or worse, crumble down into a depression like she did now every time I talked to her about Dad.

"Anything you create this summer is all mine. No one else can have it." Jude raked his fingers through my curls.

"I promise. All of my paintings are yours."

"Good. Now for your next surprise. You're going to have to be open-minded."

"I'm not doing any hard drugs."

An exasperated breath escaped his lips as he pulled out a tiny plastic bag with two white pills. Rainbows decorated both of them. He never over-consumed hard drugs and tended to only do an ecstasy pill or line of cocaine every now and then, but it worried me that one day his casual use could turn into a hardcore habit. I couldn't deal with it if he ended up like our fathers.

"Come on, Rain." He dangled the bag in front of me. "You said you would do ecstasy with me again."

I directed my attention to the balcony where the music boomed to an erratic beat. "Friends don't get friends to do drugs."

"You smoke weed."

"It's natural."

"Fucking Jamaicans."

I punched him. "You're such a racist. Not every Jamaican smokes."

"I challenge you to find me one Jamaican over twenty on this planet that hasn't ever smoked in their life, and I'll give you one of my cars."

It would be difficult. All of my mother's side had either tried it or still did it as part of their Rastafarian religion. Nevertheless, I'd find one, and he'd eat his words one day. "Deal."

He leaned over and grabbed a glass of water. "Nothing is going to happen to you. I've taken this type of pill before. It's a happy high. I know the dealer. He's trustworthy."

I snorted. "A trustworthy dealer? I'll believe that when I see it."

"T-Bone is here, watching our every more. Take one. You get a bad trip, and I'll take you wherever you need to go and calm you down." He lowered onto the ground and got on his knees as he poked his lip out. "Please, Rainy. It'll be so much fun. Come on! You're fucking perfect all school year. Loosen up."

"Nothing I do is perfect." I hid my face with my hands.

"For me, baby?" He dragged my hands away.

"Give me the damn pill."

"Yes!" He jumped up and handed it to me. "Just put it in your mouth and swallow."

I did and he followed.

"Now, back to your virginity."

I hit his chest. "Please stop. I really need you to forget about that."

"And if I choose not to?"

The music stopped. I decided not to discuss it any further. Our friendship signified the strongest and most pure thing in my life. Jude had stood by me during my worst times, just as I'd done for him. It was why I'd spent months considering the decision for him to take my virginity. I couldn't have our relationship shattered over a night of sex. And that was truly all it would be for Jude. Deep inside, I pretended like I understood that, but I really hadn't until he'd seen the apple gift bag and joked around about it as if it were no big deal, when for me it had symbolized a big moment in my life.

My first time meant everything to me. Bad memories and thoughts saturated my mind and scraped me raw on the inside. I needed my first time to be more than the usual and to bring light to my darkness. Earlier, I figured Jude was that guy for me because he'd always been my soother in a storm. But I'd been wrong.

"I don't understand why you're taking it back." Jude interrupted my thoughts.

"This is the night where history is made!" A tall chick in a mini skirt walked onto the stage with a microphone in her hand. The crowd roared. Everyone up in VIP jumped to their feet.

"Depraved Minds is here!" she yelled. "Y'all ready to party?"

Everyone screamed. I even clapped my hands and stood up. Blue light shined on Kaden's bare chest as he strummed the strings on his guitar. The audience hooted.

Kaden leaned toward his microphone. "Where's Rainbow at?"

"I told him not to do that." Jude got up with me.

"Do what?"

"Rainbow, where you at, baby?" Kaden put his hands over his eyes and searched the area. "Don't hide from me. Everyone yell with me. Rainbow! Rainbow!"

I cringed and hurried over to the balcony, waving my hands at the stage.

"Rainbow!" People jumped around. "Rainbow!"

The spotlight scanned the whole club and finally landed on me. Jude arrived at my side. I said a prayer of thanks for not feeling the effects of that pill yet. It would take time to hit me most likely, and by then, I hoped to not be on a balcony with light shining on my face and blinding me with hundreds of people watching.

"There she is. Isn't she beautiful?" Kaden stared right at me. It felt like his eyes were searing into my skin, or maybe I was imagining things.

Whistles rang out from a few guys below.

"Rainbow, you mean the world to me. Even though I haven't been in your life like I should've been, I've thought about you." He played several notes, ones that froze me like a statue of ice. I recognized them. It had been years, but I knew the song. Kaden played the intro. "So, I had to sing the song that you inspired. Any time I hear it, I think of Jack and his love for you."

Damn it. Of course he would play that song. Of course he'd have no idea how much it would hurt and stir up things that I didn't wish to be in my head at any moment.

My fingers shook as I stepped back from the balcony, searching for a place to run away.

"Ribbons of rainbows don't compare to you," Kaden sang. *"Swollen rain clouds envy the shades that shine from you."*

Drumming came in with a boom.

"At the end of a storm, it's not the clearing of clouds or the sun that brightens the sky. It's your love, your existence, the hope and happiness in your eyes."

Suddenly, my father's image rushed to my head. He strummed his guitar as he kneeled in a pool of his own blood and urine. He'd sung it to me, trying to get me to remember why I should listen to him, why I should help.

"Please, Rainbow," Dad cried. "Do it for Daddy. I can't live with the guilt."

"You're my escape when I am falling. You're my salvation." Kaden moved to the edge of the stage with his head raised up to me as he continued to sing. *"You lift me up and wipe the tears away. You're my salvation."*

"I can't do this." I rushed off, bumping into Jude and slipping away through shocked faces.

CHAPTER 5

Rooftop Promises

I ran out of VIP, not down the stairway that Jude and I had come up from, but via an emergency fire exit. The door slammed behind me. The song "Ribbons of Rainbow" faded out into the silence of the stairwell.

"Just listen to the song, baby." Dad's shaking fingers had played it again and again. *How many times had he played it that night?* It had driven me crazier than I already was. He had barely been able to keep ahold of his guitar, but somehow he'd managed until the last bullet hit him in the center of his mouth.

I squeezed my eyes shut. "No! Stop thinking about it. Stop it."

"Rain?" Jude opened the door and almost crashed into me. "Are you okay? I told him not to play that damn song."

I rubbed my eyes and blew out air. "I just need a moment."

T-Bone stepped out behind Jude. He yanked his shades off and directed his attention to me. "What can I do for you, Rain? Just let me know, sweetheart."

"Nothing," Jude said. "I've got her. I'm just taking her up to the roof." He climbed the first step, and I got behind him, breathing in and out. He looked back at T-Bone as the guard began walking up the stairs with us. "Stay here. I'll call you if I need you."

"Okay." T-Bone nodded.

After a few seconds of going up the stairs, Jude peered at me.

"Did the song trigger…you know…thoughts?" He must've noticed my bottom lip quiver. "In fact, never mind. You don't have to tell me anything. Let's just get you some fresh air."

"Thanks for understanding." I trailed behind him. We took our time.

"Did Kaden see me run off?" I asked.

"Yeah, but he played it off and started singing to the audience." Jude seized my hand as we got in front of two separate pathways of stairs. "Let's take this set of steps. They lead to the farther end of the roof. I used to come up here when I had bad head trips and you weren't here to calm me down."

Jude talked some more. I drowned his words out as I breathed in and out, struggling to get that night out of my head — the crying from Mom, the scent of Dad's blood, and the stench of alcohol on his breath. *Leave me alone. Just fucking leave me alone.* I paused on one of the steps and tightened my grip on the handrail. Tears spilled from my eyes.

Jude drew me into him, lifted me up, and carried me the rest of the way. "Relax, Rain. Nothing is happening right now. No one is here but you and me. Say that for me, Rain."

To block away the dark thoughts, I remembered the other ones I'd created in my head, one where Mom had prevailed.

Dad's body weighed down on me. It was hard to breathe or for him to hear my screams. Even though I cried out, my shrieks were muffled into his chest. My throat burned. I scratched at Dad's skin. We struggled for the gun. So much blood coated it. The metal slipped past our fingers.

"Rainy, baby. Come back to me." Jude carted me forward.

"I'm here." I swallowed down the scream that lodged in my throat and closed my eyes.

"Who's here, Rain?"

"Just you and me."

"And where are you?"

"At some club on South Beach named the Circus."

"And are you safe?"

"Yes."

"Why are you safe?" He pushed through the door and got us outside on the roof, moving quickly as if someone had been chasing us.

A cool breeze hit my skin. The night sounds of South Beach filled my ears—cars honking and speeding off, the rumble of engines, music drifting from clubs, people chatting or yelling out in delight.

"Why are you safe, Rainy?"

"Because you're with me." I buried my face into his shoulder.

"How do you feel?"

"Better."

He hugged me hard and lowered me to my feet. "If you want to go, let's go. I don't give a fuck about spending time with anyone tonight but you."

"No way." I combed my fingers through my hair. "I'll be fine soon."

He'd done so much. I had to stay.

"I just need to take a breather, and then I'm going back to get a drink."

"No drinking. You already took E." He guided me down on the ground to sit next to him. "I told Dad not to play anything from the damn *After the Storm* album."

I waved him away. "It makes sense he would play that song. He doesn't know, so it's not his fault. I can't believe I still can't hear that song without...having a meltdown."

"It wasn't a meltdown. You were just taken by surprise."

A Hispanic man in a suit stepped out. "Mr. Everett, is everything okay?"

"Yeah. Could you bring us up two glasses of water?" He glanced at me. "Do you want anything else?"

"Wine."

"No alcohol, remember? You already took E."

"Then just the water. That should be perfect."

The man disappeared behind the door. Jude grabbed my hand, lifted me up, and guided me several feet near the edge of the roof. A railing surrounded the space, but still my nerves remained jittery.

"Come on and check out this view," Jude said.

I sat down on the ground. He got directly behind me, spread his legs open, and placed me right between them as he wrapped my body in a bear hug.

He nuzzled the back of my neck. "Focus on how amazing our city looks."

South Beach glittered. Luxury hotels pierced the air and glowed in illuminating blues, pinks, and greens. Below, many strolled the streets in an eclectic fashion show typical of the city. That was the number one thing that I loved about Miami. Everybody fit in. All belonged. Some women walked in high heels. Others ambled by in flip-flops. Everything from bikinis to expensive dresses, torn shirts to high fashion suits, draped the people walking by. Dreadlocked hippies ambled toward designer suit-wearing guys with clean-cut hair and pricey shoes.

Salsa music and Reggaeton dominated the air waves as people drove through, blasting their music. So many scents rode the breeze — grilled fish and perfume, to weed smoke and the salty scent of the sea. I breathed it all in deep into my core and focused only on that moment, that instance where nothing else surrounded me but Jude's arms and our city.

I exhaled. "Thank you."

Jude ran his fingers through my curls. "I love your hair like this."

"I did it for you."

"Really? Why?"

I rolled my eyes. "To smooth you over so much so you could be excited about the idea of taking my virginity."

He chuckled. "Is that why you wore that sexy, tight dress?"

"Yes."

"And you say I'm ridiculous. You thought you had to do your hair a certain way and put on some designer dress to get my attention?"

Horns beeped below.

"I was nervous."

Jude rested his hands on my shoulders and kneaded his fingertips into all the areas of built up tension. My skin tingled all over. A wave of calm poured over me.

"I'm starting to feel better." I inhaled and my heart sped up. "I mean, really, really better."

"The pill is doing its magic."

I stretched my arms. "Maybe."

He laughed.

"What's so funny?"

"There was nothing to be nervous about. You didn't have to style your hair like this or sport a tiny dress. I would do anything for you, Rain, but making love to you isn't really going to be some huge sacrifice. I've thought about it…sometimes."

"Really?"

"I'm a man and you're a woman. Of course I've thought about it. Especially when you let me sleep next to you in your room in Sarasota."

"Now, that's going to be awkward the next time you come up."

"Things may be weird regardless after we make love, but I — "

"We're not doing anything. I'm really serious." I looked over my shoulder. "I don't think you should take my virginity."

"Why?" He frowned and had the nerve to actually appear hurt.

"I decided that I was being rash tonight."

"You're never rash. You think shit through for weeks and months. Knowing you, I bet you had a chart listing out the good and bad possibilities of us hooking up."

He was right, but I had no intention of telling him so.

"What changed your mind?"

I shrugged. "I don't know."

"You're full of it. My dad got in your head."

"No. It really wasn't him. I think it was more your whole…seeing my apple bag and just taking it all in stride as if it was no big deal and then running upstairs."

"What was I supposed to do? Jump up and down and bust out a couple of back flips?"

"Not the point." I looked in any direction except his. That anxiety from earlier tonight returned. *Why does this make me so nervous?* The whole point of doing it with Jude was so I'd be comfortable and feel safe.

He moved in even closer so that his body pressed on my back. "Give me another chance. Earlier tonight, you hoped I would be your first. I really did feel honored. I was just caught way off guard, so I fronted a little and rushed upstairs. But when I got to the top, I leaned back against my door and had to catch my breath. I couldn't fucking believe it."

I blushed and chewed the inside of my cheek. "You didn't seem shocked."

"I was more than shocked. I was rattled and shoved off my game. I'm obsessed now. I have to be your first. Asking me to do it made my fucking year, Rain."

"You're never going to let this go, are you?"

"I'll leave you alone tonight, but tomorrow or the day after that, you have to give me a chance to change your mind." He twirled my hair around his finger.

"Just say what you have to say now."

"Okay." He cleared his throat, scooted back, and sat beside me. "You would never regret me being your first because I understand you. I know what happened long ago, so I'd take my time and not pressure you. If you threw up, I would help you clean it up and wait with you weeks later to try it again."

So far, so good.

"I'd do all the girly things you would want—candles, mood music—and make sure the whole ambience is pleasing to your desires."

I snorted.

"Sure, keep laughing, but I'd spoil the hell out of you. You're my Rainy." He gathered up my hair and tossed it over my other shoulder. "I would take my time and go so slow so you could feel every push and pull within you, each lick, and every caress. I'd set your skin on fire."

He leaned into me and sucked on my neck a little, nibbling and tenderly biting it in between sucking. Heat expanded over me. I bit my lip. He could have laid me down right there, and I would've spread my legs for him.

"Let me be your first."

After catching my breath, I gave him a half smile. "Why are you so adamant about this?"

"I love the idea of being your first and knowing no one else will have tasted you but me."

"There will eventually be others."

He smirked. "Will there?"

I hit his back. "Yes."

"You would only crave me." He shrugged.

"Oh God! Just when I figured you were being serious."

"I am serious about your virginity. You opened up the whole situation with the apple bag." He raised his voice an octave and mimicked me. "Here, Jude. Look at my cute little apple. Please, oh, please take a bite."

"I don't sound like that." I giggled.

A small plane flew over so close that the roof vibrated under us as it soared high above. I lifted my face and watched the plane as it rose higher and higher into the dark sky and then finally disappeared.

"That was wonderful." I grinned.

Jude raised his eyebrows. "You mean the airplane?"

I nodded.

"Yep. You're feeling the E now."

"This feels good." My whole body relaxed. The world seemed clearer and distant all at once. The only thing that seemed odd was that my lungs felt heavy and my teeth rattled a little. At least, it felt that way.

"Don't listen to my dad." Jude interrupted my thoughts. "I mean, you do deserve the best man out there, but I'm not that bad of a guy."

I frowned. "Of course not. I think he's more saying that our friendship would change."

"It won't."

"It could."

"Never." He targeted me with his gaze. "We both love each other, right?"

We'd never said it out loud, at least not in a big declaration of love, but it was always understood. Any time I needed him, he was there, and the same went for me. Love bridged between us and was unbreakable through any strife or storm.

"Yes." I bobbed my head. "We love each other."

"Then go back to what you were thinking about, before you entered my house with that sweet little apple."

"Stop saying that."

"I can't help it." He licked his lips. "I bet it's so juicy."

"Okay. Enough with the apple comments."

"I'm going to slice your ripe fruit open and drink —"

"You're killing me."

"Shit. You're killing *me*. Ever since I got that bag, I've been having steamy thoughts in my head. I can barely even remember that blow job earlier from Vicky."

I cringed. "Please don't remind me of that. It's freaking strange how open with sex and women you and your dad are."

A blond waitress arrived with two glasses of water. "Will you need anything else, Mr. Everett?"

"No. We're fine." He handed me my glass. After she left, Jude raised his in the air. "Should we toast to the great feasting of your apple?"

"No. I refuse to toast to that." I raised my glass and clinked it against his. "To two friends sharing a special night together. That's hopefully vomit and hysteria free."

"So you're saying yes?" He kept the glass in the air without taking a sip.

I looked away to hide my blush. "Yes."

"Yes?"

I nodded.

"Okay, but we can't do it tonight. I want this to be really romantic for you, all Romeo and Juliet."

"You're not going to start screaming sonnets outside my bedroom window, are you?"

He winked. "I just might."

CHAPTER 6

The Beat and Rhythm

Jude dragged me out to the dance floor downstairs, which was odd on so many levels. He hated dancing around crowds. People gawked and pointed at him. Men held their cell phones up and recorded his movements. Women "coincidentally" bumped into him and rubbed their bodies against him any chance they could. But he knew I loved to dance, and so he donned a fuzzy Bart Simpson hat and purple heart-shaped sunglasses, snatched up my hand, and towed me to a floor soaked in colored light.

I was the beat and he was the rhythm. We swayed together, our bodies colliding into each other in perfect unison. My blood pumped with adrenaline. Sweat coated both my face and his. I didn't even care as I jumped up, screaming out the lyrics to "After the Storm," one of Depraved Mind's top songs and the best one Dad had written.

"*Though the lightning and thunder blazes the skies, I will come to you and devour all your lies!*" Kaden screamed on stage. "*My love, there won't be any place to run or hide. After the storm, I will come, and you'll never leave my side.*"

Jude lived by one main life motto: when all else fails, jump up and down and scream. So, I did until my feet swelled into numbness, and my voice transformed into a scratchy tone that hurt my throat whenever I talked.

"Twisted love. Dark and twisted like a hurricane. Baby, you keep my emotions twisting and turning in my brain!"

Jude's attention remained on me as he bopped and swung those delicious hips. Before tonight, I would have just averted my eyes and changed my view, not desiring to ogle my best friend's hot body. Tonight, all rules of propriety had smashed to the floor in bits and pieces. Hunger roamed in swirls of heat around me, traveling over my hips, brushing across my skin in sweet, feathery strokes and pumping need into the center of my thighs.

Jude tilted my way. "Stop that."

"What?"

He drew me in to him and moved his body against mine as he whispered in my ear, "You keep looking at me like you're going to eat me."

My mouth dropped open.

"I'm serious about making your first night special, but if you keep staring at me like that, I'll lift you up, tear those jeans apart, and fuck you right here in the middle of this crowd."

A tingling sensation scattered between my thighs. "So, this is *the* Jude, the guy that all the women swoon over?"

"Yes. This is him. I don't tend to have control. If you were anybody else looking at me that way, I would already be inside of you."

He pressed his lips against mine and slipped his tongue into my mouth. Chocolate coated his wet tongue. My legs gave out as he explored my mouth and nibbled my bottom lip. I moaned into him, riding a wave of pure pleasure. If I'd known he kissed like this, I may have stopped being a virgin at fourteen. He withdrew. I charged forward and hauled those lips back to me, relishing their soft texture.

"Damn, Rain." He picked me up and guided my legs around his waist. "You're not helping things."

I rested my arms on his shoulders. This close, his cologne covered me like a blanket—a pine scent mixed with the undertones of wood, something sweet, and other things from the earth. The area between my thighs ached. I tightened my legs around him and pressed my center into his groin, rubbing up and down over the hardness that appeared as soon as we made contact. I felt like I would explode right there.

I bet I could hump him until I come.

Calm down. Get hold of yourself.

"This is going to be so fucking hard." He squeezed my behind.

"You're already hard."

"I'm talking about not fucking you tonight. Stop teasing me."

"Am I?" I ground into him again.

"Oh, fuck it. Keep doing that." He groaned and stared down as I rocked my hips into him. "Does it feel good?"

"God, yes." My clitoris swelled with blood and need.

"Could you come right now?" His voice sounded hoarse.

"Yes." The pressure on my throbbing bud delivered hot sensations through me.

"I bet you're soaking wet." He moved his hands to my hips and guided me hard into him, until all I could feel was his thick dick pushing against my core.

Maybe we should do it tonight.

My stomach didn't rumble in pain like it had with other guys. All the changes in my body stemmed from the lush pressure he gave to my swollen clitoris. I let my head fall back and cried out in satisfaction.

"Right there, Rainy."

"After the storm, I'll consume you until there's nothing left. I'll make love to you. I'll put your body to the test."

The boom of the beat increased. Everyone jumped and swayed fast, pumping and winding their bodies around the dance floor. Jude and I continued rocking into each other. We were entangled into the moment—the song, the feel of our bodies, the heat radiating between us, our scents mingling together, and the mounting of an orgasm that sparked at my center and rose higher and higher, just yearning to detonate into sensual delight.

"Rainbow! Jude!" Someone tapped our shoulders.

The moment broke away. The intensity of the situation vanished. It was like I'd stepped into a freezing cold shower.

Kaden stood next to us. Sweat dripped down his face. He held his guitar and focused all of his attention to my swinging hips.

"Not now, Dad," Jude growled. His erection was stiff and unyielding. He didn't stop pumping it against me, and, as embarrassed with his father being there as I was, I didn't want Jude to end the rubbing. He could have continued, and I wouldn't have stopped until I came.

"Come on, Rainbow. Get on stage with me." Kaden yanked at my shirt, but his gaze targeted Jude. I swore rage lingered between his eyelids, but I wasn't sure.

"What the fuck!" Jude swung me around and put his back to his dad. Madness blazed in his eyes. He'd told me before that when he was on E, he never became angry; he just chilled. Apparently, this would be a first tonight.

"Don't make a scene, man!" Kaden stepped around us.

Right before Jude moved us again, I climbed out of his arms and stood back on the floor.

"What are you doing?" Jude wrenched me toward him hard.

I stumbled into his chest and shoved him away. "Stop it."

"Calm down, Jude! Let her go. You need to cool off." Kaden knocked Jude's hands down.

People looked our way. Realization smoothed over their faces as they realized Kaden had jumped off the stage and begun arguing with some guy in a Bart Simpson hat. People pulled out their phones and were recording their arguing. The music drowned out both of their words, but their faces said that nothing sweet passed between them.

This is ridiculous.

I hit Jude on the back. "Come on. We can finish later. Let's just enjoy the night."

"I don't want to fucking finish later," he countered.

"Oh, stop being a spoiled baby." I got on the tips of my toes and whispered in his ears, "And if you grab me like that again, I'm going to make your nuts regret it."

He scowled at Kaden and stepped around him. "Fine. We'll finish later."

"Okay. Let's go. I have a surprise for you, Rainbow." Kaden clasped his hand on mine, guided me past dancers with gaping mouths and onto the front of the stage. "You thought you were going to escape me tonight?" He signaled for the band to cease with playing "After the Storm" and placed the microphone to his lips. "Hey, everybody. It's time to sing 'Happy Birthday' to Rainbow."

I cringed at the name. It was one thing to annoy me in the privacy of his home with it, but to constantly yell it out in front of hundreds of strangers was another.

"Everyone join me." He set the microphone in the stand and strung out a riff on his guitar that vibrated through my whole body.

A silly grin hit my face. No matter how hard I tried to look cool and collected versus goofy, swooning fan, it didn't work. Kaden's guitar playing always melted me into a fanatical pile of mush. My whole face turned red. He strummed the chords some more with his attention on me and sang the "Happy Birthday" song. Everyone joined in.

Someone tapped me on my shoulder. A kiss to my cheek came next. I twisted around to see Jude without his furry hat, purple glasses, or even the scowl from earlier. Two of the guys in his entourage pushed over a large cart with a huge cake on the top. The cake rose three feet high and arched over in the shape of a rainbow. Candies of different colors represented each ray on the big rainbow cake. Sparkles burst in glittery flares around it.

"Happy birthday to you, Rainy." Jude landed a quick peck on my lips.

Kaden returned to the riff and screamed into the microphone. It was his signature move at the end of a concert. When he finished, he handed the guitar to me. "Tear it up, Rainbow. You're the birthday girl."

I covered my mouth with my hand. "I'm not ruining a perfectly good guitar."

"Destroy it!" he yelled into the mic.

"Destroy it! Destroy it!" the audience roared.

I got on the tips of my toes and put my lips next to Kaden's ear. "Maybe you can sign it and give it to a charity in my name or—"

He shook his head. "Destroy it! Destroy it!"

I rolled my eyes. *So mature.*

The guitar weighed heavy in my hands. No wonder he possessed those huge arms. It was a workout to just hold it. My muscles strained as I raised it up above my head. Everyone jumped out of the way.

"Rock and roll, bitches!" I smashed the end of the guitar onto the stage. Pieces of metal flew in the air. Some hit my legs. Laughter soared out of my mouth. I could barely get a grip on myself in the silliness of the moment. I beat the ground with the instrument again, slamming and banging it until it was only a shredded and destroyed image of its earlier self. All that remained was the neck and some dangling strings.

"'Rock and roll, bitches'?" Jude laughed and embraced me.

"Oh. Should I have said something more poetic before breaking a guitar like an idiot?" I ruffled the side of his hair. "Thanks so much. This is more than I could have asked for."

"You mean the world to me, girl. I had to do it big for you tonight." He nodded his head toward the back stage entrance and slipped out a small joint from his jeans' pocket. "Now, for surprise—what number am I on?"

"I'm not doing it. You know how I feel about mixing drugs."

"Just trust me. I'll be with you the whole time. I have several more surprises in store. We're leaving here and going somewhere sort of private. It'll mainly be just you and me."

"Jude, I'll be in the hospital by the end of the night. I'm not doing E and weed together."

"You're being over-dramatic. We'll drink some more water and head out."

T-Bone stepped out on stage and gestured for us. I snatched the joint and walked off. "You're like the bad guy on a 'don't do drugs' commercial."

"I try."

CHAPTER 7

Dildos, Penis Art, and Raping Swans! Oh My!

"That was just a tiny hit, Rain."

"You're the one that is always doing this stuff. I can't hang." I passed the joint back to Jude as we moseyed through a crowded Ocean Drive. T-Bone ambled behind us with a frown plastered on his face. The only thing he hated more than our drug use was our public drug use.

I'd only had a tiny smoke, nervous that I would pass out if I smoked more. Jude had started drugs at a young age with the help of his dad. Kaden had kept drugs and done them around us all the time and so his actions had made it seem like doing drugs was awesome. Luckily, my dad's actions had shown me just how badly drugs could destroy a person's life and the people around them. Usually, I was severely cautious with my drug usage, limiting it to a joint or two a month.

"Maybe you're right." Jude coughed after he inhaled. "Most don't mix this and E. I just came up with the idea one night hanging with these rappers. I've never looked back since."

"Spoken like a true addict."

A few people whispered as they passed us on the sidewalk. Most paid us no mind. The couple people that did stare at us focused all their attention on Jude's face, probably trying to figure out why they recognized him. Jude attempted to blow a smoke circle. A messy cloud of smoke fled his lips, and filled the air with that pungent, earthy fragrance of "the most blessed leaf" as my mom used to say.

"Tonight is beautiful."

"It's always beautiful here, Rain. You should never leave."

The moon never glowed as bright as Ocean Drive. The buildings gleamed with life. One building had thousands of lights on its surface that blinked off and on in the form of a woman's body as she danced back and forth to her own song. Another swirled with fluorescent pink. Others shined in blue. As a child, I had thought bright lights and vivid colors adorned all buildings in the world until I'd traveled with my parents and spotted the dreary bricked structures and dull glass towers littering other cities.

"Miamians would riot and tear the building down if it wasn't painted in a bright color." I giggled.

"Ugly buildings are bloody against the law."

"Bloody against the law," I mocked Jude. His mom was from England and had been a big porn star in Europe. He'd grown up there until he was six years old. His mom had then moved them to LA, where her adult film career slowly dwindled. She'd stopped raising Jude in his pre-teens, claiming that a growing boy should be with his dad to learn how to be a man. The few times I'd met his mom, her accent had colored every word. Every now and then, Jude slipped into his own Americanized British drawl without even realizing it. He didn't have an accent like his mom, of course, but he certainly used a few Britishisms at times.

I loved to pick on him about it. "Bloody Parliament!"

"You're definitely not getting this back. The moment you begin doing bad Mary Poppins impressions, I pretty much know you're blown out of your mind." He took a long hit. "You're done."

"Oy, me won't bat-ill wif ya, guv'nor."

"I don't even understand what language that is." He scrunched his face up in confusion. "It's like you enjoy butchering words. You're definitely done."

"Rubbish. That's the bloody British accent me mum taught me." I gave him a thumbs up. "Come on, love."

"No. The fuck. It. Is. Not." With each word, Jude dotted the air with his finger.

"I've watched years of *Doctor Who*, dude. I got the accent down."
I wiggled my hips as I walked.

"I'm starting to reconsider our friendship." He let his gaze wander to my hips and behind. "You're lucky you've always provided the sweetest sight of eye candy on this continent or I'd report you."

"Who would you report me to? The queen?" I winked.

He groaned in annoyance.

"I think both of you are done." T-Bone looked back, forth, and side-to-side as he ambled along with us. "Smoking while walking out here is just asking to get locked up. Every damn night you make my job harder and harder."

Jude coughed. "Everyone thinks it's a cigarette."

"Motherfucker, no one is dumb enough to think that tiny thing is a cigarette." He wiped the sweat off of his forehead and took off his sunglasses. "That shit reeks of stinky weed. If I raced up the block and stood there, I'd smell both of you coming."

"Race, really?" Jude leaned his head to the side. "You're not racing anywhere. Maybe more like fast walk for ten seconds and then pass out. Dream much?"

I keeled over and exploded with laughter. "Stop, Jude. Please."

A group of skateboard kids sauntered by.

"Mary Jane! We love you," one yelled, and his friends laughed.

"See." T-Bone motioned to the kids. "They smell that shit."

"We don't truly know if they are referring to marijuana or if they saw Rain and, in fact, figured she resembled a long lost love named Mary Jane." He risked another inhale, threw it on the ground, and stomped on it. "But just in case you try to continue to blow my high, I'll put it out."

"Thanks." T-Bone caught my arm and led me forward.

"Dream much?" I couldn't help it. I laughed more as he dragged me around the corner. "Oh my goodness. I missed it here. When are we going to get to this next surprise?"

We passed a twenty-four hour pizza spot that boasted the best garlic bread on the east coast. The aroma of roasted garlic wafted out of the doorway and carried with it the reggae booming from the speakers nailed over the awning. My mouth drooled.

"Let's stop and eat."

"No, Rain. Food will be where we're going. I'm surprised you're even hungry."

"I haven't eaten since breakfast."

"I don't get hungry when I do E."

"Oy, bugger that then."

He groaned.

Ten minutes later, I lay in Jude's arms with another blindfold wrapped around my eyes. Once we'd gotten close to the surprise, he'd demanded that I cover my eyes with the cloth.

"I'm starting to think that you're a bit kinky, Jude."

"Starting? I've been kinky all my life, love."

"See? English people do say love."

"I'm going to throw you down these stairs."

"You're carrying me upstairs?" I couldn't wait to see the next surprise. "Give me a hint of where we're going."

"What is the number one type of place that you're always trying to drag me to?"

"Art museum." A honey and flowery perfume entered my nose.

"Got it."

"Yes!" I bounced in his arms like a little kid. "Which one? Come on. Let me take it off. Or am I just going to be forced to smell the paint?"

He put me down. "Okay, take it off before I kill you."

I slipped the blindfold away and looked around. White walls surrounded me. Black carpet covered the ground. It didn't seem like the typical art museum I'd been in. I looked in front of me. Royal blue velvet curtains hung in front of the door. On the top, a huge black sign read: World Erotic Art Museum.

"Ha!" I clapped my hands. "You rock, Jude."

"How many times have you said we should come in here? So, I figured if I'm going to go into an art museum with you, it's going to be an erotic one."

T-Bone finally arrived at the top of the stairs. Sweat trickled on the side of his face. He panted a bit and then read the sign. "Lord Jesus."

"Stop it, T-Bone. It's going to be fun. This is probably one place Jude and I won't get kicked out of."

Even though the museum didn't close until four in the morning, I found out that Jude had rented the place for the evening so that we could tour it privately. Although it wasn't several levels like the typical art museum, it boasted a massive erotic art collection — huge sculptures of penises that started at the floor and poked up to the ceiling, nude photos of celebrities like Marilyn Monroe and the Beatles, a rocking dick sculpture that had actually been used in the filming of Clockwork Orange as the murder weapon, and my most favorite of all: a huge bed done in wood where the posts imitated large penises, and on their lengths were additional carvings of sensual scenes between a man and woman.

"I'm going to wait outside until you both are done." T-Bone slipped on his rainbow shades and escaped.

Jude nudged me with his shoulder. "I bet you a hundred dollars he's going to jerk off in the bathroom."

"Eww." Though I could see the urge for T-Bone to do so, if he was actually going to masturbate.

My hormones were on overdrive within my skin. There were so many naked images of women and men in oil or watercolor, drawings on pottery or carved in stone, black and white photography or pop art color. No person was left out — short or tall, fat or thin, and all ethnicities. Yet, everything signified beauty and took my breath away. I was a kid in a candy shop with fifty dollars in my pocket and my parents several hours away from coming to get me. Although he hated one painting that displayed a man with his penis in a meat grinder as a woman in front of him ground it up, Jude added to the moment with his captivating expressions of shock and awe as we analyzed so much art that my head went numb for a few seconds.

"I'm not getting the popularity of Leda and the Swan." Jude held my hand. "It's rape."

"Well, most Greek mythology is popular, and some would argue that she was seduced by Zeus when he took the form of the swan and made love to her."

"It's not only rape. It's bestiality."

"It's romantic."

"Twisted romance."

"The best kind." I dragged him out of the room full of many renditions of Leda and the Swan.

Suddenly, the lights shut off. Jude drew me into him. In the darkness, his hard chest pressed against my breasts. With all the art and the sensual moment we had earlier on the dance floor, my nipples stiffened in seconds. For some reason, in the dark, his cologne attacked my senses. He enveloped me with the smell of him.

Clicking, clanking, banging, and booming sounded all around me.

I jumped.

Jude laughed and tightened his grip on my waist. "Don't worry. My next surprise for you is being put together."

"In the dark?" I asked.

"Yes. They have night vision glasses on."

I rested my head against his chest. "Please say you're joking."

"Do I ever joke about surprises?"

"No. Why not just have me leave the area and then they set everything up in the light?"

"Then I wouldn't have had a reason to buy three awesome night vision glasses. Duh."

"Apparently."

"You smell like roses and peaches. It makes me want to lick your skin." He trailed his soft lips from my forehead to the tip of my nose. I trembled in pleasure. He'd done this before when we would get really messed up and crash in his bedroom. I reveled in those moments of him touching me, hoping that just one time he would capture my lips and go in for the kill, but he never had. Tonight was different.

He lifted my head and seized my mouth.

A violin played in the darkness. Jude loved classical music—well, any music—but classical topped the list. I hated it yet agreed that stringed instruments were awesome in the hands of a skilled musician.

When he finished kissing me, I whimpered.

"God, I wish I could see what your face looks like right now."

"It's probably red."

He sniffed at my neck and ran his fingers through my hair. "Do you feel like throwing up?"

"No."

"Good. I'm like the prince that wakes up Sleeping Beauty." He sucked on my bottom lip. "My mouth holds magic."

"Or the realistic and un-narcissistic reason that I don't throw up when you kiss me could be because I'm comfortable with you."

"Well, either way, it looks like the whole time you should have saved all those kisses for me. I hate to tell you I told you so."

"You were only joking back in high school."

"The hell I was." He squeezed the curve of my behind.

The lights came on. Lust burned across Jude's face. Red tinted his cheeks. I touched them. His smooth skin heated my fingertips.

"I've wanted to kiss you like that for a long time, Rain."

"Why didn't you?"

"Because I like having you around, and you know how relationships and I work out. I'm with a chick. We have sex. I do something to upset her. Later, she stalks or hates me. Most of the time, it's both."

"Yeah. I guess the last thing you would want is for me to hate you." I gave him a weak smile. "With my past, it could end pretty bloody."

His face turned from lust to sad. "Don't say that, Rainy."

"It's just a joke."

"Not funny." He separated from me and guided me into a dark room lit with sea-green candles. A table stood in the center, set with two plates, bowls of food, and more candles. A violinist stood in the background and played a song I recognized, though I couldn't think of the title.

"What is she playing?" I asked.

"'Ordinary People' by John Legend."

"Love it."

"This is surprise number twelve, I think. I've actually lost count in between the joint and the dancing at Circus."

"Doesn't matter. I appreciate everything. I'm going to have to start planning your birth weekend now just so it will be equally awesome."

His birthday was the day before Halloween which guaranteed some sort of freaky costume party and trick-or-treating incorporated into the celebrating. When we had turned eighteen, I'd left out trick-or-treating from the celebration, and he'd tripped for an hour.

"You can't celebrate my birth weekend without trick-or-treating, Rain." He'd pouted and I'd had to play it off as a joke and then quickly get his friends together for a hastily thrown together trick-or-treating event.

Maybe we'll trick-or-treat on South Beach at three in the morning. That should be interesting.

Jude steered me to my chair. "Hungry?"

"Starving."

"After this we're going to—"

"There they are." Kaden headed in with Vicky on his arm. "What the hell, man. You both rushed out of there like you all were running from the cops or something."

"You told him where we were at?" Jude glared at T-Bone as the guard marched in next.

"Your dad wasn't invited?" Kaden sniffed his nose and rubbed it. He must've done cocaine. He moved fast around the room, his eyes darting from side to side as he checked out all of the art. "Man, this is freaky."

"Sorry. You didn't tell me that you were avoiding him." T-Bone did his best at a whisper.

"It's not that I'm avoiding him. I just didn't want to share my time with Rain."

I stared at all of the plates of food and realized that Jude was right. I was no longer hungry, just happy in the moment. "It's fine, Jude. Let's just have fun."

Something crashed behind us. We all turned to see Kaden standing next to a broken sculpture of tiny vaginas. "Fuck me. I hope that doesn't cost too much."

Jude snapped to get T-Bone's attention. The guard turned his way as Jude said, "Let's try to lose him when we go to the tattoo parlor."

"Tattoo?" I shrieked. For three years I'd contemplated getting a tattoo of a fairy on my lower hip. I'd drawn it myself but never summoned enough courage to just get it.

"First we kiss some more, smoke again maybe, and then we get tattoos," Jude explained. "I was thinking it would be real cool to get the same thing. What do you want?"

"A cute little fairy sitting on a huge mushroom."

He placed his forehead on the table. "Kill me now."

CHAPTER 8

Blow Jobs Gone Wrong

*T*hey fought all night. I hid under my blankets, hugging my doll to my chest, as if the more I squeezed her the more I could quiet my dad's and mom's curses.

"This is my house!" Dad's voice boomed through the walls. Glass smashed against the wall that my bedroom and parents' space shared.

"This is our house and keep your voice down," Mom argued. "You don't get to come in here if you're drunk and high off of whatever you're messing with now. Get out!"

"Fuck you! I bought this house — "

"We bought it. You take your shitty-ass money with you if you think you're going to walk in here smelling like whores and drugs and think you're going to lay down with me."

A door slammed. Another did after it. Footsteps banged by my room.

"I'll call the cops!" Mom screamed.

"Call them, you grimy tramp. Call them like you always do. I'll fucking be upstairs in my bedroom, wanking off since my wife is too good to do it for me!"

I had to pee, but I stayed in my bed. The bathroom was across from my doorway. I pressed my legs together to calm it.

"I'm on the phone with them now!" Mom called out from downstairs.

"Oh, yeah? You'll be dead before they get here!" Dad stomped through the hallway to the stairs.

No. Don't kill Mommy.

My nerves flared. Urine ran down my leg as I cried into shivering hands.

"Rain." Someone shook me. "Rain."

I pushed the hand away and opened my eyes. Salty sea air brushed against my skin. "Stop, Jude. I'm awake. Quit shaking me."

"The sun is coming up, Rain. You told me to wake you before you missed it."

"I did?" I scanned the area around me.

We lounged on the front of Jude's new Bugatti. As far as I knew, he was the only one that owned a custom-built, four-door Bugatti. It must've cost Kaden a lot of money to spoil his son with it, but then again, many corporations gave or leased him items with the promise that he would make sure to be seen on TV or in the news with them.

My back lay against his windshield. The beach surrounded us. Jude had driven as close to the shore as he could without getting water in the car. His tires were probably messed up by now. I hoped we wouldn't need a tow truck to help us out.

"Yeah. You did." He smoked his joint, coughed, and handed it to me.

My mouth was dry. My waist ached and stung. The memory of getting my tattoo rushed to my mind. I yanked down the waistband of my pants and stared at it in shock. "Wow. I thought I asked for a fairy on a mushroom."

"You changed your mind after we took a quick smoke. You drew that and were screaming about how we both should get it."

I strained to get a closer look. Instead of a fairy, a different tattoo greeted my eyes — a ripe, red apple rested on a coiled gold and sea-green snake. Its tiny tongue stuck out and formed the word "Jude."

"Holy fuck! I've got your name on my body?"

"I told you that you would be pissed when you came down from your high, but you insisted."

"Yeah, right. I bet you were just *so* fighting against me putting your name above my panty line."

He snorted and lifted his shirt. "Well, I wasn't against it. I thought it would be cool too, which is why I put your name on me."

I directed my attention to his glorious six-pack and laughed. Right next to the delicious path of blond hair that traveled into his jeans was the exact tattoo that I had, except the snake's tongue formed the word "Rain" instead of "Jude."

"Do you remember what you said in front of the tattoo artist as he drew it on me?" he asked.

I covered my face in horror. "Oh God. What did I say?"

"'Now, when groupies give you a blow job, they'll see my name.'"

"Awesome." I slumped back with embarrassment.

He watched me. "Any regrets on the tattoo?"

"No." I checked mine out again. "This actually is cooler than the fairy. Plus, the fairy was just something I liked, whereas this symbolizes so much more. I'm glad I got it."

"Well, I'm glad you're not upset. Now, any regrets on the hot and steamy sex we had in front of everybody at the tattoo parlor?"

"What?" I looked down at my clothes. They didn't appear messed up at all.

"Just joking."

"You could've kept the joke going. Clearly, I don't remember much after we left the museum."

The sun crept up over the surface of the ocean, layering the sky into dark oranges and golden rays that pushed away the darkness above it. It was beautiful. Waves crashed against rocks as we continued to watch. Birds flew by, traveling through the sky as it transformed from night to day right before our eyes.

I exhaled and leaned my head on Jude. "Good idea. I may not punch you in the balls for waking me up now."

"This was your idea while we tried to sneak away from my dad who started preaching to me about the misfortunes of fucking a good friend."

"That would be me, of course. The good friend?"

"Yep."

I yawned. "Where's T-Bone?"

"You thought it would be funny to run from him too. He's going to whip your ass when he sees you next."

"So not my fault." Another yawn fled from my lips. "Did we ever escape your father?"

"Sort of."

I closed my eyes and rested a little, promising myself that I wouldn't fall back asleep but instead take a few minutes to chill. Time passed with just the sound of birds talking to each other and the waves traveling back and forth.

"Dad thinks I'll treat you like shit after we have sex."

Well, that woke me up.

I opened my eyes and peeked at him. "Will you treat me like crap after we have sex?"

He sucked his teeth. "I can't believe you have to ask me that."

I shrugged. "You do tend to sleep with women and never truly deal with them again."

"I couldn't do that to you. Who the hell would I call at night and talk on the phone with? Who else would deal with my crap?"

"Good point."

He put the joint out on the surface of his car.

"I can't believe you just did that."

"Such is life." He flung the joint out on the sand.

"You ruined an almost priceless car's surface and littered at the same time. You're going to hell."

"You'll be there with me."

I tensed. He'd been joking, of course. Yet, I often wondered if I would, in fact, go to hell for all the things I'd done in my life.

"What are you thinking about?" he asked.

"How spoiled you are."

"You sound like Dad. He kept on saying that I could sex any woman I desired, so why hook up with you?"

I squinted my eyes and stared at him. "Your dad is really getting to you, isn't he?"

"Why do you say that?"

"You never go on and on about something like this unless you're bothered by it. Are you thinking about backing out of this? It would be fine if you did."

"No." He leaned all the way back on his windshield and tucked his arms under his head. "When I said I've considered sleeping with you, that was an understatement. If my spank bank ranked the most-viewed fantasies in my mind, it would be hot ones of you riding me."

That woke me up completely. I cleared my throat. "Me riding you?"

"Yes. With your hair splayed all over your shoulders and those big breasts bouncing up and down. I wonder what color your nipples are."

I stiffened in shock. "Do I say anything?"

"My name, but it's weird. You do it in your mom's Jamaican accent. Sometimes your mom is there too."

I hit him. "Okay. I don't want to hear any more. You're disgusting."

"Oh, like you don't touch yourself to dirty thoughts." He turned his head my way and laid it on his hands. "You ever touch yourself thinking of me?"

"Maybe."

"Tell me more."

"Do you have any water?" I closed my eyes.

"I'll give you some water if you tell me what you picture me doing to you." His voice held the same sort of excitement as when he was opening a gift or really hyped up about something.

"It's no big deal." I stretched my toes, suddenly realizing I wore no shoes. "We don't even have sex. At least, not the way it is defined."

"Boring. Give me some details."

"I have my legs open and you're between them."

"Are you naked?"

I struggled to not blush. "We both are. I'm touching myself— "

"Where?"

I bit my lip. "My nipples."

They hardened as I imagined the thought. The car moved under my legs. Jude moved closer to me. I opened my eyes as his hand snapped the top of my jeans open.

"What else?'" He pulled the zipper down inch by torturous inch. "Don't worry. We won't have sex. I just want to…"

"What?"

"Get us familiar with each other."

"That's it?"

"I don't know. All I can think about right now is having my fingers inside of you. Blood is no longer flowing in my brain right now. It's somewhere else. Now, tell me what else I do."

I swallowed. "You stroke yourself right in front of me."

He dove his hand into my pants and slid his fingers into my panties.

I gasped. My heart pounded in my chest. My fingers balled into tight fists. I didn't know what he was going to do, but I damn sure didn't want him to stop. Relief flowed through me. There was a reason why I hadn't let anyone touch me. The very thought of other guys placing their fingers anywhere on my skin made me break out in hives. But Jude's touch inspired the opposite. I moistened right as his finger tenderly stroked me.

He scooted over to me and kissed my cheek. "What else do I do?"

"You rub your penis—"

"I don't have a penis, Rain. I have a dick. Say it." He gently bit the curve of my neck. Shivers of bliss waved through me. His stroking moved in a circular rhythm.

"You put the head of your dick on my clit and rub it over and over until I come."

"Hmm. You're so nasty." He entered his finger inside of me. "I love it. Tell me more."

I arched my back and could only whisper, "Mmm."

"You want to come right now?"

"Yes." I rocked into his fingers and felt ready to pop.

"You think you can handle my tongue right here." He glided his thumb over my aching bud.

"Yes."

"I'll lick you right now if you take off these jeans as well as promise me that you'll keep your moaning down so you won't wake up Vicky and my dad."

I scrunched my face up into confusion. "What?"

"They're in the back, knocked out." He sucked on my neck and slid his finger in and out of me.

I moaned and forgot what he'd even said as hundreds of shivers stimulated all of the cells in my body and awakened desire in my core.

He rubbed his cheek against mine. "Not too loud, Rainy."

"Actually, we're up and enjoying the show. Be as loud as you want," Kaden said from behind us.

I shoved Jude away, which was difficult with his finger still working deliciously over my clit. "Stop it."

"Why?"

"Your dad."

"Fuck him. I don't want to stop."

I punched his arm. "I do."

He wrenched his fingers away. "Sorry. You're just so fucking wet."

Rage curled in my chest. I tried not to show it, but I couldn't stop from frowning. Plenty of times before, he'd told me about the crazy things he and his dad did with women. They'd had sex with twins in a McDonald's bathroom once. Thankfully, they had done it in different stalls. Last Christmas, he'd called me from Russia at three in the morning, crying about how he'd taken acid with his dad and thought they'd had a threesome with some Russian waitress on a pool table after the restaurant closed. As we talked, he began to realize that the memory was false. Sure, they'd shared the same waitress, but not at the same time. The whole moment ended up being a bad head trip, yet Jude thought that horrific scene could be his future if he continued using too many drugs with his dad as they hooked up with women. From then on, he kept a decent distance from Kaden.

"Are you mad at me now?" Jude's voice came out in a low whisper.

"I'd rather not do stuff in front of your dad." I made sure to not say, "Or with your dad," hoping that was understood.

"Me either. You're not the type of woman I'd share with him or anybody else. You've got to know that." He touched my ear with his lips. "It's just that you started talking about imagining my dick when you touched yourself, and it made me stop thinking for a few minutes. It won't happen again."

"Okay." I zipped my jeans back up, inched over to the side, and jumped off of the car. "You still could have told me they were behind me."

"I forgot you didn't know."

Sand smoothed against my bare feet. I trudged to the passenger side of the car, happy that Kaden didn't say anything else and further embarrass me. Glasses wrapped around his face. Fake jade diamonds bordered the glasses.

I bet those are the shades T-Bone gave me for my birthday. I just had a hunch. "Are those my glasses?"

"They were in wrapping paper." Sun reflected off of the dark glasses. His face tilted in my direction. "So, you're going to do it?"

"What?" I opened the front passenger side and climbed in.

"Give him your virginity."

I groaned. "I think the best part of getting this virginity thing over with is that I won't have to hear you bring it up anymore."

He laughed for a minute.

The car swayed from side to side a little. I figured it was Jude getting off of the hood, but he stayed there with his gaze glued to the sky. I glanced over to the back seat.

Kaden grunted.

What the hell?

Vicky's head was positioned in his lap. It moved up and down. Her red head whipped back and forth as she worked her mouth. He fisted her hair in his hands and pushed her down some more. Choking sounds ensued. She moved faster.

The car rocked. I should have turned away. I didn't. My body already throbbed in need from Jude's lips and fingers. I kept telling myself to turn around, that it was weird to watch, and what would Kaden think. I peeked at his face for a few seconds, and what I saw froze me in my seat. He'd taken the glasses off, as if he wanted me to know that all of his attention was centered on me. He licked his lips and my nipples tingled. I spun around, not really sure what else to do. I looked at Jude. Snores rumbled from his chest as it slowly rose and fell.

Of all the times to fall asleep, this is definitely not one of them. What the hell did he smoke to make him pass out like that in seconds?

Kaden groaned. "Yeah. Right there. Suck it harder."

My whole body was set on fire. I couldn't decide if the heat came from desire or straight up embarrassment. I curled my toes. My panties moistened and my jeans felt wet.

How sick am I?

"Oh fuck." He grunted again. "I'm close, sweetheart. Don't stop."

I should jump out and go…anywhere. Wake up, Jude. If I just get out quickly, will it even be a big deal? But then what would I say when I come back?

Either way, the situation balanced on the edge of unpleasant and uncomfortable. I set my hands in my lap. Kaden released deep, guttural moans. The urge to touch myself itched in my fingertips, but I couldn't. What the hell would he think, or Vicky, or especially Jude, if he woke up and saw me finger-banging myself to his father's moaning?

What is wrong with me? Is it odd to get turned on by the sound of sex right next to me? How the hell could anybody not be turned on?

The car's rocking sped up.

"Fuck yeah!" he roared. "Take it all. God damn you!"

I closed my eyes, happy that they were almost done.

Vicky giggled. Movement rustled behind me.

I tapped my toe on the leather floor mat. *I'll give them a minute or so and then I'm waking up Jude so we can go. I'll just have to convince him to let me drive.*

Vicky coughed and made a big show of spitting over the edge of the car, which made me uncomfortable. Or maybe I was just disgusted by her giving a public blow job, or by Kaden watching me the whole time, or by my own fit of voyeurism.

CHAPTER 9

Indecent Proposal

When I decided enough time had passed, I fumbled with the door handle and escaped.

"Wait, Rainbow." The sound of Kaden zipping up his jeans sounded behind me.

"I'm waking up Jude." I made sure to not turn back around and see him doing anything else.

"Let him sleep. I'll call us all a cab. Just chill out, Rainbow."

How can he call me Rainbow after he just had his dick out? No wonder Jude is always stepping over people's boundaries. He never learned them from his dad.

"Okay. Just yell for me when the cab comes. I'm going to take a walk over…there." I hurried off.

A car door banged. "Rainbow."

Oh God. If he thinks we're going to talk like regular people, seconds after he came, then he's dead wrong. At least give me a few minutes to get over the uneasiness of it.

"Rainbow?"

"Yes." I continued moving forward.

"Hold up."

"Why?"

He captured my arm. "Come on, give me a minute."

I gestured to his hold on me. "Seriously? You don't find this weird at all?"

"Me grabbing your arm, or shooting a load into Vicky's mouth in front of you?"

"Oh God! Let go of me."

"I'm sorry. Should I have said something more romantic?" He let me go and followed me as I rushed off.

"I'd rather you give me a few minutes to process what just happened." Sand skittered under my feet as I marched toward the shoreline. Cool water washed over my toes. Being this close to the water gave me the opportunity to lose myself in watching the sea. And that's what I hoped to do — escape beneath the waves and forget what had just happened.

After a minute of silence, Kaden broke it. "You're so dramatic."

I ignored him.

"You have your legs wide open, close to being taken by my son on the hood of his car, right in front of me — "

"I didn't know you were behind me."

"Sure you didn't."

I ceased from walking. "Are you trying to say I did?"

"Fine, you didn't." He placed his glasses over his eyes. *My* glasses.

"I didn't know you were behind me!"

"Okay. Okay." He raised his hands in the air. "But you have to admit that you stared at me while Vicky sucked me off."

I glared at him.

"Just admit it and I'll leave you alone."

"I kind of looked for a minute," I muttered.

"What was that?" He cupped his ear and leaned my way. "I can't hear you, Rainbow."

"Yes. I watched, and stop calling me Rainbow while we discuss you and blow jobs." The more I walked, the deeper my feet sank into the sand, and water pooled around my feet. It soaked the bottom of my jeans.

"I bet it made you wet."

I flinched like he'd slapped me. "When I got into the car, why didn't you stop?"

"Stop what?" He quirked his eyebrows. "I hope you don't mean stop getting a blow job. It's damn near impossible when she'd been sucking on me for that long."

Disgusting.

"Why didn't you stop looking?" he asked.

Because I was horny and you're hot and most women's fantasy, including mine. And clearly I'm just as sick and perverted as you. Anybody with an ounce of decency would have fled from the car, right?

"For the record, watching Vicky give you a blow job was not tantalizing at all. It was sort of like seeing a stray male dog humping a female one and getting his penis stuck in her. You know you should look away, but you just stare all the same."

"You're full of it. Give me the real reason."

I sighed. "I don't know why. And I did look away."

"Eventually." He chuckled to himself.

I stopped. "Jude's right. You have to pick the role you want in people's lives. You did this big declaration on how you wanted to be my friend, and now it sounds like you're trying to hook up with me."

"Oh, I get a role with you now? I've been trying to be in your life for years, and you avoid me like I'm some old, degenerate nutcase."

"Well, you're not old, but the jury is out on you being a degenerate nutcase."

"You're not funny." He stepped closer to me. "So, you're saying that getting a blow job in front of you was unusual?"

"You know it is or you wouldn't be out here talking to me right now." I crossed my arms over my chest. "And you were looking at me while you were getting it."

"Because you were watching me. I'm only a man, after all. Vicky's lips were wrapped tight around my cock. I'd already heard you moaning with Jude then you brought your sweet little innocent ass in the car and stared right at me like you wanted to join the fun."

I edged away. "I didn't."

He pressed his lips into a straight line.

"Don't look at me like that. I didn't. You're my dad's friend." I snapped my fingers next to him like I was trying to wake him up. "Remember? That would be seriously twisted. And Jude would go bananas."

"Would he?"

I didn't really know. Jude and his father had a strange relationship, one with few limits and definitions. I assumed he wouldn't have liked me sleeping with his dad due to the way he'd reacted about Kaden hitting my behind. But, Jude relished being my protector. He could've just been trying to save me from one of his dad's advances.

"I have no idea how Jude would feel about us messing around." I pushed a seashell away with my toe. "Not that I would ever need to find that out."

"Well, maybe he would." Kaden shrugged. "He thinks you're more innocent than you actually are."

"Oh, really? More innocent than I actually am? You really have me all defined, don't you? Since I'm such a slut." I stormed off. My hair blew and rose in the wind. My Oscar the Grouch T-shirt waved against my skin.

"No. You're not a slut, but you're not a nun either."

"I never claimed to be, Uncle Kaden." I spat the last two words at him and glanced over my shoulder. The car was far away and appeared small from where we were walking. Vicky had climbed out and was studying us as we argued.

"You're no longer allowed to call me Uncle."

"Is that due to the freaky blow job?"

"That and your moaning, and maybe other things." His gaze traveled down my body. "Like your strutting around me half-naked."

"That dress wasn't for you, so it doesn't count."

"Doesn't matter. You've been sauntering in front of me with that ripe body, just waiting to be…"

I peered at him. "You might as well finish. You've already hit the record for boundary pushing today."

"You're not innocent of anything either, Rainbow." He caught my arm and spun me around. "Your best bet this summer is to stay away from Jude and me. You're playing around with fire, and the only person that's going to be burned is you."

"I've known Jude all of my life. He won't hurt me. And you obviously must be high and drunk. It's one thing to finish off a blow job behind me, but it's an entirely sicker thing to openly state that you want to hook up with me."

"Hook up with you?" He chuckled. "Rainbow? I'd spread you wide open and consume your soul. You'd have nothing left to give to another man."

Curiosity coursed through my veins. I battled with not getting excited. It was wrong for me to be interested in him or what he said. *How pitiful have I become?* Kaden hit me hard with the truth. I was flirting with disaster and seeing just how far I could go without being destroyed in the process.

"Look at that face." He grinned. "You're considering it all, aren't you?"

"No."

"It's sad to see you try to deceive yourself, because you're definitely not deceiving me."

"So, is this what you meant last night when you were cooking for me and talking about Dad? Is this your definition of being in my life?"

He looked away. "Clearly, things aren't the same."

An exasperated breath left my lips. "What the hell happened from then to now that would cause such a huge change from Dad's crazy friend to creepy old guy trying to sleep with me?"

He smirked. "Creepy old guy?"

He stepped close to me. His stiff chest pressed against my hard nipples, setting off a rush of hormones which were begging me to take my shirt off and do more than just touch. He inhaled and groaned. "Shouldn't you be backing away from the creepy old guy?"

I swallowed and inched back.

"I won't lie to you. When I opened the door last night, my dick surged. I hadn't been that hard in years. I thought God had blessed me with a new adventure. But then you spoke, and I recognized that voice as my little Rainbow, so I ordered my dick back down and tried my best to shift into the guy I should be." He moved forward so that we slid against each other again. "Then I discovered you're a virgin, and the hottest things ran through my head. Still, I tried to leave it alone. You walked around in that tight dress—"

"I'm…going back to the car."

He caught me and pulled me back, encasing me in his arms. "No. You asked me why I desire you now, so let me tell you."

"I don't want to know."

"Because it's not proper?" He imitated an old English accent.

I shoved him away. "Yes. This is improper on so many levels. I don't have time to list them out."

"But the problem here, Rainbow, is that you would let me fuck you if we were alone and no one could see you being so bad. You would happily bend over and show me that sweet little pussy and let me lick it, wouldn't you?"

"No." I bit my lip.

"I could make that happen. We could meet somewhere private. No one would have to know but us." He inhaled me. "I just want to lick you and see what you taste like."

My heartbeat banged in my chest. "No."

"Please, Rainbow. It would be so good if you gave it a chance." He brushed his erection against my thigh. "I'm rock hard again, just because you're next to me. You have no idea how bad I would like to tear that damn shirt off."

I stumbled back. "I can't...and Jude would—"

"Jude will just hand you over to me after he's done anyway."

My breath caught in my throat.

He targeted me with a hungry gaze. "Change your plans for this summer unless you want my cock inside of you by July."

I blinked. "I-I'm not just going to—"

"I want you. It's wrong, and that could be why my cock twitches in my jeans every time you walk by, but the fact still remains that I want you, so give me some fucking time away from you."

I combed my fingers through my hair. "You're crazy. So you're saying avoid you—"

"And Jude."

"Why Jude?"

"If you think he won't shred your heart into tiny little pieces, then you're crazier than me."

"You don't know him like I do."

"Yes, I do. He's my boy. Like father, like son. Breaking beautiful women's hearts runs in our family. My father did it. I do it, and Jude does it every damn day. It's not intentional, but it's what happens."

He shook his head. "If you were anybody else, I wouldn't care. I'd slip in the bed right after he's taken that sweet little pussy, but I see the way my son looks at you. He cares about you. You're important to him, maybe even more than me. If he hurt you and then eventually lost you due to his stupidity, it would crush him."

"He won't hurt me."

"He will."

"First of all, I promised him my whole summer. You're barely here. So you should leave."

"I'm not going anywhere. Jude's starting his music career. I've never been able to teach him much in life, but music is something I know I can show him. I'll be here until the album is done." He dug his hands into his pockets and edged back. "Fine. I won't convince you anymore. In the end, I crave you as bad as he does. It's only a matter of time."

I was too scared to ask, but I did anyway. "It's only a matter of time before what?"

"Before you're drowning with nothing around to save you." He walked off back to the car but called over his shoulder, "If it's not me hurting you, then it'll be Jude."

CHAPTER 10

Cruel Intentions

Hours later, Jude and I lay in bed together. I had my back to him as he held me. I'd ended up calling Thompson to pick us all up because Kaden never called the cab. He'd simply returned to the car and passed out next to Vicky. Jude had remained snoring on the hood. By the time Thompson had arrived, it had taken me several minutes to wake all three of them up and steer them into the town car. The whole time, I'd sat on the phone with a tow truck to haul Jude's car back to his mansion. When we'd gotten to their place, I'd intended on going straight home, but Jude had begged me to come up. I reluctantly had.

And there we lay in the bed in my designated guest room. I'd taken a long shower and stepped out of the bathroom to see Jude half-naked and lounging under the covers. We usually didn't sleep together. The only times we had was in my dorm room, because there was no room for him to sleep anywhere else, and for some reason Jude had refused to get a hotel. He'd claimed he enjoyed roughing it and hanging out like the college kids did.

"You smell so good." He buried his face into my damp hair. "I'm going to get tubs of that fruity shampoo and make sure it's in your bathroom every time you stay with me. What scent is this, mangos?"

"Strawberry surprise."

"Delicious."

"Umm hmm." I drifted toward sleep.

"Is everything okay?"

"Yes."

"You seemed really uneasy during the ride home."

Because your father spent the whole drive back here ogling me as he fondled the tops of Vicky's breasts.

His gaze had forced me to turn my whole body toward the window and keep my view centered outside the door instead of on Kaden's fingers.

"Did Dad do anything?"

"Nope." I cleared my throat. "I'm fine."

He tossed my hair over to the front and planted kisses on the back of my neck. "You sure about that?"

"Yes." I shrieked as he bit my skin. "Ouch."

"Sorry. Serves you right for smelling so sweet." He released me and turned me on my back. "Vicky said you and Dad were arguing."

What was Icky Vicky trying to do, get me in trouble or something? I sucked my teeth.

"She said Dad ran over to you when I was sleeping, and you both looked like you were yelling at each other, and then later she thought maybe you were making out."

Yeah right.

"We weren't fighting or making out." I turned around and faced him. "She's being nosy and trying to start something. If she doesn't keep my name out of her mouth, I'm going to snatch those red strands out of her skull and choke her with them."

"Calm down. I told her to stay out of anything where you're concerned. I explained it wouldn't be healthy to mess with you."

"No, it wouldn't."

"So, what actually happened, and what did he need to say to you?"

Should I tell him?

I'd planned on not saying anything and just avoiding Kaden for the rest of the summer. It wouldn't be difficult. He liked to stir things up, and then when he became bored, he left. At least that was the man I remembered.

Jude studied me as I pondered what to do. "Is it that bad?"

"Promise you won't get mad."

He shook his head. "No. Fuck that."

"Oh well then." I closed my eyes. "Get some sleep."

He shook my shoulders. "Now you have my attention. What did he say?"

"Promise me you won't get mad at him or me. No arguing or fighting with him."

"What did he do?" He sat up and shifted his face into a neutral expression.

"We both kind of did something." I sighed. "Remember when I hopped off the hood of the car and sat in the back?"

He nodded.

"Vicky was giving your dad a blow job in the back seat."

"Yeah. I know."

"You knew?" I lightly punched him on his arm. "That was so awkward."

He remained with that stiff gaze. "Did you join them or something?"

"No. Hell no. Why would you ask me that?"

Still, he didn't relax his expression. "So?"

"I kind of watched for a few seconds. It was like I couldn't look away, and your dad was kind of staring at me the whole time."

"And?" The muscle in his jaw twitched.

"That's pretty much it. I turned around. They finished. I left the car, and he followed me out to the beach. He claimed I should get away from both of you before I got hurt."

Jude averted his eyes. "Maybe you should."

"You think you're going to hurt me?"

"I don't plan on it, but clearly Dad has some ideas in his head. What else did he say?"

"He said he wanted me." I couldn't even look at Jude, but I made myself do it. "And he said that he knew I wanted him too."

"Do you?" He studied me.

My fingers shook a little. I placed my hands under the blanket as his gaze seared into my flesh.

"Tell me the truth, Rainy."

"No. I'm not interested. It would be crazy and wrong and just really not a good thing. Plus, that would complicate everything, and who does things like that? Not me. I'm—"

"You're babbling." He frowned.

"I'm not."

"You babble when you're nervous and lying."

"This topic makes me nervous."

"Because you like him or at least would love to have sex with him." He lay down next to me. "Just admit it. I'd rather you not lie to me. I hate when people lie to me."

"I don't like talking about this."

"Okay. If, back in the day, your mom had cornered me in a room, tore off all her clothes, and tried to sex me, I would've lain down and let her." He rested his face on the pillow right in front of me so that his eyes were level with mine. There was no humor on his face. It seemed odd to see him not smiling or winking and being witty. "Would you have sex with my dad?"

"You're sick."

"Yes. I am." He captured my lips and sucked on the bottom, but still, his eyes had an edge to them, one I wasn't used to seeing. "So, tell me the truth. You ever imagined having sex with him? Did you let him touch you on the beach today?"

"I don't like this conversation."

"So that's a yes." He lowered to my neck and kissed it. Earlier, the touch of his lips was sensual and soft. Now, he pressed down hard on my skin. "Tell me. You let him kiss you like you let me kiss you?"

I refused to say anything else and didn't enjoy his line of questioning.

"Why are you so quiet? What is my dad doing to you when you think about fucking him?" He yanked my shirt down in a rush of rough movement. It tore at the top.

"Your dad isn't doing anything to me." I shoved his hands away. "Stop it."

"Is he rubbing his dick on you like in your dream of me?"

"No."

He wrenched the shirt down again and dipped his tongue between my breasts. I gasped as he sucked on my left breast hard, so hard it stung a little.

"Stop that." I slid away from him.

He glared at me. "Tell me what my dad does."

"No."

He lifted his right lip up in a sneer. "Why not? Is it that bad?"

Who is this Jude? He's never acted like this around me before.

He rolled over onto his back. "Why are you so quiet and pushing me away?"

"I'm sorry. I'm not excited about you kissing me while you ask me how I masturbate to your dad."

"So you do?"

"I-I didn't say that. I'm —"

"You do. It's written all over your face, Rain." He put his hands under his head and rested on them. "I hate when people lie to me. Just tell me the truth."

I swallowed. "I have once."

"Or twice?"

"Maybe. And it's not that I'm lying to you. I just don't want to freaking admit things like that. It's okay for people to have dark thoughts and not share them."

"Not when it's you and me. We don't keep secrets, and we don't lie to each other."

"I'm tired. Let's go to sleep."

"It's really not a big deal." He turned away from me. "If you want him, have him."

"I don't."

"You're lying."

"Even if I was, I wouldn't have sex with your dad. I can't even believe we're arguing about this."

"We're not. I'm perfectly fine with you fucking him."

Yeah right.

I scooted over to him and held him from behind like he'd done with me earlier. His body tensed under my arms.

"That wouldn't be cool. I would never do that."

"We're just friends, Rain. I wouldn't have cared if you'd joined Vicky and him earlier." He moved my arms away. "You can do anything you'd like to do. You're my buddy, not my girlfriend or wife. We have fun and don't set up a bunch of rules."

"Well, I care. I wouldn't want you to do that to me."

He laughed. "Dad is right then. You probably should stay away from us, because if your mom propositioned me like my dad did you, I would have fucked her right there on the beach without another thought."

It was my turn to sit up. "Are you joking?"

"No."

Silence passed for a minute. My mind clouded in confusion. Part of me felt relieved that he wasn't mad about me fantasizing about his dad. The other part was pissed he had admitted to having no problem with hooking up with my mother. He'd said we were just buddies, and that was true, but I couldn't pretend that for some weird reason I thought I meant something more to him.

What had I thought we were?

I realized that I wasn't his girlfriend or anything like that. I'd watched him hook up with girls and take them home so many times, and it had never been a big deal. I'd never had a boyfriend or even a date that hadn't ended in total failure, but I imagined if I had, Jude would've been cool with me dating and been nice to the guy.

Still. We're not just friends.

I guess deep down inside, I believed I was special to him. He'd confided in and told me secrets that no one ever knew. Once, he'd confessed that a twenty-year-old woman had taken his virginity on his fourteenth birthday, all at the order of his father. Kaden was high one night and had decided it would be awesome for his son to finally experience a woman. The groupie had snuck in his room and woken him up with a blow job. Afterward, Kaden and his friends had burst in there, hugged him, and declared that Jude was finally a man.

I remembered the night like it had happened yesterday. Jude had snuck over to my house the next day, waited for Mom to leave, and told me all about it. The oddest part to me about the whole confession was how unsettled he'd seemed, as if he was unsure if that was a good thing for a father to do or not. He'd plastered on a weird smile as he'd given me all of the sick details, and at the end, he'd lain next to me without speaking another word. At fourteen myself, I hadn't known what to say and had just hugged him the rest of the day until finally my mom had come, and he'd had to sneak out through my window.

Jude glanced at me over his shoulder. "What's up, Rain? I thought you wanted to go to sleep."

"I was just thinking."

"About my father?" He frowned.

"That's not funny."

"Oh God." He rose, threw off his blankets, and got out of bed. "You overthink everything, Rain. Just have fun."

"Just have fun? How, by being shared by both your dad and you?"

"It doesn't matter if we share you, as long as you enjoy being shared."

"I'm not interested in it."

"Sure you're not."

"And I'm not overthinking."

"Yes, you are. If you want to hook up with my dad, then do it."

"I-I don't."

"Whatever." He headed to the door.

"Where are you going?"

"Are you my wife now?" He raised his eyebrows at me. "I have an erection due to kissing and being next to you. It's not like your innocent little self is going to do anything about it right now, so I'm going to yell for Vicky."

Fury boiled within me. "Your resident slut?"

"At least she understands what she wants and goes after it." He opened the door and slammed it shut.

"What the hell does that mean?" I called back and scanned the guest bedroom, searching for a sane person to explain to me what had just happened. Hadn't we been cuddling and talking like friends? Then the next minute, all of a sudden, we're arguing about his dad, and he wants to leave?

Vicky understands what she wants? Give me a break.

I decided to yell out something mature. "I know exactly what I want. To not be friends with a dickhead!"

Yep. Totally mature.

"Vicky!" Jude yelled near my door. He had to be standing right in front of it, which was ridiculous. His bedroom stood several feet away from my guest room. There was no need to be calling out to her where I could hear it.

I formed my hands into tight fists. He was lucky I'd left my purse in the town car with Thompson, or I would've maced him right there.

"Vicky!"

Is that really necessary? Does he have to make sure I hear him going after her?

"Vicky!"

Female giggling ensued from a distance. A door opened and closed; at least, I think that was what I'd heard.

"What's up, baby?" Vicky's footsteps stomped past my door.

"I need you to take care of me." Jude's voice sounded right outside of the damn room. Right outside of it!

I gritted my teeth when the sound of slurping came next. My door banged, likely from him leaning her against it.

Don't do this, Jude. Don't do this to me.

"Take off your shirt." His voice held an edge.

Is he going to really have sex with her right here?

Vicky moaned, and I cringed and rushed out of bed, putting on my pants as fast as I could.

Why is he doing this? What is he trying to prove? What the hell happened to make him so mad? Or was he even mad? Maybe this was the Jude that women dealt with. Perhaps this was the Jude I didn't see when I stayed in the friendship category. Possibly this was what other women experienced each time they had sex with him.

Moody, sick asshole.

The door banged against the wall's frame, I assumed due to him pounding into Vicky, as he grunted and groaned. And, completely ashamed of myself, my eyes watered with tears, my stomach balled into knots from hurt, and I couldn't admit to myself why. He was just my friend. I shouldn't have been mad or upset, so full of hurt and crying like a baby. I wasn't his wife or anything else but his buddy.

But is this what you do to a buddy?

"I guess," I muttered under my breath, marched to the door, and opened it.

Vicky screamed as she fell back.

Jude cursed as he crashed to the floor with a bang.

"My back hurts." Vicky rubbed it.

"Good." I stepped over her and hurried down the hallway.

"What the fuck, Rain?" Jude yelled at me.

I checked behind me to see him grabbing his dick. Unfortunately, I got a good look at his impressive equipment. He was as big as Vicky had claimed, and I hoped I'd injured it somehow.

Maybe it's broken, and he'll need a cast and can't use it for the rest of the summer.

"You could have hurt us!" Jude roared.

"That's what I was hoping for, dick weed! What did you think I was going to do, lie in bed and listen to you fuck her?" I ran down the stairs. "I may not be your wife or girlfriend, but you don't have to treat me like I'm nothing!"

I stormed the rest of the way to the front door in angry silence.

Downstairs, Kaden peeked out of the kitchen with a v8 in his hand. "Everything okay?"

"Oh, go ram that v8 up your sick ass." I threw up my middle finger. "You're right. I need to stay far away from the both of you."

He chuckled like the evil bastard he was.

I got out of there like my sanity depended on it, because frankly it did. Jude, Kaden, and even Vicky were on another level. If I personified the uptight category of people in the world, then they were the highest plateau of open-mindedness that I knew I could never reach. *Never.* I believed in boundaries and limits. I thrived on them. Most of all, I could never imagine hurting Jude, no matter what.

I pulled out my phone and dialed Thompson for the second time that morning. *Poor guy.* I made a note to get him a gift this summer.

CHAPTER 11

Paparazzi-Filled Apologies

The rest of the day blurred as I drifted in and out of sleep. Jude called several times as I slept but didn't leave a message. An unidentified number showed up on my phone too. I figured it was Kaden. I was surprised Mom didn't add to my missed calls list. I ignored them all. Once I got up, rather than deal with them all, I shut my phone off and planned my day. I bought a ticket to the opening of a play I really wanted to see, made reservations for one of my favorite restaurants, and headed off to the spa for a mani, pedi, and massage.

I just needed a break from Jude's world — the parties, drugs, sharing women, and doing or saying anything they wanted, like driving on a beach in a car worth six figures, or traveling down a taboo path just because they needed to see how far it would go, or even having sex with a girl against my guest bedroom door so I would have to listen.

When I saw him again, I would simply explain that having sex with him would not be an option. *That would be after slapping the shit out of him and stabbing a fork into his groin. In fact, I'd better wait until I calm down before I talk to him again.*

His rudely fucking Vicky against the door of the room I sat in had kicked my thought process into overdrive. A simple truth filled my head: Jude and I saw sex, respect, and relationships differently. To me, sex was this intimate act, something that you shared with a special person. At least, that was what I imagined for my first time. Sure, maybe later I would become more comfortable with having sex. I'd be more casual and relaxed.

But I hadn't considered the fact that maybe Jude would sleep with me, then jump up after that special moment, and an hour or so later sleep with Vicky or whoever else walked around their mansion at the time. And naturally, he had every right to do it. We were just friends. But it would still hurt. I became jealous just thinking about it. Maybe I wasn't being real with my feelings for him. Jude considered me just a buddy. Perhaps I thought of him as something more or even hoped that after we shared that night, that something bigger would flow between us.

I wasn't insane. I didn't think we would be girlfriend and boyfriend or that my vagina would be the one to snare him into monogamy when others hadn't. But, I had imagined that maybe we would make love again and that he'd show me respect, that things would remain the same between us yet change in regards to our relationship becoming deeper.

Oh God. Who am I kidding?

I might have dreamed of us being together a little. I should have left it all alone. Our friendship surpassed anything else in my life. We truly loved each other. We spent all of our time together. There was no need to yearn for more, especially with Jude. I doubted he could even give me more or give the respect that I required.

Just stop thinking about it. Don't let that great, relaxing massage go to waste.

I took a hot shower after my massage and dressed in a new white sundress I'd bought. Once I finished, I placed my phone to my ear. "Thompson, I'm ready."

I headed toward the spa's front exit. There were several secret ways to leave the spa due to the huge celebrity client list that the place boasted, but I'd made sure to keep out of the spotlight. Despite my parentage, I was hardly a celebrity anyone ever recognized, so I left the same way normal people did. A few paparazzi who sat across the street perked up when I opened the door and then sat back down when I stepped out onto the sidewalk, probably figuring I was just a nobody and wouldn't garner any excitement from a magazine or newspaper.

My dinner reservations started in an hour. I'd planned to drop by the book store, grab a new sci-fi book I'd been excited to read, and check it out while I ate. No complications tonight. No over-sexed fathers or inconsiderate friends. No riled up memories of my dad before his death. Just a yummy meal, a great book, and an awesome play.

The first thing that told me my night wouldn't go as planned was the fact that Thompson sped away in my mom's town car instead of jumping out and letting me in. I rushed outside and waved my hands. "Thompson! I'm right here! Where are you going?"

Jude and T-Bone pulled up in front of me in another car. I had never seen this one before, so it had to be new. T-Bone drove and avoided my eyes, which tended to be what he did when he knew Jude was going to do something stupid. He wore a new pair of shades, orange ones with palm trees on them. That was another bad sign. A switch of glasses in the middle of the week signaled a bad mood or a trip.

I crossed my arms over my chest and scowled at Jude. "Did you tell Thompson to leave?"

"I gave him a thousand dollars and told him that T-Bone and I would be driving you around this evening." Jude jumped out. He wore black pants and a white button down shirt that was open at the top. He could have been stepping onto a runway instead of heading toward me. His blond curls moved with the breeze. "I'm sorry about earlier today. You look beautiful, by the way."

From across the street, chatter among the paparazzi started up; they must've been racking their brains for why Jude looked familiar.

"Thank you for apologizing, but Jude, I already made plans tonight. I'm sorry, but I can't cancel. Besides, I'm still pissed. All I will do is fight with you right now."

"Sure." He bobbed his head as if he understood. "What're you doing?"

I dug in my purse for my phone so I could tell Thompson to return. "Things that I'm excited about and things that are not with you. I'll hang out with you next weekend."

"Next weekend?" He moved my purse away and pulled my hand out of it. "You're playing with me, right? I'm not waiting until next weekend to see you."

"Then tomorrow."

"That won't work either."

A crowd of teenagers strolled by. One whispered and pointed to Jude. The girls in the group giggled. They must have recognized him. He put on a fake smile, waved, and gestured for me to get in the car.

I shook my head. "I need a break."

"From who, me?" He leaned his head to the side. "You need a break from me?"

"I'll see you later." I inched back and returned to getting my phone.

"I said I was sorry."

"I heard, and thank you. I just want to hang by myself."

"No."

I paused and glared up at him. "No, what?"

"No, you're not getting a break from me tonight. No, I won't wait until next weekend." Anger was clear in his eyes, but at least he kept his voice down. "You get a break when you go back to Sarasota. You've only been in Miami for one damn day. I want to hang out with you."

"Too bad. I don't stop what I'm doing for people who try to hurt my feelings." I pulled my phone out and dialed Thompson's number.

Jude snatched it out of my fingers.

I sighed. "That's not funny."

"What are you doing tonight?"

"Besides going to the courthouse to get a restraining order?" I tapped my feet several times.

"The courthouse is closed now, and I don't think they're open on the weekend. You'll have to wait to get a restraining order against me. In the meantime, I'll be stalking you the rest of the evening."

"Funny." I looked at T-Bone. "Could you control Jude for me please?"

"I'm out of this," T-Bone muttered.

"Good, then you won't step in the middle of this when I punch him in his nuts." I formed my hands into a fist.

T-Bone choked a little as he laughed.

"Are you hanging with someone else tonight?" Jude asked. A serious expression remained on his face.

"Yes."

The muscle in his jaw twitched.

I checked my watch. "And I don't want to be late."

"You told me I had your whole summer. Now you have a date with someone else? Did you lie to me?"

"You do have my summer, but surely you couldn't mean every minute of my time. There will be moments like these where I'm going to be doing something else."

"I made plans for us tonight."

"Then hang out with Vicky. Let her *take care of you.*" I extended my hand his way. "Give me my phone."

He put my phone in his pocket. "I'm not interested in hanging with Vicky. I made plans for you."

We stood there in silence. Cars drove by. People traveled the sidewalk. I was sure the receptionist inside the spa had been ogling the whole event. I needed to get out of there before our simple conversation was posted to the Internet. One of the paparazzi across the street had already started focusing his camera on us and was snapping pictures. I shuddered to think about what gossip magazines or blogs would come up with. *News Flash: Top Party Guy Jude Everett and legend Jack Kenner's daughter were spotted outside of a high-end spa, arguing about her pregnancy.*

"Rainy. Please forgive me for earlier today and spend some time with me. I was an idiot. I shouldn't have disrespected you like that. Now, let me make it right."

"Cool." I tapped my foot some more. "Let's do whatever you want to do tomorrow night."

"No. I'd rather not."

"I don't care."

"I'm sorry."

"Good."

"That was stupid and immature and…fucked up."

"Yep, but I'm still not hanging with you."

A camera flashed on the side of us. I turned to see a guy in regular jeans and a shirt, snapping pictures with his camera. It was the same photographer from across the street.

Most likely not wanting any more pictures taken of him, Jude captured my waist and slung me over his shoulder as I screamed out curses and beat his back with my fists.

"This is stupid. Put me down. T-Bone, please make him put me down."

"Not in it," T-Bone replied.

"Who's this, Jude?" The guy snapped another picture and almost pushed the camera in my face. "Is this a new girlfriend? What's her name?"

T-Bone finally rushed out of the car and pushed the paparazzi forward. "Get back and give Mr. Everett some space."

"Could this be the one, Jude? You were with actress Polly Michaels last week," another man with a camera yelled as he crossed the street.

I froze as I hung like a ninny on Jude's shoulder.

"Come with me, Rain. It'll be fun." Jude carried me over to his car, opened the back door, put me down, and gestured toward it as if no one was even around. "Please, get in."

The two guys took more pictures and barraged Jude with questions. "When is the album coming out? Who is this? Will she be featured on the album? Will your father be singing on some of the tracks?"

More people began to surround us, just passersby probably wondering why the two men were photographing us, and it made me nervous. Even though T-Bone had good control of the forming crowd, I felt trapped.

How the hell does Jude do this every day?

I tucked my hair behind my ears, dug my hands into my purse, and pulled out my birthday glasses. I'd swiped them from Kaden when he was asleep in the back of the car and then later disinfected them to rid the glasses of the pervert's germs.

Ignoring them, Jude targeted me with that deadly blue gaze. "Please, get in."

I jumped into the car and slammed the door, shielding my face the whole time.

He hurried to the other side and stepped around everyone. "Give me a break, guys."

"Come on, Jude. Answer a few questions," one of the photographers yelled as T-Bone climbed back into the driver's seat.

"Short interview, please," another begged.

"Do you see the lady I'm with?" Jude chuckled. "Would you want to stand with you all and answer questions, or ride off with her?"

The men snickered.

Jude hopped in and closed the door. T-Bone sped off. Loud blues music blasted out of the radio. Any time T-Bone drove, he enforced one rule: the driver gets control of all music. So I wasn't surprised that he played blues.

When Jude and T-Bone had met, it was years ago in a studio somewhere in Georgia. T-Bone had told me the story one night. Jude had fought with some pianist over writing credits. He'd held his own until the opponent's band mates joined in. T-Bone had been recording a blues demo, heard the racket in the studio room next door, and scurried over there to break it up. T-Bone had ended up getting hit. The next thing everyone knew, he was slinging bodies into keyboards and drums, slamming trumpets against legs, and yanking Jude out of the pile of bodies, recognizing who he was. T-Bone's demo had never gotten any interested responses from record companies. Somehow Jude had found out and offered him a two-fold deal—he would fund T-Bone's first album as long as he served as his bodyguard during the whole time. Now it was three years and no T-Bone albums later. I had no idea if he was interested in being a blues singer anymore, but he sure loved playing it.

"Thanks for not making a big scene." Jude rubbed the sweat off of his forehead and tilted his body my way.

"I wouldn't do that to you."

"I know, but thanks anyway." He continued talking as T-Bone stopped the car at a red light. "I'm so sorry, Rain. I was a dick. I get that."

"Okay. But I'm still not hanging with you tonight." I turned away from him and stared straight.

"Because you made plans?"

"Yes."

"With someone else?"

Is that what this is all about?

I rolled my eyes. "Actually, I'm just going to do a me night."

"Book, dinner, and a play?"

"How did you know?"

"That's what you do when you're not with me." He tilted my way and kissed my cheek. "If you really are excited about whatever play you're going to, then we'll do that. I'll take you to get your book and watch you eat. I miss you and feel like shit for doing what I did earlier today. I just got so mad, and Dad trying to have sex with you pushed me over the edge. I should have just punched him in the face."

"I'm not interested in him."

"You're lying, so let's not discuss it."

"I'm not—"

"How much more do I have to beg you to let me come with you? Are you going to punish me so I can get it over with and spend some time with you?" He brought his face forward. "Slap me."

"Dear Jesus," T-Bone muttered. "This white boy has lost his mind."

"I'm not slapping you." Even though my hands itched to paint his lovely cheeks with pain.

He kept his face in front of me. "This is the agreement. You slap me as hard as you can, and then all is forgiven."

"But you'll just do something like this again."

"I'm not fucking perfect, Rainy. And you can't see the future. Just fucking slap me so we can be friends again!"

"Are you sure?" I rubbed my hands together. "Because I'll do it. I've been thinking about it all day."

"Do it." He closed his eyes.

I reached my hand back and used all the force I could as I slapped him with no mercy. A loud smack sounded, then a red hand print stained his face.

He swayed back a little and rubbed it. "Goddamn that was hard. Really? Have you started lifting weights, or something?"

"No." I stuck out my lip and pouted.

"Why are you freaking looking sad over there? I'm the one with the injury." He scooted my way. "Will you kiss it for me?"

"No."

He formed his lips into a frown. "Do you forgive me?"

"Yes." I leaned back like a conquered fool. Jude had me right where he wanted me. I forgave him just like that, and even worse, I no longer felt like being alone.

"I should be driving you both to a mental facility." T-Bone chuckled and turned up the song.

Jude ignored him and focused on me. "Are you still trying to get rid of me?"

"No."

"Are we going with my plans or yours? I never finished giving you your birthday surprises. T-Bone, grab that thing for me please."

T-Bone unclasped the glove compartment, pulled something out, and handed it to me.

I opened the tiny booklet and saw my picture. "Why do you have my passport?"

"If we do my surprise, then you may need it, so I brought it along just in case."

"How did you get into my house?"

He winked. "Your housekeeper, Lisa, is in love with me. Okay. Decision time. Is it my surprise or your play?"

I chewed on the inside of my cheek. "No more ecstasy, right? Last night I was so high I blacked out."

"No pills or weed. Just a little wine."

"How are we getting there? Do I need to pack?"

"Everything is taken care of."

"Okay. Fine."

"Take us to the airport, T-Bone."

Out of nowhere, T-Bone did a U-turn. A few cars honked. Drivers yelled curses out of their windows. He sped off, turning up the blues music even louder.

"He's no good! Oh Lord, he's no good!" The woman's voice came out loud like a scream but couldn't exactly be defined that way because it had a harmony to it. A harmonica rang out a harsh tune with fierce guitar notes adding pain to each word. *"Lord, show me your plan. 'Cause I can't get over this man."*

"We'll need to take my dad's private plane to get there." Jude set his arm around my shoulders. "It should be less than an hour and a half. You can eat something small when we're up in the air, but don't ruin your appetite."

Unease settled in my gut at the mention of his dad's name. "Will it just be you and me, or will Vicky and your dad be coming?"

He chuckled. "Just me, Rainy. No Dad or Vicky. Just you and me, like it always should be."

"I check on him daily. Make sure he ain't running around. Oh Lord, I check on him daily. Make sure he ain't running around. Came home one night, Lord. He was laying two women down."

I laughed at the lyrics.

T-Bone joined the woman's singing. *"Oh Lord! He's no good!"*

CHAPTER 12

One Bite

About ninety minutes later, we landed on one of the islands in the Bahamas. After I stepped outside, I caught a glimpse of the early evening sky and breathed in the fresh island air. Jude slapped a blindfold over my eyes and carted me off into another vehicle.

"I'm starting to feel traumatized by all these blindfolds." I tugged at it a little to get a peek of my surroundings.

Jude tapped my hand. "Oh, quit complaining, Rain. You love my surprises."

It took us another five minutes to arrive at the next place. He helped me out and wrapped my hand in his soft fingers. Blind, I walked wherever he led. Piano music played in the background. A cool breeze brushed by, bringing a natural salty fragrance with it, so I knew we still had to be outside. I could hear the crashing of waves too.

Okay. We're on a beach or near the sea somewhere.

"Take off those sandals." Jude squeezed my hand. "Do you need my help?"

"No." I slipped out of them. Cool sand slid under my feet.

Okay. We're definitely on a beach.

He lifted me up and carried me. I shrieked and then fell into a fit of giggles. "Why did you ask me to take off my sandals if you were just going to carry me?"

"Just be quiet and enjoy the ride."

"Gee, you're so bossy right now."

"I'm more impatient. I really want to do something and it's driving me crazy."

"What is it? What do you want to do?" I rested my head on his shoulder. He didn't answer. I exhaled a long breath. "So we're on the beach. That's a good sign."

"Why?"

"I've always had good things happen around water. I think I have a strong connection with it."

"You and every other human."

I stuck my tongue out and blew.

"I'm really sorry about this morning, Rain."

"Forget about it." I nuzzled my head against him. "Did I hurt your penis?"

"I don't have one, remember? The art geeks you hang with in Sarasota have penises. I have a dick."

"Penis."

He paused. "Say it, Rainy."

I bit my lip. "Dick."

"And who has one?" He pressed his lips against my cheek.

"Jude has a dick, apparently as big as a wine bottle, according to Vicky."

An explosive laugh fled his lips. He continued carrying me to wherever we were going. "Vicky should stop doing drugs. She's hallucinating."

"So, did I hurt your dick?"

"Hurt what?"

I grinned. "Your dick."

"I love when you say that and, no, everything is intact."

I wondered if it was a good time to tell him that I no longer desired him to be my first. Things were flowing well right now. We'd laughed and joked on the plane as we sipped on martinis. He'd listened to all my boring stories about college — trying to pledge a sorority and giving up in the middle of pledge week, how my art history teacher had embarrassed me in front of the whole class because I'd mistakenly emailed him one of Jude's dirty jokes instead of my homework assignment, and even the failed dates I'd had with guys that creeped me out. The whole time, he'd sat there watching me with this fascinated expression, as if my regular life entertained him.

"Okay. Here we go," he said.

The piano music sounded closer. Fabric pressed against the soles of my feet. He lowered me onto a blanket, I assumed, and captured my lips.

I tensed and moved away. "I think we shouldn't kiss anymore."

"I think that's a bad idea." He nipped at my bottom lip.

"Aren't you going to take off the blindfold?"

"No." His breath tickled the skin on my shoulder. "Why do you want to stop kissing me?"

"I think that it would be a smart idea." I raised my hands to remove the blindfold.

He stopped them and pulled me into his embrace. "Are you thinking of taking back your offer of giving me your apple?"

"Maybe." I arched up as he dropped several delicious kisses near the top of my sun dress.

His lips touched me in slow, seductive movements along my chin and down toward the curve of neck. My nipples grew hard. He slipped his hands over my breasts and rubbed them both with his fingers. Sparks of desire burst all over me.

"I know I messed up, but give me another chance."

I leaned away from his hands. "Let's talk about this without the blindfold."

"No way. You have to keep the blindfold on for a while. We'll have to talk about it later. This surprise is about the senses."

I grinned. "You're really scaring me right now. The senses?"

"Yes." He slipped his hands down the sides of my waist, by my thighs and legs, and finally stopped at my bare feet. He massaged the soles. "I love this color on your toes. What is it called?"

I relished his hands' attention so much that it was difficult to concentrate. "Brandy wine."

"Beautiful." He spread my feet apart. "Did someone massage your feet at the spa today?"

"Yes."

"Did they do your whole body?"

"Pretty much."

"Were you naked?"

"Pretty much."

"Did a man or woman massage you?"

"Does it matter?"

"For my sanity, it does."

"Meaning?" I moved my feet away from his hands and tried to remove the blindfold again.

"Keep it on, or I'm going to tie up your hands."

"You wouldn't."

"You don't truly know me, do you?"

"Apparently not." I blew out a long breath. "I had no idea about this blindfold fetish you have."

He removed his hands.

Movement sounded at my side. My heart stopped. I didn't enjoy not knowing where I was or what he was doing.

He kissed my ear.

I jumped with a shriek.

"Relax, Rainy."

I extended my hands out to touch him. His silky skin yielded under my fingers. I traced the hard bridge of his nose, the arch of his eyebrows, and the outline of his full lips. The whole time, he groaned. Sensations fluttered in my chest. I knew we should end this and not go any farther.

But I can't stop touching him.

He trapped one of my fingers within his lips and sucked, encasing it in the moist warmth of his mouth. As much as I tried to keep it in, a whimper fled from me.

He released my finger. "Open your mouth."

I swallowed. "Why?"

"Because I really need to put something in it."

I covered it. "If you put your penis into my—"

"I don't have a penis."

"If you put your *dick* in my mouth—"

"Stop thinking so naughty and relax. Open your mouth for me, Rainy." His voice warmed my body, flustering my senses.

How haven't I realized how sexy his voice sounds? Maybe his face and lush body drowned out all of my focus.

I parted my lips and hoped for the best. If Jude did something stupid, I couldn't just call up Thompson to pick me up. I'd have to use my credit card. Mom's accountant monitored all of them and notified my grandmother of anything out of order, so it would be my last resort.

"Good girl."

I rolled my eyes under my blindfold.

"I really wish I was putting my dick inside that sweet mouth, but this will have to do."

Something warm and wet slipped between my lips. Caramel and a fruity juice coated my tongue. It was a piece of pineapple dripping with caramel. Smiling, I ate it.

"Was that so bad?" He stroked me with something soft and light.

I gasped, trembling under its light touch. "What is that?"

"A feather." He ran it down to my chest.

My breasts longed for release. They felt heavy and swollen with need. I squirmed a little as he glided it across my shoulders and down my back. "You're really taking this to the next level, aren't you?"

"I'm trying to show you that you can trust me to please you." He placed a chocolate covered strawberry on my tongue next.

"Well, you're doing a good job so far." I hummed in pleasure.

"You like that?"

"Yes."

"I had a catering group whip up some treats for you so that we could have a little picnic on the beach."

"A blindfolded picnic?"

"Yes."

More sweet fruit came. I recognized other blends—banana in powdered sugar and cinnamon, melons slathered in a berry sauce, tiny circular cakes soaked in rum. The whole time, the piano played romantic tunes with sensual harmonies that pushed visions into my mind, like slow sex under stark white sheets in a luxurious beachside room where the window stood open, letting the air flow through. Each time Jude fed me, I nipped at his fingers and heard him grunt with desire.

Why did I wait so long to try Jude? Goodness. He has me going crazy.

Once I'd held up my hands and said I was full, he exchanged the fruit for his finger laced in warm milk chocolate, and then his caramel coated tongue. I sucked on it hard. All earlier thoughts about not sharing my first time with Jude evaporated into the sea air. I yearned for him so badly that my body rocked with desire. I craved him. Even I could smell my arousal in the air.

He whispered in my ear, "Tell me why you're squirming like that."

"You know why." I licked the last bit of caramel on my lips.

"I guess I do." I heard him sniff and whimper next to me. "You're so wet. That perfume is filling the air. Every time I inhale, I get harder and harder. I wish I could lock your scent up and put it in a bottle." He laid me down on my back and kissed me some more. "You really think that you can convince yourself that I'm not the one to taste your apple?"

"I'm not sure." I writhed under his hands as they traced my whole body.

"All these years we've known each other. I think it was always meant to be." He glided the straps on my sun dress down but didn't lower it to expose my breasts. Instead, he slid his lips across my skin, making me shiver in delight and speeding up my pulse. My heart boomed in my ears. He licked a path over my shoulder to the tops of my breasts, and with each inch of licking, he nibbled and sucked until I was wriggling beneath those fingers and grasping for the blanket under me.

"There won't be another man that will take your virginity." He pulled the blindfold off of my eyes.

It took time for my sight to return. When it did, he appeared above me. Hunger creased every inch of his face. Above him, lavenders and pinks, turquoise blues and shades of gold merged into dark blue and painted the sky. Palm trees swayed around us on the beach. Crisp white sand spread across and connected with a clear blue and turquoise ocean. We lay on a green silk blanket. A large tray of tiny clay pots with various sauces rested next to the plates of fruit and cake. I turned my head. A black man in a suit with a blindfold over his eyes sat in front of a piano as he played. No one else was on the beach but us and the piano player.

"I rented this portion of the beach just for us."

"This is an amazing surprise." I directed my attention back to him and ran my fingers through his silky blond curls.

A neutral expression covered his face. "Did you hear what I said? There won't be another man."

"We should…talk about this later." Right now, I had no idea what I desired. One minute I didn't want to take our friendship out of our cozy existence. Next, I lay on my back with his delicious lips all over me. I tried to get up.

He shook his head. "Don't avoid this. Being with you means too much to me."

"Can we at least talk about this with me sitting up?"

"No." He placed his hands on my waist and pulled me in closer. "I don't think you can think when I'm next to you like this."

"So you'd rather I didn't use my brain when considering you as my first?"

"There's nothing to consider, Rainy." He raised the bottom of my dress. Air slipped against my bare leg. He dove his hand under my dress and caressed my thigh. "There won't be any other guy before me. I decided that earlier this morning when you ran off."

"That's what *you* decided?"

"Yes."

"You don't get to decide for me, Jude."

"Then maybe your body will decide for you."

I wriggled a little as his fingers journeyed up to my panties. Although my body burned with excitement, my hands and arms transformed to wobbly jelly. I suddenly didn't know what to do with them, so I forced them to remain at my side while I froze under his touch.

"Relax. I just want to touch you."

"So, earlier you said there won't be any guy before you." I slowly breathed in and out as his fingers danced on my skin. "Before you? It sounds like you think our having sex is inevitable."

"It is." He slid his fingers under the band on my panties, and inch by inch, he pulled them down. "Let's not pretend like there has never been any sexual attraction between us. Why not act on it?"

"Because we may end up hurting each other or..." I paused as he yanked my panties down my legs.

"Or what?" He guided his fingers between my thighs.

Dear God.

"I forgot what I was going to say," I mumbled.

This feels like heaven.

"I won't hurt you." He toyed with my clit as it swelled under his fingertips. "Do you believe me?"

I moaned and lifted my hips into his hands. Every brain cell focused on the pressure of those magical fingers, touching me the way I'd always dreamed someone should, caressing me the way I'd tried to do myself but never truly could get it down like this. If I'd been wet before, now I bathed his hand as he worked me to a bundle of shivering nerves.

"Rainy?" he whispered and dipped his tongue into my ear. "Do you believe me?"

"Yes," I moaned, having no idea what he was saying, just knowing that he couldn't stop or I'd die.

"Then tell me that it will only be me." He removed his hands and I whimpered. "No more backing out or saying you're undecided. I want to hear you say that no other man will be between those thighs. Only me."

Even though he'd removed his fingers, my body clenched with pleasure. I squeezed my thighs and felt moistness between them, dripping down my skin.

"Only me," he said through clenched teeth.

I raised my eyebrows. "Are you mad?"

"Please say it." He averted his eyes from my view for a few seconds, as if to calm down.

"Only you."

"No other man." He pierced me with an intense gaze.

For some reason, that scared me a little. "No other man what, Jude? No other man to take my virginity, or no other men period?"

"No other man." He took off his shirt, unbuckled his belt, and completely undressed.

I couldn't help but drool. He was all tanned flesh and tight muscle from his abs to his thighs. He wore no underwear. A thick and long erection greeted my eyes. My mouth dropped open. Suddenly, I wasn't confident about him putting it inside me anymore. He wasn't as big as a wine bottle, but he wasn't small either.

How bad will it hurt? Are they all this big? Maybe I should start off smaller and then work my way up?

"Fuck. The way you're looking at my dick makes me want to do naughty things right now."

I drew on all the courage I could find. "Then do it."

"Say what I want you to say." He took off my dress. The fabric moved down my body with ease. He groaned as he undid my bra, and my breasts fell heavy in front of him. My dark nipples pointed right at his face, pleading with his mouth to come to them. "Say it for me, Rainy. No other man."

"You're the only one that will take my virginity."

Tossing me a wicked grin, he climbed between my thighs with his dick in his hand. "That's not what I asked you to say."

"Then explain what the whole '*no other man*' statement means."

"Stop overthinking it."

"Stop being vague."

He placed the tip of his erection on my clit, and I melted into the beach right there. I fell into that one part of my body his dick touched as he circled it around me, gathering up moisture, and drenching me in arousal. I cried out in delight.

The piano song skipped a few notes and paused for a second. The player fumbled with the keys, gave up, and began playing a new song. "I'm sorry, sir."

"No problem." Jude massaged me with his mushroomed tip. "I wouldn't be able to play a song either if I heard that moan."

I blushed in embarrassment, but I had no time to think about it as he focused all of his dick's energy to massaging my now swollen clit.

"Touch your nipples for me just like in your fantasy."

I brought my fingers up and teased them a little. Desire flickered on each pebbled point. My calm breathing transformed to desire-hungry panting. A murmur of something left my lips. I had no idea what I'd said, just that I would be coming soon and hard.

"How does it feel?"

"So good," I moaned.

"Do you want me to keep doing this or do you want more?"

My hands shook as I pinched my nipples, but I couldn't back down, not when every cell in my body burst with lusty craving. "More, please."

He lowered down until he lay on top. His muscular chest pressed against mine. His cock lay between my thighs so close to my opening, I almost cried out with hysteria for him to pierce me. He lapped at my right nipple and then sucked on it hard. I crumbled into nothing but ecstasy.

When he stopped, he gritted his teeth and almost growled as he whispered, "Say it for me, Rainy."

"Oh God." I squirmed under him impatiently. "Please fuck me, Jude. Stop talking and put it inside of me."

A strangled moan came deep from his chest. "Damn it. You're driving me crazy. Just say it."

"What the fuck do you want me to say?"

"No other man."

"Why?"

"Because I need to hear it."

I loudly exhaled. "No other man."

In that moment, he entered me, inch by inch. I gritted my teeth from the initial pain. Digging my nails into his shoulders and crying out, I tensed from the invasion.

He paused for a few seconds. "How bad does it hurt?"

It was in that moment when I realized that my face had scrunched up in horror. "It's freaky, but…I like that you're inside of me."

He licked his lips. "Trust me, I love it too. Can I go in some more?"

"There's more?"

He chuckled. "Stop it. You're cracking me up."

"Okay. Give me some more." I spread my legs out and breathed deeper as he stretched me out to fit him.

"Maybe this will help." He encased my nipple with his moist mouth and played with my other one as he penetrated me further.

Mmmm.

The pressure seemed so foreign and so very necessary at the same instant. It hurt and felt good. It split me open and saturated me in heavenly waves of pleasure.

Oh my God. He filled me with himself, and I could find no escape.

Our bodies formed into one entwined link, one grinding sensual movement of skin upon skin. Laboring breath skimmed across shivering flesh. Sculpted muscle molded against stiff nipples. The area between my thighs knew no pleasure till that moment. We collided, and all I could do was hold on.

Jude dominated me, and he did it in the most delicate movements — tortuously slow. He took his time. The piano played, the notes mingling with the sweat of our sex, the crashing of the waves, and the sound of my cries. Dear God, he took his time, until flickers of an orgasm turned into a bomb of passion that detonated inside and exploded through me.

"Ah!" I dug my nails deeper into his shoulders.

"Are you coming?"

"Yes!"

"Sweet Rain." He slid in and out at that slow, delicious pace.

"Oh, baby." I rocked into him.

"Who's your baby?" He increased his pace.

"Jude." My body spasmed with the strongest orgasm I'd ever had. No vibrator or even my fingers had ever brought me one so intense. When it was over, my eyelids drooped lazily as I tried to catch my breath.

"Hell yes. Now, my turn." He pounded into me.

Shocked, I held onto his shoulders.

"Fuck." He paused for a second. His lip quivered as he stared at me. "Does that hurt? I almost forgot this was your first time."

"No," I murmured. "Don't stop."

"Ever since you grew breasts, I've wanted to ram my dick into you like this." He pierced me so hard I shrieked.

He bit my shoulder, and I cried out again. Even after my own orgasm, his dick still felt so good, and his teeth in my flesh made me feel like he was marking not just my pussy, but my whole body. He softly held onto me some more with his teeth, shifting to suck the bite, and then licked the marks before rising up and gazing into my eyes.

"All these damn years, you strutted this sweet pussy around me. And now, I finally get to have you."

He slammed into me and groaned. I spread my legs out wider. Another grumble left his lips. The piano player stumbled over some notes but quickly recovered.

"Fuck!" Jude gripped me tighter, raised his body, picked me up, and balanced on his knees. The whole time he still moved inside of me. "No man before or after me. Say it."

My eyes widened.

Everything was happening so fast. He moved me around like I weighed nothing. I clung to him, and still he slammed into me with no mercy. My breasts bounced against his chest. My hair blew in the wind as it rushed by us. He planted his hands under my behind and squeezed.

"Say it!" He moaned loudly over sound of the piano.

"No man...before or after you."

"Never?"

I looked into his eyes. "Never?"

"Never!" He groaned, thrusting into me in one violent stroke and then collapsing beside me in complete exhaustion. Laughter spilled from his mouth.

Uninjured, I sighed and couldn't wipe away the large smile that spread across my face.

He laid his head down in the sand. Too lazy to do anything else, I snuggled against him.

"So that was sex. That's what all the fuss is about in songs and books?" My voice dripped with sarcasm.

"Yes." He cupped my behind and tenderly nibbled my other shoulder.

I yelped.

He licked the mark. "I wish I could eat you up."

I glanced to the side of the green blanket we lay on. Crimson drops decorated the sheet and my thighs, symbolizing the loss of my virginity and passage into adulthood. By most standards, I was now a woman. *Well, old standards back in time.*

He hummed in pleasure. His warm chest vibrated under my face. "So sex is no big deal, right?"

I thought back to what had just occurred. A delicious tremor passed through me. "No big deal at all."

CHAPTER 13

He's No Good

Hours later, we sat in our suite's massive tub. Bath beads made the water lavender scented and silky. Rose petals floated on the water's surface and mingled with bubbles upon bubbles. Jude had turned off the lights and lit a few candles around us. They gave off an herbal scent that soothed me. He figured I'd be sore and should soak for a while before we flew back to Miami. I agreed.

"Never?" I quirked my eyebrows. "What did that mean?"

He slid black sunglasses on his face, gulped his beer, and leaned back onto his side of the huge tub. "Never? What are you talking about?"

Why did he put those sunglasses on?

I squeezed the sponge over my shoulders. Jude's teeth imprints decorated my skin in that area. I touched one of them and shivered at the thought of his teeth on my flesh. "When we were having sex, you said that there won't be any man before or after you and then you screamed out the word *never* like a lunatic."

Candlelight flickered off the surface of his black glasses. "I don't remember that."

"I do."

"Then forget about it." He took another sip and set the beer on the edge of the tub. "Sometimes I yell out crazy shit when I have sex. It's no big deal."

No big deal?

I wasn't sure how I felt about that. I'd brought up the question because it seemed so odd for him to say during sex. I figured it needed addressing, but his response also made me feel strange. It seemed like he was lying, or maybe that was what I wanted to think.

Did I want more now? Did I like the idea of no other man having sex with me but Jude?

"What are you thinking about over there?" He rested both of his arms on the edge and let his head fall back. Rose petals stuck to his skin.

"Nothing."

"Bullshit."

"You're one to talk."

He snapped his head up and formed his lips into a straight line. "Meaning?"

"Nothing." I shrugged.

"Fine. You want to talk about what I said during sex, then let's talk about it." He combed his fingers through his wet curls. "During the moment it just seemed...intense and emotional. This idea got in my head that I didn't want anyone else touching your body or sucking on those beautiful breasts or just experiencing everything I was feeling, so I yelled that stuff out."

"And now you don't feel that way anymore?" I focused on the bubbles wavering in the water. I didn't like the way my heart beat faster as I waited for his answer. This situation should have been free and fun, not have me on edge wondering how he felt about me.

"Unfortunately, I feel the same way or at least something like that. I still don't like the idea of another man with you, but that's life. I'll have to get over it whenever it happens."

I doubt it'll happen any time soon.

"So it was intense to you as well?" I formed a heap of bubbles between us into a mountain that boasted a sharp point at the end. "Do you have a lot of intense sex like that? I mean...should I expect my experiences to be similar with other guys?"

"I hope not," he muttered. "And, no, sex is never like that for me. I think it's just because of our feelings. We've known each other for a long time. We love each other. Usually I don't know the chick or her name, so all I'm thinking in my head is, 'Awesome! Boobies!'"

"Those are really deep thoughts."

"I guess I'm a poetic type of guy." He mimicked a karate chop sound and sliced through my mountain of bubbles.

"Asshole."

He winked. "You love me."

"So." I made a new bubble mountain. This time I placed it closer to my side, put my back to him, and got between him and the bubbles. I gathered a few petals and sprinkled them on top of my lovely creation. "Are we going to have sex again?"

He didn't say anything for a while. I couldn't explain it, but I felt his gaze on me, burning through my skin. He touched my wet hair on my back and twirled the ends for a few seconds. Our shadows flickered and danced on the wall next to us. Again, a weird sensation hit my gut as I balanced on the edge of nervousness.

"Did you hear the question?" I asked.

"Yes. It's just hard to answer."

"Why? You won't hurt my feelings." I tried not to sound anxious. "Just tell me."

"I don't think we should have sex again."

My heart dropped into my stomach. It hurt to hear that. It shouldn't have, but it did. I had hoped he would say that he craved me and couldn't get enough of my body. That he'd rather die than not touch me again. It was how I felt. Plus, that's what happened in all of my romance novels. The hero and heroine met. Electricity charged between them, and then they made love. Don't get me wrong. Jude and I would never be in love like a man and woman in a relationship, but I guess I yearned to be pined for.

Did he hate the sex that much? No. It couldn't be. He claimed it was intense and emotional. Just stop thinking about it. He said no, so be cool with it. We're back to how it used to be.

"Rainy? Do you understand why?" He broke through my scattered thoughts, leaving my insecurities to flood my head.

"No. I don't understand." I pushed my rose-petaled bubble mountain away and watched it drift and then smash into the other side of the tub. "But in the end, it's your choice. I won't hold it against you."

"It's not that you weren't fucking amazing, because you totally blew my mind. I'll be thinking about tonight for the rest of my life, but…I don't like it that…intense. It makes things complicated."

Complicated.

I'd heard him say that word before for reasons why he didn't call a female back again.

"She's too complicated," he'd claimed. How many times did he yell that out before dismissing the woman? And now, he'd written my name down on the complicated female list only a few hours after sex.

"I'm not complicated," I countered.

"Yes, you are. The whole time your wet pussy was tight around my dick, I just kept thinking that maybe I'm not good enough to be inside of you."

"That's insane."

"I know, but it's what I thought at the time, and even afterward when I carried you back to our car. All these doubts filled my head. I've never felt that way before. Usually, when you're around me, I question the person I am, but this time…after the sex, I felt like I'd wasted so much time with others…"

"Others?"

"I don't want to talk about it anymore."

"Okay." I twirled the water in front of me with my fingers until it looked like a whirlpool that I could sink into and hide. "I'm complicated. Fine."

"I do think you're amazing."

"Cool."

"You don't believe me?"

"I do."

He captured my waist and pulled me into him. Water swished around my body and spilled out of the tub. His erection pushed into my behind. "Do you feel that?"

I more than felt that. I longed to have him back inside me, even though I was sore. "Yes. I feel it."

"So trust me when I say that I really want to fuck you again." His grip tightened on my waist as he blew out a long breath. "The more I pushed into you, the more I didn't want to leave. I could have stayed out on that beach with you until we died."

He glided his right hand down my waist and to my center. "Even now, I'm reconsidering my answer."

I arched into his hand. "If we're never going to have sex again, then you should stop."

He stroked my clit. It swelled in response. "Make me."

"I don't want to. In fact, I'm disappointed that you don't want to make love to me anymore." I rested my head on his shoulder, forgetting about the bubbles and anything else. He placed his fingers on the sides of my throbbing bud and traced tiny circles on it.

Goodness. Now I get why Vicky and other girls have sex all of the time. This is what I've been missing.

I focused on his wonderful fingers. "Make love to me just one more time."

"I can't, Rainy."

I sucked my teeth. "Please, make love to me."

"That's the other problem." He shoved a finger into me and grabbed my breast with his other hand. "I only made love to you tonight because it was your first time. I usually only fuck, and there's nothing slow or gentle about what I like."

"Show me."

He groaned and pinched my nipple hard. "You're sore."

"I'm fine."

"Fuck, Rainy." He nipped at my shoulder and rubbed his cock against me. "You're a good girl. Stay that way. We have a good thing going right now. We're friends. We hang out and never argue that much or anything. Let's keep it that way."

"What does arguing have to do with fucking me?"

He released my clit and pushed me forward so he could get up. Spinning around, I stopped him by placing my hands on his shoulders. "Just one more time, please. We can just fuck and nothing else. We don't even have to talk about it again, just keep our little secret. What happens in the Bahamas, stays in the Bahamas."

His gaze traveled down to my moist breasts. "Promise me that you'll tell me to stop if it gets to be too much."

"What? The sex or the intensity?"

"Everything."

"Okay. Now you're scaring me. Is it BDSM or something?"

He scrunched his face up in horror. "No."

"So no whips, chains, or knives?"

"Knives?"

"Do I need a safe word?"

"Hell no. Safe word? What the fuck do you read in college?"

"I like dirty books."

"Now you're scaring me, Rainy." He drew me forward and pressed me against his body. "Do I have to take away your library card, Miss Kenner? What happened to all the sci-fi and fantasy books you used to read?"

"I still do. It's just sometimes the alien chains the sexy human female up and whips her a little." I straddled his waist. I did the kiss that he'd been doing to me for years by kissing his forehead, his left cheek, right cheek, the tip of his nose, and a tiny one on his chin. "Sometimes the vampire likes to bite the innocent heroine on her special place."

"You're no longer allowed to buy books without my supervision." He guided me down on his dick. He was right. I was still sore, but who cared? Not me. I yearned to have him, if only for one more time. The head of his cock pierced my tender opening. I bit my lip as the tiny sting merged with pleasure.

"Damn, you feel so good." His body tensed. "Why the fuck do you always feel so good?"

I tried to take off his glasses.

He moved his face out of the way. "Keep them on."

I lifted up a little and slid back down on his cock. "But I want to see what's going on in your eyes."

"There's nothing to see." His face shifted to serious. He stopped me from moving on him. "This is only sex right now. Nothing more."

I waited for him to laugh or say he was joking. It never came out, and his dick slowly softened inside of me.

"Now who's being so intense?" I said.

"I just don't want you to…I don't know."

"Relax. I'm not going to rush out and buy matching Mr. and Mrs. Everett T-shirts. Just fuck me."

Neither one of us moved. He just studied me through his sunglasses. It shoved me right back to the edge of uncertainty. I had no idea what he was thinking.

"Get up, Rainy."

"What?"

"Let's not do this."

"But—"

"Let's just end it here as far as sex goes. We stay friends without sex. Okay?"

I sighed and rose off of him. His body trembled as I moved away, but I paid it no mind. In the end, he'd refused me, and I wouldn't push it.

He climbed out of the tub, reached for a towel, and wrapped it around him. "We should leave soon."

All of a sudden he's in a rush to leave? Or is he in a hurry to get away from me?

"Okay." I stood and grabbed the towel he handed me. The whole time, he avoided looking my way, as if I was disgusting or grotesque, or even worse—as if he was afraid.

He combed his fingers through those wet curls. "I have a big day tomorrow, so I'll just drop you off at home. Lots of work and stuff."

Sure he had a big day. *Liar.* He'd never had to use the word "work" in a sentence before. If he'd claimed he was busy, then it meant parties, women, and writing music. It was funny that earlier today he'd begged me to spend time with him all summer, and now after having sex with me, his schedule flooded with activity that didn't involve me.

Whatever.

I hadn't expected more than this, but I had hoped that his reaction would've been better. My heart sank in disappointment. I waved it away, dried off, and kept my head high as I strolled out of the bathroom. If he expected a meltdown or tears, sadness, or a fight from me to spend time with him, then he'd be disappointed. I never longed to claim him. Jude would never really belong to anybody. Plus, he'd chosen *rock star* as a choice for a career. My dad and his father, Kaden, represented my definitions of rock stars, which never served as the type of man I dreamed about falling in love with.

I had imagined myself settling down with a quiet guy, the type that could sit next to me and read his own book, and it wouldn't be weird or uncomfortable while I was reading mine. My dream guy wouldn't shy away from me. He'd understand everything he craved. He wouldn't be moody and close up.

Maybe it's good that we didn't have sex again.

I dressed and kept my face as neutral as possible.

"Is everything okay?" Jude climbed into his pants.

"Everything is fine." I tossed him a smile and turned my back on him as I finished with the rest of my clothes. "Thank you for tonight."

And I meant it. I'd asked him to take my virginity, and he had with a flight to a secluded and exotic island, a pianist, and awesome food. He'd made my first time as special as it could be and imprinted in my mind and on my body a moment that would never leave.

Isn't that what I'd asked for all along? Not for a relationship or more sex afterward, but for the most memorable first time of my life.

After I finished dressing, I headed over to him with determination in my step and a huge smile on my face.

Everything will be fine. We were never meant to be anything more. We were always only friends, and I like it this way.

Fully dressed, he stood next to the bed. His shoulders appeared stiff and full of tension. Those sunglasses stayed right over his eyes, shielding them. "What's up, Rainy?"

"You rock." I tackled him with all my weight, shoving him forward. We crashed into the bed. The headboard bounced against the wall. I tickled him under his arms.

Chuckles burst from his shocked face. "You're insane!" He rolled me over and held me down, laughing some more. "What's gotten in to you?"

"It seemed weird a few minutes ago. I didn't want to have the whole plane ride be awkward." I collapsed back on the bed. "I just wanted to tell you how amazing you are, and thanks so much for giving me a great first time."

"No regrets?"

"None."

"Yeah?" He looked relieved.

"Yes." I pushed at his chest. "Now, let me up."

He stared at me for a few seconds and then got up. "I don't deserve you."

"Maybe I don't deserve you either." I gathered all of my hair and put it into a big ponytail so it wouldn't dry into a large mop of fuzzy curls. "And I understand that you're busy tomorrow, but let's do something this week. Pick a day. I'll paint. You write."

"Okay." He watched me as if he was unsure of what to say next.

We finished putting our stuff together and left the hotel in silence. I figured he would've been back to normal after my tackling him, but still he acted odd and kept distance between us. Usually when we walked, we held hands, even before he'd taken my virginity. Tonight, as we left the hotel and headed to T-Bone, who was leaning on the side of the car, I tried to grab Jude's hand. He moved away and put it in his pocket.

"You're being weird." I twisted my lips to the side. "Why?"

"I don't know." He dug his other hand into his pockets.

"Did I pussy whip you?" I headed to the door.

He snorted, and in that moment I believed things would return back to normal. He was my Jude, and I his Rainy. *Nothing more. Nothing less.* But still, quiet continued on the drive to the airport. He sat in the passenger seat next to T-Bone instead of in the back with me. It pissed me off. He had never sat up in front when T-Bone drove. Blues music blasted from the speakers, and this time, the lyrics weren't funny to me. They just made me sad and regretful. That same song that T-Bone had put on earlier was playing again from his iPod.

"He's no good! Oh Lord, he's no good!" the blues woman sang. *"Lord, show me your plan. 'Cause I can't get over this man."*

"You okay back there, Rain?" T-Bone gazed into the rear view mirror.

"Of course." I leaned back into my seat and threw on my own sunglasses. T-Bone had given me a new pair, of course, possibly to commemorate my virginity being taken away. I don't know when Jude told him about everything, but clearly he had, because all over my new glasses were little apples with a bite taken out of them. Knowing T-Bone, he'd gotten the glasses before we'd left the States since he had helped Jude plan all of the activities in the Bahamas.

"He come sniffing around at night, eating up all my honey. Oh Lord, why he come to me every night, eating up all my honey?" The harmonica streamed in with the woman's voice. *"By morning time, he's gone and I ain't got no more money."*

This time, I sang with T-Bone and the singer. *"He's no good! Oh Lord, he's no good!"*

CHAPTER 14

Grave Cake

"I don't have any regrets, but I am worried that he's going to act different. I think if we hadn't had sex last night, then we would be hanging out today." I cut a slice of the cake, set it on the paper plate, and put everything in front of my father's grave. "Instead, he's avoiding me, or maybe I'm just imagining it all."

Sunlight seeped through the tree branches that hovered over Dad's gravesite. A guitar carved in white stone served as his tombstone. His name glittered in gold letters formed by his actual guitar strings. Flowers already scattered the ground. His fans still came to show their respect throughout the year, but hoards visited around his birthday. In order for me to have this time to myself, I'd worked with the cemetery owner to visit two hours before the public was given access.

"In the end, it doesn't matter." I cut another slice of cake for Kaden like I'd promised him days ago. "If we never return to how we've been, then I'll just find new friends and maybe another guy. What I truly found out last night is that I am capable of being touched by a man."

I'd tried in high school, but the emotional wounds had been too deep then. My first kiss with Clayton Jenkins had ended in a fit of tears and vomit. My second kiss finished with nothing but vomit.

After that, the word had spread all over school that Rain Kenner ranked high on the freak scale. Not even hanging with Jude had eased the harsh jokes and ridicule. When college application time arrived, I'd picked art schools far away from home, my private school, and all of my dark memories. Jude hadn't appreciated my leaving, but he'd understood. Somehow he'd convinced me that Sarasota would be the best place for me, due to it being far enough away from Miami for me to get some distance but close enough for him to fly up and whip someone's ass if they messed with me.

With a new past and an image to create that wasn't connected to my junkie father's, I had started dating again at art school, only to discover that hives rose on my arms when I thought of my dates touching me. My school therapist had explained that all of my body's reactions came from anxiety at being touched. I disagreed. She'd assumed I'd been molested or raped since I wouldn't tell her what my real problem was. But no one had inappropriately touched me in a sexual way during my childhood. Eventually, she'd diagnosed me with post-traumatic stress disorder.

No shit.

She had suggested taking my time when dating, work on building trust with the prospective guy, and then doing breathing exercises before I finally decided to kiss him. It had freaked me out that all of that was required for just a simple kiss. Meanwhile, when I had gone back home and visited Miami, Jude's lips and fingers touched me constantly with no effect, except shivers of desire that crept up now and then. Months ago, I'd woken up from a dream where Jude and I masturbated together on a stage in front of everybody. The idea had hit me then: Jude should take my virginity.

"And it worked, Daddy." I formed my lips into a smile. "There's nothing wrong with your little girl. I'm not as broken as Mom and I thought. I'm perfectly capable of having an intimate relationship. Just in case…you were wondering up there, wherever you are."

Tears spilled out of my eyes. I barely cried when I visited him. Today, my emotions were all jumbled, uncoiling and stretching through old thoughts and insecurities. *Why am I feeling so crazy today?* I wiped my eyes and cheeks.

"I'm not as broken as Mom and I thought. I'm stronger than you. I'm fine. You gave up on me, but I still survived. I'm not broken." I rose from the ground and turned around.

Kaden stood right there with flowers in his hands and a six-pack of Red Stripe that was probably for him and Dad. Vicky lingered farther off, checking out other gravesites as if she was strolling a store, looking for a shirt to purchase.

His mouth parted, but no words left them.

I gestured to the extra slice of cake. "There you go. He's all yours. I'll leave the rest of the cake just in case Vicky wants it, or you can take it home for Jude."

"Thank you." He dropped the beer next to the cake.

I walked off.

"Rainbow," Kaden called after me.

I spun around. "Yes?"

"Don't ever say you're broken again." He rushed the few feet between us and embraced me.

I kept my arms to my sides, completely caught off guard.

He held me tighter. "Do you hear me?"

"Yes," I whispered. "You don't understand. I was telling Daddy I was okay."

"It was more than that. I'd ask you, but you wouldn't tell me, huh?"

"Tell you what?"

"Why you would even think you were broken in the first place."

I kept my lips shut tight.

"I have questions for you, Rainbow."

I flinched at the name. So close to my dad's decaying bones, I couldn't even deal with that name. "I may answer you if you stop calling me that name. If you must call me it, do it away from here."

He nodded.

"Go ahead."

"Why did you run away when I sang 'Ribbons of Rainbow'? He wrote the song for you."

"It gave me bad memories."

"Will you tell me of what?"

I gave him a weak grin. "No."

"The day Jack killed himself, he called me and left a message."

My feet wobbled under me. I stumbled back and Kaden caught me, dragging me toward him. My heart beat so loud; I bet he could hear it.

What had Dad said? Did he tell on us? No. That's impossible. He couldn't have.

Kaden continued to hold me. "Do you want to hear what he said, or should I leave all of this alone?"

"It's too late for that." I climbed out of his arms. "Go ahead and tell me."

He rubbed at a worry line on his forehead. A red mark remained after he removed his hand. "Jack's message said, 'That evil woman took them all. I finally jumped off the cliff, and I can't stop falling. Not even Rainbow can save me this time. She's falling too.'"

But Dad was wrong. I stopped falling.

"Bye, Kaden." More tears threatened to fall from my eyes. I hurried away.

He ran after me. "Rainbow — I mean, Rain — wait!"

"Leave me alone, Kaden. Go have your beer with my dad and rehash the good old druggie years of rock and roll." I made it to the gate in no time.

"Rain!" Kaden's voice sounded close.

Thompson jumped out of the town car and hurried over to us. "Everything okay, Miss Rain?"

"I'm fine."

Kaden snatched at my hand.

Thompson got between us. "It doesn't look like Miss Rain wants to talk to you right now, Mr. Everett."

I waved the remark away. "I'm okay, Thompson."

"Can we talk in the car?" Kaden asked. "I won't keep you long."

"For what? So you can give me more awesome messages from my dead dad?"

"Okay. Clearly, that wasn't smart, but I don't know what the hell it means."

"And naturally, all you can think about is yourself. Poor Kaden Everett can't decipher a message. Maybe he should go to Jack's fucked-up-in-the-head daughter and remind her about that night." I approached the town car and got in.

"Wait. You're not messed up in the head."

Wrong again, Kaden.

He slid in next me. "I'm sorry."

"Get out."

He slammed the door. "Let me talk to you."

"What role is it today? Are you my uncle or Dad's best friend, or are you Jude's dad, or even better, are you the guy that would love to fuck me on the beach? Who are you today?"

He leaned back in the seat. "I'm — "

"Sorry, yes. I gathered that. You're so sorry."

"What happened?" He didn't look at me. He stared straight ahead. "You're mad, and I know I messed up, but not that much. What happened?"

"Nothing."

He faced me. "Tell me."

"Why?"

"I have a right to know how Jack really died."

How Jack died? Like Dad deserves the pity.

The tears fell. I lost all control of myself. Sadness burst into rage. Fear collided with pain. "He grabbed his gun, put it in his mouth, and pulled it. We all know this story. And because he was such a great dad, he did it in his daughter's bedroom." I spat the words out and for once, everything seemed clearer. I'd never talked bad about Dad and had tried my best to think of the good times. Jude hated him and never liked when I brought him up. Most of the time, he refused to go with me to Dad's gravesite.

"He would've never killed himself without some serious reason," Kaden said. "We'd just been planning a tour and a new album. The week before, we were partying and writing music, beautiful songs filled with happy stuff. The next week I wake up to find out that he's dead, and he'd killed…were they fighting or something? What happened that night?"

"It has been five years. Get over it." I slapped my forehead. "It's like you only exist in your world. Your friend left a wife and destroyed child to deal with his body and blood, and all you can think about is your pain and where you were at."

"What do you mean he left his wife? She's gone, and I don't understand why he did it. After all these years, I just don't understand."

"Get out!" I screamed at the top of my lungs. I tightened my fingers into fists and dug my nails into my palms. There was no escape.

I could run out of the car like a crazy woman. If I fled, Kaden would follow. I had no doubt about that. He thought he deserved the truth. He longed for closure and the answer of why his childhood friend would leave him in this world by himself.

But if he hears the truth, where will I end up? Behind bars or in a mental facility?

"Rain? Just tell me."

"Please leave me alone." I hugged myself. Thoughts entered my mind. Bad ones. The sky, the roof, and everything around me felt like it would tumble down onto me. I almost covered my head to protect myself.

Kaden kept talking and talking and fucking talking. "Jack's message said he's falling and you're falling. Then you're at his grave, trying to prove to a dead man that you're not broken." He scooted closer. "I've even asked Jude, and he gets all angry with me any time I want to talk about it."

Why does it even matter anymore if Kaden knows? Why do I have to keep all this pain in my chest and lock it away? Why? Because then my life would be over. I will be the one that's dead.

I swallowed and prepared to tell the lie I had practiced over and over before the police and ambulance had arrived. Once the cops had come, they saw my tears and the gun in Dad's hand as he lay dead on the bedroom floor. Then they found the suicide note.

Yes. That's how it happened.

They didn't ask any questions and since they had been to our house so often, they probably figured that the next time they showed up, Mom or Dad would be lying in a pool of blood. I hadn't slept for days after the coroner had left. Instead of planning a funeral, I'd been packing my bags and discreetly gathering cash and fake IDs. I was going to run off, escape, flee, never come back.

Mom would understand.

Jude was the one who'd talked me in to staying, and when the medical examiner's report came back, we were relieved. It was declared that although Dad had died from gunshot wounds, the angle of the bullets seemed to coincide with a suicide. The next day, my grandmother had flown in and tearfully given an official report about the tragedy to all media networks.

"I just don't understand what happened in that house that night."

Fine. I'll tell him what he wants to hear, even if it's a lie.

"He was drunk and high that night. That's what happened." I tucked my feet under my thighs, sat Indian-style on the seat, and leaned my head on the window, away from Kaden. "Dad was worse than any time I'd ever seen him. He fell down the stairs before he could get to the second flight. When he did, he stepped into my room and lay down in my bed, calling me my mom's name and touching me the way he would touch her."

Kaden's intake of break was loud in the quiet car.

How easily the lies slipped out of my lips. I turned around. "What's wrong? You wanted to talk about your great Jack. A great guy that would never kill himself. Well, Jack thought I was his wife that night, and no matter how much I screamed and cried—"

"Rain, I didn't know. I didn't have any idea." He reached out to me and quickly pulled his hand back when he spotted the look of disgust on my face.

"And before Dad could finish…what he was doing to me, Mom burst through the door. I don't know how she heard me crying, but she ran in there and started hitting him. That was when Dad finally realized that he'd been…with me the whole time. She saved me because she loved me so damn much. She came to the rescue, and I wasn't alone."

My vision blurred with tears. At least the crying was real. I cried for my dark soul and the ease I had at being a manipulative liar. I cried for how simple it was to slip into this new reality and not have to deal with the actual one that haunted my past.

"He just kept saying 'Rainbow' over and over and over. I covered my ears and screamed. Mom ran off and came back with her gun. I was so scared. I thought she was going to shoot him, but instead she told him to get out. He did."

"You don't have to—"

"No." I shook my head. "No. You don't get to turn this off like a faucet just because it displeases you. You asked questions. Here are your answers."

Kaden's face reddened.

"Mom put the gun on my dresser, ran to the bed, and held me. But you see, Dad didn't leave the room completely. And instead of getting out of there, he grabbed the gun. Only I saw him. Mom was too busy crying and rocking me in her arms. He stared at me as he walked over to my bathroom on the other side of the room and closed the door. A few minutes passed and then the gun blasted, and his body hit the floor."

Kaden squinted his eyes, as if he was confused. "But how could your mom have been with you? I thought they found her in the basement."

"The police lied about that to protect her from suspicion with the press. You know how underhanded newspapers and tabloids can be."

He froze for a few seconds. His Adam's apple slid up and down his throat as he swallowed. "Rainbow, what are you talking about?"

"Mom held me until the police got there. She told me that everything was going to be all right. She kept me from looking at all of the blood." I frowned. "There was so much blood. It was everywhere."

"But...your mom—"

"Is amazing." I shrugged. "I know we don't always get along or haven't spent much time together since that night, but she's doing just fine."

Kaden shut his eyes.

"Dad thought I was broken and couldn't be fixed." I touched my chest. "He didn't even try to pick up the pieces that he shattered. He just fucking left because life wasn't fun anymore, and his little girl wasn't the same anymore. Mom stayed and took care of everything."

He leaned over and held me.

I struggled with getting away, realizing I'd taken the lie too far. The last thing I needed was him holding me. I didn't deserve it. Plus, he reminded me of Dad. It made me question why I found Kaden attractive. Why I sometimes touched myself with his image in my head. It reminded me of how truly broken I was after all.

"Don't touch me." I pushed at him.

Commotion exploded outside. It sounded like someone was fighting or arguing. Then the door on my side burst open.

Jude stood outside. "Let her fucking go!"

"I was just trying to console her—"

Jude reached his hand out to me. "What the hell did you say to her to make you think you needed to hold her?"

"I didn't know that she was...crazy." Kaden shook his head from side to side. "I had no idea."

"She's not crazy. What did you tell him?" Jude studied me with sad eyes and I hated it. I didn't need anybody's pity.

"I told him what I needed to."

Jude nodded, probably understanding that his father hadn't heard the truth. Only two people knew what had really happened: Jude and me.

"Come here, Rainy. Let's go." He motioned for me to go to him.

I waved him away. "I just need to be alone. Both of you, please leave."

This time, Kaden had no problem hurrying out of there.

Jude leaned inside the doorway. "Rainy—"

"I'll talk to you later." I turned away from him. "Could you tell Thompson to get me out of here?"

"Can we talk just for a minute?"

"I'm done talking." I shrugged.

"Then can I just ride with you to wherever you're going?"

"No."

He hadn't wanted me around him today. There was no reason now to sit around me out of pity. "Please, just get Thompson."

Jude sighed and closed the door.

My phone rang. I knew it would be Mom without looking at it. Her assistant had my name on Google alert. Any time my name showed up online, the news went to the assistant's email inbox and then was forwarded to Mom.

I'll have to make up a reason for why I was here today. She'll hate that. Mom thought it was bad for my mental health to go to Dad's grave or be around his friends. I was slowly understanding why.

Thompson finally got in, and the town car sped off.

CHAPTER 15

Mommy's Keys

I fumbled the keys in my hand and they dropped to the floor. I froze and waited to hear if Dad had woken up. Nothing came from upstairs, so I slowly picked the keys back up and tried each one on the basement door. Mom cried from the other side.

"Shh. Mom, don't cry." I kept my voice as low as possible. "I'm coming. You'll be out soon."

I was on the fifth key by now; so many of them hung on Dad's key ring. They all looked the same—gray and dipped in blood. Fog spread around me. I stood there putting keys into the keyhole. Each time, none of them worked. Over and over I stood there with wobbly knees and tears streaming down my cheeks.

Mom's cries grew louder.

"Please, Mom. You have to be quiet." Then all the keys melted in my hands and dripped through my fingers.

Mom screamed, as if she knew that there would be no escape. She screamed and I cried with her as I fell to my knees, searching through the gray, murky liquid for maybe one key to still be there.

I just need one key, then I can save her.

I woke up with screams ripping through my throat. I'd gone a whole year without this nightmare.

Why did it come back? Will the others return?

I thought the melting key dream was the worst of them all. It made me think of what would have happened if I'd never found the key to free my mom. My heart sank at the thought. All those damn memories that I'd managed to not think about for a year surged back into my head.

Dad had gone on an acid binge for two weeks. Out of all the drugs he took, acid had scared me the worst. Cocaine had sent him into the studio to work twenty-four-seven. Marijuana had calmed him down and kept him in a relaxed mood. Some of my most favorite times had been hanging with him while he smoked from his bong. But, when he'd done acid, I stayed away. He acted crazy. It wasn't unusual to catch him twirling a sharp knife in his hand while he talked to himself, or for him to sling darts at my mother and I as we walked by, explaining that a demon lurked near us.

The last two weeks of Dad's life, he'd been varying his drug usage between smoking angel dust and eating acid strips. He didn't sleep or eat. During the day, he and Kaden had sat in the studio behind the house, partying, tripping, and writing music. Jude had hung with me a lot, calming me down when he could with his stories of what girl he'd banged or the next girl he was considering. At night, however, there'd been no distractions. Mom and he fought. She would call the cops and kick him out. He'd return the next morning in the same clothes, with flowers, saying he was done with drugs and ready to change. By the afternoon, he would be high again.

Four nights before Dad died, he woke me up at four in the morning with a flashlight shining in my face and a gun pointed at my head.

"Are you a duppy like your mother, or are you my Rainbow?"

My body froze. I held in my scream. "I'm your Rainbow."

He glanced over his shoulder. "I told you it's okay. Rainbow didn't fall."

I checked to see who he was talking to. No one was there. For some reason, his talking to imaginary people scared me more than the gun to my head.

"You know what a duppy is, right?"

The cold metal dug into my flesh. "Yes, Daddy."

"Tell them, so they'll believe you." His eyes widened in fear. His skin grayed in patches around his eyes and forehead.

What's on his skin?

He checked behind him again. "Damn it! Give her a chance. Just give her one chance. Go ahead, sweetheart. Tell them what a duppy is."

I swallowed down my fear. "A duppy is a bad spirit. We all have two souls, one good and one made from the earth. When we die, the spirits up in heaven draw the good soul to them and give it to God to judge."

The gun shook against my head. "What happens to the other one?"

"It stays on earth inside the dead body. If certain prayers aren't chanted and herbal arrangements made, the soul could leave and transform into a duppy."

Dad waited and nodded every other minute as he took council with the shadows in my room.

My heart pounded in my ears. I knew I was being judged by his imaginary people. They assessed me, analyzing if in fact I was a duppy like Mom. The gun was too close, my dad too strong. I could only lay there and wait to either live or die.

But what scared me the most was that he'd said Mom was already a duppy. I couldn't hear her in the house. Did that mean he'd already killed her?

I gripped the sides of my head and screamed. "Stop thinking about it! Stop thinking about it!"

Footsteps sounded downstairs. Banging fists hit my door.

"Miss Rain, are you okay?" Thompson rattled the door knob.

"Yes. I'm fine." I hid back under my covers. "It was the television. I just turned it off. I'm going back to sleep."

I decided to just change my thoughts. The brain is a powerful thing. What I perceive is only what my brain perceives. I can change it all like it never happened. I can rewrite that night.

And so I did. I shut my eyes tight and pictured a slightly better night, one that didn't end with blood everywhere.

After several long minutes, Dad removed the gun and cried into his hands. "They said you are okay. We're safe for now."

I sat up.

He jerked back. "What are you doing?"

"Nothing, Daddy." I tensed and remained where I sat. "I'm just waiting to find out what we should do next. You said Mom is a duppy."

"That's what they said, but I couldn't kill her."

I dug my nails into my skin. "Where is she?"

"I locked her in the basement and nailed rosary beads on the door. We should pray for her soul for three days, and if the duppy does not leave her body, then we'll have to kill her." Tears spilled out of his eyes. "You shouldn't have to go through this, my Rainbow. You shouldn't. But God's plan is never known to us. You understand?"

I cried and wiped away my own tears. "Yes. I understand."

"Pray for her."

"Okay, Daddy."

"I love you, Rainbow." He fell asleep in front of my bedroom door inside my room with the gun in his hand, and I never went back to sleep.

I sat in the corner, in my own urine, waiting for him to let go of the weapon. Once he woke up an hour later, he ordered me to clean myself up and relieved all of the staff for the rest of the week. I was no longer allowed to go to school or down to the basement to see Mom. He claimed we needed my prayers all day and that the strength of my chants would lessen if I was far away in school. He locked away my phone and computer. All the other phones in the house were hidden too. I had no way of contacting the police. He even turned on the house alarm so that he would know if I tried to leave.

If it hadn't been for my friendship with Jude, my mother and I would have never survived. After a few days of me not answering my phone calls, he came to the house, pissed. My dad made excuses for why I couldn't see him, saying I was sick, sleeping, and wouldn't be in school for the rest of the week. Jude left without another response.

At midnight, a knock sounded in my room. Thinking it was Dad doing something crazy, I gripped a steak knife in my hand and kept it behind me. I'd sneaked the weapon earlier while Dad and I had eaten a nerve-racking lunch. The knock came again. I realized it had to be coming from the window and rushed over to see Jude balancing himself on the ledge.

"Why aren't you answering my calls?" he said through the glass. "I know you're sick, but I was worried—"

I shook my head and held my finger to my lips. He closed his mouth. The realization that something horrible was going on dawned in his eyes. I motioned for him to stay there, tiptoed to my desk, wrote down a message on a sheet of paper, brought it back, and showed the paper to him. It read: "Dad locked Mom in the basement and me in the house. Call the police."

He climbed down without saying goodbye or that he'd be back.

The police showed up in less than thirty minutes. Dad answered. I stayed in my room with the door cracked open, listening as my dad laughed with the officers and suggested that whatever kid called must've been prank calling the cops. They left without even checking the place. They left because rock legend Jack Kenner answered the door, and all of his stardom radiated out of his skin, making them mishandle Mom's and my safety.

The door slammed closed. "Rainbow, get down here."

"Yes?" I hurried his way with the knife behind me.

"Did you tell anybody about us praying for your mother?"

I acted shocked. "No. How could I, Daddy? You have my phone and computer."

He laid his ring of keys on the end table where Thompson usually placed the mail. "There's more going on here."

"There is?" I inched back and realized that he no longer had his gun.

"Someone else is working against us."

"Who?" I could stab him and run out.

But will I make it? Can I hurt him? What would he do if I stabbed him? He'd put me down in the basement with Mom, and then there would be no way to get us help.

He grasped at his hair and pulled. "I don't know. I don't know. There could be more duppies surrounding us. I could barely breathe this morning. How about you?"

"Yes. I also had trouble breathing," I lied.

"I have to go back and think about this." He rushed up the stairs, and I got out of his way. "I need to talk to them."

I stood there, not shaking any more like I had been days before. My body turned into numb flesh. I checked the alarm next to the door. The red light flickered on and off.

The alarm's on. I can't run out without him knowing. How far can I make it before he grabs me?

The next mansion was half a mile away. Even if I made it, I'd need to somehow get through the locked gate. I glanced at the end table.

The keys.

I got to them in seconds, quickly tiptoed through the kitchen, and hurried down the stairs to the basement. I was scared to leave by myself, but with Mom, I was ready to do anything. Together, we could figure out an escape or overtake Dad.

Two has to be better than one.

I arrived at the door. The keys fumbled in my hands. "It's me, Mom."

"Oh God, Rain," she cried.

"Shh. Dad is upstairs." My fingers shook. The keys clinked against themselves.

I could have sworn I heard footsteps upstairs. Had Dad come down to the main level to look for me? On the third key, the door opened. My mom stumbled to me. Her kinky curls sat in a crumpled mess on top of her head. Dark, purplish shadows ringed her swollen eyes. Blood was dried under her nose. She held me so tight, sobbing into my shoulder and smelling like crushed flowers and sweet things that I could no longer remember.

"Mom, don't cry." I didn't want to let her go. I didn't. She felt like home. Safe. She felt like Mom. "We have to go."

She bobbed her head, choking on her own tears. No fear swam in those beautiful brown eyes, just regret. I grabbed her hand and tugged her up to the main floor. She seemed so weak and tripped almost every other step.

"Where is he?" she asked in a low voice.

"In his bedroom, I think." I approached the door as I held her hand. "He has the alarm on. He changed the code to something else. I tried so many number combinations. None of them worked. Can you run?"

"Barely. Where will we go?" She trembled next to me. All the hope I'd experienced when I'd opened the basement door earlier vanished. I'd thought Mom would have the answers and lead the way, but in that moment, I discovered that she was just as lost at me. Even worse, she'd slow me down.

How could I have been so stupid?

"We could…run to one of the estates next door or…" I had no real answer but to run and scream for help.

"You don't have your phone?"

"No."

"He hid them all? What about the one in his studio?" she asked.

"I don't know. Probably. I wasn't allowed to go out there."

"I bet that's where they're at. He always hides them there."

Always? How long has he been doing this? How long have Mom and Dad kept me out of these crazy fits of insanity?

"You run to the studio and search for a phone." She snatched the steak knife from me. "I'll stay here. If he comes down to check on the alarm, I'll stab him and hold him back."

"Mom, I don't think this is a good idea."

She wiped tears away from her swollen eyes. "If there isn't a phone in the studio, run out the back entrance and keep on running, girl. Don't you stop no matter what, you hear?"

I stiffened, understanding what she was saying and not wanting to do it.

"The whole time I sat there so scared that he was hurting you. Get out of here." She unlocked the door, opened it, and triggered the alarm. "Run, Rain. Hurry!"

The siren blared. I raced away so fast that I passed the corner and forgot to go to the studio. Instead, I headed to the front gate. A shot boomed behind me.

Mom!

Not thinking, I ran back, but not to the front door. I scurried to the side entrance where the staff usually entered. The lights in the house shut off all at once. Dad must have cut the power. Depraved Mind's latest album blasted next.

Hands seized my arms. I screamed, hitting and kicking.

Jude's face appeared in front of me. "Rain, it's me."

"Oh my God." I hugged him, almost climbing his tall body as if it was the safest place on earth. "I got Mom out. She wouldn't run with me. Then I ran. I heard a gun shot. I think Dad killed her. The music. It's everywhere."

"Calm down, Rain." He kissed my cheeks and hugged me. "Listen. Calm down."

I breathed in and out at a fast pace, gasping for breaths that didn't seem to be there.

"My car is parked outside the gate. I saw the cops leave without your dad, so I climbed back over to see where you were at. Come on." He tried to drag me away. "Let's get the cops."

I shook my head. "She'll be dead by then."

"We can't—"

Footsteps stomped outside, over the music. We ducked into the bushes. Mom screamed as Dad dragged her against the concrete by her feet. He held the gun in his right hand. Blood smeared the pavement in a trail behind them. Jude looked at me right as Dad towed Mom past us.

And then everything happened so fast. Jude jumped out of the bushes and charged Dad. They crashed to the ground. The gun fell. I rushed out to pick it up. It felt cool and heavy underneath my fingers. Mom lay there on the ground, soaked in her own blood. Scrapes marked her back and arms. Dad punched Jude in the gut. Jude kneed Dad.

"Stop!" I screamed. "Stop or I'll shoot you!"

They both froze.

Dad gazed at me and relaxed. "Oh, sweet Rainbow. Give me the gun, baby. Give it to Daddy."

I backed up. "Get away from Jude, Daddy, or I'll shoot you."

He untangled himself and stepped away from Jude. "Would you really shoot me, baby? Not my Rainbow. Don't fall into your mother's evil ways. Don't fall, baby."

He moved closer to me with his hand out. "Give me the gun, Rainbow."

"Don't move, Dad. Jude, go call the police." After all those days, I stared at my dad and faltered for a second, but it was only a second.

My dad stepped my way.

I pulled back the trigger. A bullet pierced his chest. The pressure of the shot shoved me back, and I crashed into the ground.

Jude ran for me and helped me up, taking the gun out of my hands and placing it on the ground. "Are you okay, Rain?"

"Jude." Mom picked up the gun and pointed it at him. "Go take Rain somewhere safe."

Worry creased around the edges of Jude's eyes, but he nodded his head. "Okay."

"No. I want to be here when the police come."

"Take her away for me, Jude." Mom pointed the gun at Dad. "Get up, you son of a bitch! Now it's time for you to go into the basement."

That's what should have happened. Mom would have been fine if only things had gone this way.

In the real world, my phone buzzed, pushing me out of my dark re-write of memory lane. I yawned, checked the glowing screen, and saw Jude's text.

Why aren't you answering my calls? ~ J

It's six in the morning. I'm sleeping. ~ R

Can I come over later? I'm sorry about Dad bothering you at the cemetery. Is everything okay? Have the nightmares or the blood come back? I haven't talked to you in days. ~ J

I'm fine. ~ R

I shut off the phone, placed it on the dresser, and gripped my blanket hard in my fingers. The fake emeralds sewed on top of the cover pressed against my skin. I stared at my bathroom door. Blood dripped down from it. In my mind, I knew it wasn't real, but I jumped under my blanket and squeezed my eyes together anyway. Sometimes that happened; blood spilled onto my hands or pooled around my feet.

It's not real. It's not real.

Jude thought I should see somebody. I didn't think it would help when I would only be lying to the counselor the whole time.

I'd never tell them that I killed him. I couldn't tell.

Nevertheless, I did go to a therapist at my school in Sarasota. She never pried, but she knew something had happened. I never told her about my visions.

Clearly, I'm crazy, but how insane am I?

I'd gone to her when the blood visions had plagued my whole week. I hadn't gone to class, left my dorm room bed, or eaten. I'd just cleaned. My room reeked with the odor of bleach. One of my teachers had shown up at my room covered in blood, at least in my eyes. She'd asked me how I was doing. I'd lied and said, "Fine." My teacher didn't need to be a genius to see something was wrong with me — I wore a rain coat with plastic foot covers, and had a bottle of bleach in my left hand and a wet cloth in my right.

She'd told me I had to go to the therapist and then took me there herself. I had refused to change out of the rain jacket and just left with her. Luckily, no one snickered, whispered, or pointed as I'd walked through campus. Half of them were probably as crazy as me.

The art world provided an excellent occupation for crazy people. According to some scholars, mental illnesses flooded the art world and other forms of creativity. Van Gogh had probably been bipolar and battled with it, as was seen when he'd hacked off his ear. Michelangelo had endured obsessive compulsive disorder. Pollock had struggled with alcoholism and mood swings. Clinical depression had cursed Georgia O'Keefe, Picasso, Munch, and many artists, writers, and entertainers had dealt with even more mental problems.

Jude and I had argued so many times about whether creativity and mental illness had a connection. *How could they not? Artists tend to see beauty when it isn't there. We love to experiment with a normal person's concept of the world and present it in a new light.* Jude had opposed my suggestion, not appreciating the idea that if he was a musical genius, then he, possibly, was also mad.

I, on the other hand, was comfortable with being insane. I didn't mind the blood or odd thoughts, the weird occurrences during intimacy, or the nightmares of keys. I rejoiced in being alive, no matter how fucked up a day could be. What scared me was a therapist seeing through all of my lies and slowly figuring out the truth.

Yet, the therapist had helped. I hadn't told her about the visions of blood or about Dad. Instead, we'd talked about my lack of intimacy.

It had given me a focus. After a few weeks, the blood had disappeared. My sex drive had returned and thoughts of losing my virginity had drowned my brain.

Would it be weird to call her now and ask her why the blood has returned?

"Okay. My virginity is gone. The blood is back. Now what do I do?" I gripped my blanket hard in my fingers and stared at my bathroom door as more of the crimson liquid leaked down in several lines.

Kaden dragging me down memory lane and this damn house is bringing the blood back. I have to get out of here. I would have never come back this summer if I'd known I'd be at home so much.

I jumped out of bed and started packing, keeping my thoughts on the plan ahead. Every now and then I would risk a glance at the door behind me. Finally, once my suitcase was packed, the blood disappeared.

Get out of this house, and I'll feel better.

CHAPTER 16

Road Trip

"Thank you, Thompson." I squeezed his hand one more time before I released it and stepped away. "Thanks so much for letting me borrow your car. I swear to God that when my trust fund comes, I'll buy you a new one and write you a check."

"I don't need the money or a new car." He frowned. "I need you to come back here in one piece. I need you to make good on your promise that you'll call me every day to check in and eventually return."

"Okay. I just need a few weeks to myself."

He dropped the keys in my hand. "I'll go get your bags from the house."

"Thanks so much."

"Don't thank me yet," he muttered.

Why not?

The booming of a song sounded far off in the distance. Mansions littered my neighborhood and provided living spaces for several professional athletes, so a car blasting loud music on a Tuesday morning wasn't odd at all. However, the long black luxury motor coach that sped down the road toward my house was out of place. It turned into my long driveway and barely fit behind my mom's town car and

Thompson's Toyota. No signs or words decorated the bus. I had no idea who, what, or why it would be coming to my mom's place. I just hoped Mom wasn't going to step out of it.

The door opened.

Jude jumped off like a crazed man and stomped my way. "You were just going to fucking leave without saying anything to me?"

"Why do you have a bus?" I almost dropped Thompson's keys.

"Stop avoiding my question," he said through clenched teeth. "We make love one night, and you think you can bugger off whenever the mood hits you?"

I scrunched my face in confusion. "First of all, stop yelling at me, and second, my leaving has nothing to do with you."

"I didn't say that. I'm saying that now, because we hooked up, you won't come to me when you need me."

Thompson came out with his attention focused on the ground as he carried my bags to the bus.

He must've told Jude that I was leaving, or maybe Jude had made him say it.

I rolled my eyes. "What did you do, bully my driver into telling you where I was going?"

Jude closed the distance between us. "I didn't have to bully him. He called me and told me you were taking a bloody road trip across the damn country! He obviously cares about you and knows I care about you too!"

"Stop yelling."

"Fuck you."

My mouth dropped open. "Why are you so mad?"

"Get on the bus."

I flipped him off. "You can't just rush up here and talk to me any way you want to. This trip was about me, not you."

"Then we'll do this the hard way." He picked me up like a caveman and slung me over his shoulder with no further word.

Thompson gaped at us.

Jude ignored my punching and yelling as he marched over to the coach, climbed the stairs, and set me down on my feet next to a shocked bus driver. Clearly, the poor guy had not been informed that Jude was executing an abduction.

"Hello, Miss Kenner." The bus driver tipped his black hat and quickly averted his eyes.

"Hello," I said.

"Keep going." Jude snatched Thompson's keys from my hand, slung them outside, and pushed me forward.

"Stop shoving me! I know how to walk, and this is just us talking. Nothing else. I don't even know why you have a bus, and why you threw those keys outside and—"

"Just keep moving," he snarled.

"Asshole." I walked through the slits in a black curtain and entered an area decorated in all white from the carpet to the walls. A huge leather couch with a TV and video gaming system was on the right. T-Bone chilled on the other side with his feet propped up on a foot rest while he read a thick book with ferocious dinosaurs adorning the cover. The aroma of pizza and something sweet drifted in the space.

Jude grumbled behind me, "Go ahead, Rain."

I kept moving. "Where are we going?"

"In our room to talk."

I paused in front of a white door. "Our room? How is this *our* room?"

The coach moved. The floor vibrated under my feet. I lowered and leaned to look out of the window. *Damn it.* We were backing out of my driveway.

"Have you completely lost it?" I tried to step around Jude, but he acted like a brick wall and wouldn't let me by.

"Keep on moving, Rain. If you think you're getting off this bus, then you're dead wrong. If you think you're going on some road trip as a beautiful young woman on a lonely highway by yourself, then you're more insane than me. Get in the back so we can talk, or I'll pick you up and take you there myself."

"Where are we going?"

"To the back."

"I'm talking about on this bus, asshole! Where is this thing going?" I crossed my arms over my chest and tapped my foot.

Jude stared me down, and what I saw in his eyes made me shiver in fear. He looked like a man that would tiptoe along the ledge of a roof twenty stories in the air. Fury pooled within his eyes. He cracked his fingers on his right hand and took a few breaths, as if to calm himself.

"Where are we going?"

"Apparently, we're going on a bloody road trip!"

I scanned the area. A duffle bag lay next to two boxes of pizza and a big bong with musical notes at the top.

"When Thompson called me early this morning and told me that you were packing your bags and had asked to borrow his car, I told him to stall you until I could call him back and let him know I was coming," he said.

"No wonder it took him six hours to finally bring his car to the house."

Jude nodded. "I rented this since I figured I couldn't convince you to not want to drive out of Miami."

"What happened to you avoiding me Sunday? That's why I didn't call you to tell you I was leaving."

"You're so full of it. I've been leaving messages on your phone since yesterday. I texted you this morning. You said a few things and then ignored me."

"You avoided me before so I decided to avoid you." I shrugged.

It had made sense at the time, but now it just sounded petty and stupid. In the end, I was just angry. It didn't matter at who or why. I'd been fuming since I started having all those horrible dreams.

This morning, I'd been forced to talk with Mom, and boy was she pissed. She'd seen footage and articles of me all over the Internet—partying at South Beach on Friday night, arguing with Jude in front of the spa on Saturday, and running away from Kaden at the cemetary on Sunday. The Internet speculated that I had slept with both Kaden and Jude. Others claimed I'd broken Kaden's heart by cheating with his son. Blogs named me the Slut of the Year. To say Mom was horrified was an understatement. She'd described my actions as being immature, reckless, and detrimental to me and her. I had a feeling she was going to cut off my credit cards and lock down my bank account if I didn't fix this.

After our conversation, all I could do was scream.

I'd spent all these years trying to be good and keeping her secrets, only to be labeled as bad. What was the point of trying to do the right thing when people treated me how they wanted to anyway and pushed me down whenever the opportunity arose? So the plan to escape had popped into my head, to just get in Thompson's car and drive until I became tired. Just leave. I'd taken out as much as I could at an ATM, returned home, and waited for Thompson to return with his car. Mom had many cars I could use, but if I took any of them, who knew what she would do. I left all my credit cards in her bedroom.

What was the point of bringing them if she'd just cancel them anyway?

"I want to be there for you like you've always been there for me." Jude interrupted my thoughts. "So if you want to leave Miami, then fuck it, we leave Miami. But it happens together."

"Whatever."

"I'm going to interpret 'whatever' as a big, fat yes. And by the way, I wasn't avoiding you Sunday. I just needed space."

"Space from what? It's not like I was crowding you."

"Let's talk in the back." He formed his hands into fists.

"And will you be beating me behind closed doors?" I motioned to his fists.

"No, but I can't say if mirrors and walls won't be harmed during our conversation."

"Whatever." I turned around, opened the white door, and walked through it. An opened door with a bathroom inside stood on my right. A poster of a naked woman hung on it. She had her legs spread open and her hand stroking herself. I glanced at Jude.

"We have a bathroom in our room with a shower, so I designated this one for T-Bone. I let him hang up the nude girl." He placed his hand on the middle of my back and guided me forward. "This is my studio on the left."

It looked like a big walk-in closet with only glass walls. A microphone stuck out from the ceiling. Two stools had been nailed to the floor in the center. Buttons, switches, knobs, and glowing lights were on all the walls.

More black curtains swayed ahead of us. I assumed that was the location of "our room." I pushed through them. The walls were painted yellow—Jude's favorite color. A huge bed sat in the middle. My painting of the beach near Jude's house adorned the wall behind it. Art supplies were stacked on a tiny desk in the corner.

"Thompson put your bags in the compartment under the bus. If you need anything, you can go down there when we stop to eat, or you can borrow my shirt." He pulled his off and handed it to me.

I let my gaze drift down every row of muscle on his stomach as I took the shirt. "You should probably rest. Thompson said you didn't sleep last night, that you screamed a lot and that this morning you just walked around the house yelling at things to yourself and talking about blood."

Thompson has a big mouth.

I walked out of the room and through the curtains.

He came behind me, turned me around, and pulled me back to him. "Why would you decide to just leave like that?"

"I needed a break."

"From what and who?" His voice came out in a low growl.

"From everybody."

He gently pushed me into the glass walls outside of the studio and molded his body into mine. "You don't get to have a break from me."

"I got one yesterday and Sunday. Get off of me."

"Those were my stupid moments of insanity. I won't be giving you any more space." He lifted me up and wrapped my legs around him.

My body melted into his. I hadn't been expecting this. We were supposed to be just friends, no more intimate touching. But there we stood in the hallway with him holding me up and his body and lips so close that I couldn't think of anything else but him moving inside of me and shoving all of my earlier depressing thoughts away.

"I thought I needed a day or two to get my head right," Jude whispered. "I had to get you off my mind and clean up all the confusion the sex brought to my brain."

"Well, holding me can't be helping." My hands shook. "Please put me down."

"No." He kissed me. His soft lips caressed mine. His tongue tasted like wine and some sort of candy.

I gasped as he slid his hand under my shirt, thrust it under my bra, and seized my breast as if it was the only thing that could keep him alive. I panted and squirmed in the grip of those big hands. "Why were you so mad?"

"I hate to see you go through this."

"I'm not going through anything."

"Yes, you are. I bet you're seeing blood again. Thompson figured as much. I wish I could just fix it." He pierced me with his gaze. "I wish I had a formula or pill or song or anything to make whatever you deal with go the fuck away."

"I-I'm fine."

"Don't ever try to leave me again." He buried his face in my neck and sucked, then set me back down and opened up his studio door. I figured he needed time alone, but he grabbed my hand and pulled me in. "I want you to listen to something."

He flipped a switch and pressed some buttons. "Promise to give me your honest opinion on this."

And just like that, he had shifted to a new mood, and I found myself not pissed at him, but happy I was with him. *Why does he have so much power over my emotions?* He knew what emotional buttons to push and which ones to ignore. Once I realized he rented the bus to drive me around on my crazy whim of a road trip, I had to forgive him. I'd planned on driving out of Miami as fast as I could, escaping all those dark memories and the very idea of my life for a few days. I didn't even have a notion as to where I'd be going. I just knew I had to get out of the city. But now, Jude stood in front of me, ready to comfort me as I went through a stressful situation, and I couldn't figure out why I hadn't thought about asking him to come with me before.

"Okay." He turned another knob.

"What is the song called?"

"I'm not telling you."

The sound of falling rain filled the studio, and not a pitter patter, but an all out assault of water on pavement. A simple beat rushed in next, making me bop my head to the rhythm. An electric violin played a melody that complemented the beat and the sound of the rain. Then came flutes and a piano. I'd never heard anything like it. Everything merged together in a perfect harmony of pleasing noises and tempo. It created an ideal fusion of experimentation and progressive rock.

I grinned. "This is crazy good."

He placed a single finger in front of his lips. I stuck out my tongue, sat on the stool next to him, and listened some more.

"Her love is liquid. It drenches my skin. I can't find where I start and she begins." Jude's deep voice flowed out of the speakers. *"I'm drowning, baby, with a smile on my face, in the center of a monsoon. Her love's a heavy shower, a cloud bursting in an explosion of water, rain dancing under the moon."*

Jude put his back to me, as if he was worried about my reaction.

"I pray the rain never ends, no trickle into a drizzle of her without me." His voice sounded so sad and beautiful at the same time. *"Let the storm come — her love, her pain, her joy, her sorrow — let it all fall down on me."*

My body tensed. Naturally, any mention of rain in his song made me think he'd written it about me. But I tried not to assume. I just listened. His lyrics and the captivating mix of raining and music imprisoned me in the moment. I absorbed it into my skin. I'd never experienced a sensation like that before. I felt high. Intoxicated. Drunk off his voice. I could have collapsed to the ground, wrapped the song around me like a blanket, and dwelled there for eternity, just me and his song.

When it was over, I felt hollow and empty, kind of like after Jude had moved inside of me days ago in the Bahamas and then slowly, inch by inch, left me. A void existed in my core.

He faced me with a neutral expression. "Do you like it?"

I tried to gain control of my breaths, feeling as if I'd been running at top speed for hours. "It's all-consuming, Jude."

"Stop it. Tell me the truth. No lies."

"I'm so serious. It's like a drug." I rose on the tip of my toes and hugged him. "I can't believe you wrote that."

"I named it 'Downpour.'"

"It's fucking amazing."

"Obviously you were my inspiration for it."

"Obviously?" I quirked my eyebrows.

He glided his hands down the outline of my body. "After I dropped you off on Saturday, all I could think about were your moans and the way your body felt. I just wanted to memorialize that moment. I needed something around me that I could look at, touch, or hear in my darkest times and remember that there was an instance in my life where everything was pure and flawless. So I wrote this song."

I had no idea what to say or how to react, so I said nothing.

He placed me back on the stool and devoured my lips with unhurried dips of his tongue. I groaned into his mouth, unable to hold back.

"What do I do about us, Rainy?" He lifted me up. "There's no way I'm not fucking you while you're on this bus this whole trip and laying next to me. I can't even be around you for a few minutes without trying to taste you."

"We don't need to do anything." I held on to him. "All these years I over-thought every move I made. This whole time I kept secrets in my head and tried to be the best daughter and student and friend and whatever else I needed to be. But I don't think any of that ever matters. The world just goes on. Everything continues whether I fuck up or not. Now…I don't want to think or plan out anything anymore."

"So no thinking when it comes to us?" He kept me up by gripping my thighs.

"Exactly." I let go of him and pulled off my shirt. "We just have sex when we want to."

"And what about when we'd like to have sex with other people?"

I unsnapped my bra and gave him a wicked grin. "Then we have sex with other people."

"I don't know. That sounds like we're playing with fire." He set me down and unbuckled his pants. "Lucky for you, I can't think right now. My cock is in so much pain from being so hard and not being able to feel your pussy around it."

I hurried to take off my jeans and pointed to the glass walls of his studio. "What if someone sees us?"

He reached behind him and pressed a button. It beeped. Solid black curtains slid over the walls. His jeans fell to his ankles. Once again, he wore nothing under them. His cock popped out in a stiff erection that tinted pink toward the tip. "Turn around."

My mouth dropped open. "Why?"

"Because I'm going to fuck you from behind."

"Not in my…actual behind, right?" My bottom lip quivered.

"No overthinking this, remember?" He chuckled.

"No putting anything in my behind either." I twisted around. Right as I bent over the stool, Jude picked me up in the air by my hips so I was forced to flail my arms out to try to maintain balance.

"What are you doing?" I planted my hands on the walls where the buttons were as he kept my feet off of the ground and my ass in the air next to his cock.

"Press the red button near your hand." He propped one of his legs on the stool's foot rest so that his leg held up one of mine. "I have an idea for another song."

I steadied myself on the wall, making sure the top half of my body remained up as Jude held the lower half close to him. The microphone dropped in the center. A screen turned on with bright blue lines that dragged over the display like one would see on heart monitor machines in hospitals. Jude rubbed the tip of his erection along my center, drawing squiggly lines along the wet lining.

"Hmm," he hummed. "You're so ready for me. When did you start getting wet, Rainy? When I kissed you or when I brought you into the studio?"

"When you kissed me." The lines on the screen shifted into a wavy pattern each time I said a word. "Are you recording this?"

"Yes. I want to record you moaning." He thrust inside of me with no warning or time to comprehend his answer.

Oh shit.

He pounded into me with no mercy, filling me with all of him, and it was a lot. My entire body felt full with his cock inside my tunnel. My pussy moistened more with each delicious plunge. Ribbons of bliss uncoiled, stretched over my flesh, as my aching nerves trembled in wet desire. Shocked, I realized I was already so close to coming just from a few seconds of him inside of me.

"Jude!" A ragged moan followed.

"Oh, Rainy. You take my dick like a good girl should."

Slapping noises rose in the studio as he pumped into me at a steady pace. He spanked my ass. I shrieked. He increased his speed and slipped his hands over to my clit, bearing those succulent fingers down on my throbbing bud and teasing it until I screamed.

"Jude! Oh God!"

"You want me to stop?"

"No, don't stop! Oh, please! Don't. Stop."

"I love you, Rainy."

That was all I needed. My body ignited into fragments of the person I used to be. His cock repaired me, as odd as it seemed. He mended me with each pound, freeing my spirit. I ceased thinking about the crap in my past or the rough days to come in my future. I only focused on him, his cock, and my body's earth-shattering responses.

"Oh! Oh!" An orgasm tore into me, racking my brain with blind pleasure.

"Damn it. You already have me coming." Jude trembled behind me and groaned so loud I could have sworn the glass around us shuddered.

Liquid dripped along my thighs as his strokes dwindled down to exhausted pushes and whimpering grunts. Seconds later, he pulled out of me, yet his presence still remained inside of my body as if he'd never left. He whipped me around to face him like I weighed nothing, his arms wrapping around me in a tight hug. I felt safe and loved for the first time that day.

"Thank you."

"For what?" He nibbled my ear.

"For everything."

He planted kisses on my shoulders, breasts, and lips. "Don't ever try to run away without me again. I'm here for you, Rainy. No matter what. I'll be there. Just me and you against the crazy world. Don't ever fucking forget how much I love and care for you."

"I won't," I whispered. "I won't."

He carried me to the shower with a shirt draped over me just in case T-Bone spotted us in the hallway.

After Jude made love to me under hot water and rising steam, I lay down to take a nap, thinking about him and hoping that this new level of our relationship would work out.

I need a break from disorder. No conflict. No problems.

I'd barely closed my eyes when my phone beeped, signaling that I had a new text message. I had assumed on Saturday that the unrecognized number was Kaden's. Now, I was certain.

> I'm sorry about pushing you to talk about your parents at the cemetery. Do you forgive me? ~ K

> I forgive you. ~ R

> Can I see you tonight? Dinner? Movie? Concert? A passing of a joint among two good friends? ~ K

Unease hit my gut. I had to take precautions when dealing with Kaden. He'd proclaimed he desired me as well as that he would consume my soul if given the chance. I didn't take that lightly at all. Not to mention, he was Jude's dad. I had no intentions of doing anything to hurt or disrespect my best friend.

Are you still there? ~ K

I'm doing a road trip right now. I'm no longer in Miami. When I come back, maybe we can do something together. ~ R

Are you with Jude? ~ K

I sighed and had no idea if Jude wanted his dad to know his whereabouts or not.

Yes. He's with me. ~ R

What's the next city you'll be heading to? ~ K

I'd told Jude I needed to grab some of my art stuff from my studio in Sarasota. We planned to spend the night there and then head out the next afternoon. The tattoo that Jude and I shared had inspired me to put it on a huge canvas. To Jude's dismay, I hoped to incorporate our bodily fluids into the piece. It would be our blood, of course, to form the red in the apple. I'd ordered Jude to provide me with as much semen as he could. He'd claimed he masturbated at least once a day. I challenged him to shoot the semen into a jar designated for my painting and have me a good bit by the time we reached my place.

I'm dropping by my art studio in Sarasota tomorrow morning to get some supplies. We're resting there that night. ~ R

I'll meet you there. ~ K

Wait. I'm not sure if that is a good idea. ~ R

Trust me. It is. Will you paint me? ~ K

I shook my head, wondering what he was trying to do now?

Yes. I can paint you and Jude together. ~ R

I'll be at your studio with a robe on
and nothing underneath. ☺ ~ K

I'll call the cops if you come to my studio
with no clothes on! ☺ ~ R

Fine. You can paint me with clothes on.
I'll see you there at 12 in the afternoon? ~ K

Fine. ~ R

Bye, Rainbow. ~ K

I slung my phone into my purse, climbed out of bed, and headed to Jude as he wrote in his studio. *I probably should let him know now and prepare for his moodiness.*

I knocked on the glass. His gaze centered on his tattered notebook. He slid his pen over the paper like a frantic artist, staining the white page with black swirls and scribbles.

"Jude." I knocked again.

He snapped his attention to me and opened the door. "What's up, Rain?"

"Your dad texted me."

"How did he get your number?" he said through clenched teeth.

Happy to pissed in seconds. I have a gift.

I shrugged. "I thought you gave it to him. I don't know."

He returned his attention back to his notebook, but he didn't write. He just stared at the page. "What did my dad text you for?"

"To meet up. He apologized, so I told him that we were on a road trip and were heading to Sarasota."

"Why?"

"I feel bad about what happened in the car. I screamed at him, said a bunch of mean lies about Dad, and basically —"

"He attacked you with questions about a fucked up night. Don't feel bad. He did the same to me before he left for the cemetery. It had made me mad that he still can't seem to let it go, but then I got worried he was going to run into you at the gravesite, and that just pissed me off."

I placed my hands on my hips. "Are you mad that I invited him?"

"No." He drew a line on the right side of his page and doodled along it. "So, what are your plans with him?"

"Correction. What are *our* plans with him. He asked me to meet him at twelve tomorrow at my studio and if I would paint him."

He peered at me from under those messy blond curls. "Will you?"

"If it's okay with you." I leaned my weight on the right side of my foot.

"What the fuck does that mean?"

"Last time you got upset—"

"I don't care anymore."

"No?"

"No. You can fuck him if you want to."

I raised my eyebrows and snorted. "Hold up. I'm talking about painting, not sex. How did we get on the topic of sex?"

"Anything my dad does involves sex in some way. If he's coming to see you, then he's expecting something more."

"I'm not interested."

"Whatever." He rubbed his eyes, got up from the stool, and set the notebook on it.

"I'm not." I backed up to let him out. "And just in case you're right, I would like you to let me paint the both of you together. It would be amazing to have dad and son in one painting. Have you ever done anything like that—photographs or art—with the two of you?"

"No. There are not many things we agree on. The things that we do agree on involve drugs and women. We're not the type to sit down for a family picture." He ran his fingers through my hair.

"You promised me earlier that I could paint you both."

He twirled one of my curls around his finger. "I'll do the painting with him for you though."

"Thank you. It'll be fun." I got on the tip of my toes and kissed him.

"Sure, it will be fun. Either that or we'll be fighting over you."

"I doubt that."

"Don't be so sure, Rainy. Don't be so sure."

CHAPTER 17

Three's Company

I stood in the center of my studio and studied all of the supplies that littered the room while Jude pissed into a cup in my bathroom. His urine was for my painting. My process of creating art never started when charcoal glided over a crisp white sheet or a paint-soaked brush slid down an empty canvas. My system began with the supplies. Normally, I spent days playing with the technique and the media to use in expressing whatever concept I had pushing against my brain.

I used blood a lot in my works. It was the only time I could see and smell it without going crazy. Somehow, working with blood in my concepts didn't injure my mind like my visions did. It was a normal occurrence to find me carrying buckets of animal blood from my local butcher's shop into my studio. No one called the cops or worried as drops splattered to the ground in front of my dorm room. Artists had been using blood since the beginning of time. That crimson liquid boasted a striking tone that regular red paint could never capture. It stuck to any surface with ease.

Plus, blood symbolized almost everything in life. I incorporated the liquid in spiritual works due to its great use in religion—Christians symbolically drank it for salvation; some Muslims re-enacted Abraham's offering up of his son Isaac to God by sacrificing an animal;

for years, blood had been spilled in Indian villages for local Hindu deities; and even near my own city of Miami, followers of Santeria practiced rituals involving animal sacrifice. Energy charged through blood. It created life and showed up at death. One could see it during pain or even the deepest moments of love, like when Jude had taken my virginity, causing red drops to adorn the sheet we'd made love on.

I'm definitely using blood in the painting of Jude and Kaden.

I opened the huge fridge in the right corner and remembered that I'd gotten rid of all the small containers of preserved blood I'd grabbed from the butcher since I wasn't going to be here this summer. "Do you feel like grabbing me some blood?"

"Hell no, Rain," Jude called out from the bathroom. "You already got me jacking off and pissing into jars like a serial killer. I stop at handling animal blood."

"You suck."

"You're a weirdo. Sexy weirdo, but odd all the same."

The door behind me cracked open. Kaden stepped through, holding a bottle of wine and two glasses with skinny, violet stems. He wore leather sandals and dark red pants that hugged his muscular thighs. A black shirt draped his upper body. "Rainbow?"

"Hey." I checked my watch. "You're an hour early."

"I had to make sure you didn't run off."

"Where's Vicky?"

"I gave her a ticket back home." Fresh cologne drifted from his tan skin, reminding me of cool water on a hot summer day. It gave off an aquatic scent, if that was even possible. I loved it. "Vicky wasn't serving her purpose anymore."

"And what was that?"

"Getting my mind off of you."

"I never thought you would resort to corny lines. What's up with the wine?" I gestured to the bottle and glasses.

"To set the mood." He placed them on the table near some of my tubes of paint.

"Set the mood?"

He headed to me and encased me in warm muscle. "I love this soft dress. The white material is thin enough for me to see those beautiful nipples."

"Really? We're just going to start right off with unapologetic flirting as soon as you step through the door?"

"Would you expect anything less of me?" He slipped his hands to my waist. "Are we alone?"

"No."

"Where's my son?"

"In the bathroom, providing me with his urine. I'm painting you both. Have you drunk a lot of water? I need yours too."

"Wait a minute. Did you just say he's giving you his urine?" He took a few steps back but still grasped onto my hips.

"Yes. He's giving me his urine." I picked up a tiny metal can no bigger than my hand. "And you will be too. Now go ahead and piss into this can. I'm incorporating it into the work. There is antibacterial soap in the bathroom along with gloves to handle it."

His face scrunched up into disgust. "I never thought someone could surprise me, but I'm actually at a loss for words over here. You've managed to shock me, and I've seen some sick stuff on the road, but playing with people's pee is on a whole other level."

"I won't be playing with it." I handed the can to him. "Now hurry. I don't want to paint this all day. I would like to catch the sunset on Siesta Key."

He turned the can over a few times and analyzed it, as if it held some special secret. "My urine?"

"Can you be a little more mature about this? Artists use urine all the time. It's perfectly normal."

"Name one artist who does it and I'll run in there as soon as I can."

Did he forget that I freaking go to art school?

"Andy Warhol did it in his *Oxidation* series. He had people urinating onto a canvas of metallic copper pigments so the uric acid would oxidize into abstract patterns. Andres Serrano's *Piss Christ*. He submerged a crucifix into urine and then took pictures of it. Ofili did an image called *Virgin Mary* all in elephant dung. Do I need to continue? I can do this all day."

"None of that sounds like art."

"Nevertheless, all of it is considered art. It just might not be to your taste. Kant said people think things are beautiful because it elicits some form of pleasure in us. The piece stimulates our emotions, intellect, and/or imagination in some way."

I didn't tell him my reasoning for using it in a painting of them. Since urine was waste expelled from the body, I was hoping that by incorporating it into their portrait, I'd likewise rid myself of the fucked up situation I'd found myself in where Jude and his dad were concerned.

He leaned his head to the side and smirked. "So, for you, piss on paper stimulates your mind?"

I held my hands to my forehead. "Would you just go piss in the can?"

"Where's the bathroom?"

I turned to the doorway and gestured to the area. Jude stood there, leaning on the post and gazing at Kaden's hands as they still grasped onto my waist. I moved away from his gripping fingers and stepped to the side. "Jude is done. You can go in now."

"Hey, Dad." Jude walked over with his own can and didn't even glance Kaden's way.

Kaden nudged Jude's back. "Is she serious about the urine, man?"

"Dead serious. Surprisingly, the paintings actually end up looking good too. She's done several of me in blood."

"You mean the red ones over your bed?" He smiled.

"Yeah. Those." Jude put his back to him and set the can on the table.

"I love them. You're talented, Rainbow." He sucked in a breath of air and then turned to leave. "Okay, I'll follow you down the rabbit hole to see where it goes," he muttered as he headed into the bathroom.

"Thanks," I called back and faced Jude. "Everything cool?"

He dug his hands into his pockets and kept his back to me. "Of course everything is cool. Stop worrying about me. I get that you're not mine, and I'm not interested in anything more. We're just friends, Rain."

"You keep saying it like our painting is something more than just that."

Turning around, he came close to me and brushed his lips against my ear. "I know my dad better than you. He assumes I'm going to share you because we always do it. This is how it starts off. Wine, fun activity of some sorts, as well as him and I hanging out with the woman. He even gave me the sign that he wanted us both to take you at the same time."

"What sign?"

"When he held your waist, he looked at me and blinked his eye twice."

"Creepy."

He stepped back. "What do you think about him wanting to have a threesome with you?"

"I'm not interested."

"Are you sure about that?" He gave me a skeptical look.

"Yes. I'm sure. Let's drop this and get back to the painting." I returned to scanning my stuff.

He slipped in behind me and pressed his erection into my ass. "As you can feel, I'm down for whatever."

Yeah, right.

"I doubt my mind or body can take both of you at the same time or even in the same life." I climbed out of his grip and gestured to the stage. "Take off your shirt, sneakers, and socks. Keep your jeans on. I think a portrait of you both with no shirts and barefoot is quite enough for me. I don't need to jump into an orgy or anything."

"So you *are* attracted to him?" He yanked his shirt off.

I picked a brush up with lots of silky hairs flaring out of the stem. "I thought we established that already."

"No. You never admitted it. I just assumed as much." He lowered onto the stage, laid his legs out in front of him, and leaned back on the white wall behind him. His face had a neutral expression. He raised one of his legs and balanced his elbow on his knee.

I wished I could see what he was thinking in that head of his. This situation teetered on the edge between fun and chaos. Jude had declared he didn't care about things, and then in the next moment, he did something rash. I needed this moment to be about the painting and all of us enjoying each other and creating new memories to fill my head with. One thing I'd realized from that night hanging with Kaden in the kitchen was that I missed him and that part of my life. I couldn't run from Daddy's rock past or my childhood anymore. I had to start embracing my true life instead of running from it. At least, I figured that would be the best way to heal.

Would Mom approve of this?

"All done." Kaden came out with a can wrapped in paper towels. "Rain, this is by far the grossest thing you've done around me. I remember that time when you had me eat dirt pies. It took me hours to get those tiny pebbles out from between my teeth."

"You were an adult. You would think that you had enough sense to not actually eat a dirt pie." I pushed the huge canvas against the easel. "Kaden, I need you to take off your shirt and shoes, but keep your pants on, of course. I would like you to sit on Jude's left side and lean against the wall just like him."

"Yes, ma'am."

After lighting a few rose-scented candles, turning on some jazz, and putting on latex gloves, I began with huge brushes, dipped each one in their cans of urine, and spread the golden hue all over the canvas. A saxophone rang out an upbeat tune from my small speakers. For Jude's urine, I spread it in side-to-side horizontal lines. With Kaden's, I brushed his on in vertical lines. Each boasted their own rich color. A golden checkered pattern emerged in different shades.

"I can't believe you're using piss." Kaden laughed. "Is that what your generation sees as art these days?"

"My generation? You're talking like your whole lot didn't have its share of ridiculous contributions to the world."

"Be careful, Rainbow. I've already threatened to put you over my knee once. You'll get no more warning."

I finished with the background, dropped the urine as well as the cans into hazardous waste bags, and put the bags and gloves in a garbage container I used for getting rid of blood.

Okay. Here we go.

I reached for smaller brushes and studied both of their complexions—Jude's skin held a darker tint than Kaden's.

"Since the candles are lit, maybe we should dim the lights in here and turn on some slower music." Kaden rested his hands on his thighs.

I powered up my iPod and switched on a playlist I'd named "the chill out room."

"What about turning off the lights?"

"I can't see if it's dark in here. I need light to paint."

"Do you need that dress on while you paint?"

"Yes." I mixed a few colors on my palette that I believed represented the tones in their skin. "We're not having a threesome, Kaden, so stop trying to set the mood."

Jude burst out laughing.

"Well, since you brought it up." Kaden formed his lips into a frown. "Why not?"

I peered at him from the side of the huge canvas. "Do I really need to answer that?"

"You'd love it."

"Leave it alone, Dad." Jude rubbed his eyes. An odd grin stretched over his face, like he was forcing the whole playful smile.

"Sure, Jude. Of course you can say leave it alone." Kaden waved his comment away. "You've probably already gotten a chance to experience sweet Rainbow, where all I can do is sit here and beg. Besides, you're the reason why she's hesitant about it."

"That's not true," I interjected. "I'm also saying no because of common decency."

"Says the girl playing with urine."

"Be quiet. I'm painting your mouth now," I lied.

"She's scared to do it because she thinks you'll be mad." Kaden turned to Jude.

"I know." He stared at me. "I get why. I tripped a little when I heard about both of you on the beach. But, I think…I wouldn't be mad if she wanted to."

I quirked my eyebrows. "Do you both discuss everything? Are there no limits with you two?"

"He doesn't tell me about most stuff when it comes to you, and that's the same with his music. Those two things he keeps to himself," Kaden said. "Everything else, we pretty much share."

Jude leaned his head back on the wall and closed his eyes. "So what do you think, Rainy? If I didn't get annoyed, would you say yes to us? That's what all of this is about, right, Dad, to get us all together so we can fuck?"

An exasperated breath fled Kaden's mouth. "Someone's in a bad mood."

"I'm not in a mood. I'm just tired of the bullshit pretending. You couldn't care less about Rain painting you. Let's be real about this. You came here to try and have sex with her."

"That's never been a secret."

My brush slipped from my fingers and dropped to the floor. I cleared my throat and picked it up as if Kaden and Jude hadn't rattled me. "Okay. How about we stay silent for a while?"

"Let's take a break. I'm going to smoke." Jude rose and stormed off without waiting for my reply. I hated when he did things like that—turn from easygoing to pissed off in seconds.

Why couldn't we just sit in my studio and do a nice portrait? Why did sex have to be mixed into it? Can't they simply just hang out with a woman without sleeping with her?

I considered the girls that Jude had talked about in the past. None popped to my head that were similar to our relationship. In fact, I couldn't think of any female he talked to on a strictly friend basis. Even worse, none of their female relatives came to my mind, either—not cousins or aunts, grandmothers or female friends of the family. Jude's mother barely came to Miami to visit, and according to him, her relationship with Kaden had only been a one night stand.

Maybe they really don't know how to deal with women without sleeping with them.

Granted, Jude's and my relationship had only ventured into sex due to me, but he really had no other women as just friends.

"Do you have your own art in this studio?" Kaden disrupted my thoughts right as Jude walked out and slammed the front door. "I would love to see it."

I set my brush down and washed my hands, since apparently both of my subjects were done with the portrait for now. "You see the room separated with the black curtains and on the right of the bathroom? That's my private gallery."

"Yeah, but come on and show me some of your stuff. We can let Jude cool off. Let's forget about all of this other mess for now." He headed toward my art work.

As if you two odd guys in this situation are easy to forget. And they call me crazy.

Kaden stepped into my gallery in front of me. The curtains swung behind him. I followed him into the dark room, but before I could switch on the light to my right, he trapped me with his huge arms, drew me into him, and captured my mouth with his.

Oh my.

My body heated with each dip of his tongue slipping in and out. He grunted as he pulled me in closer.

Oh my God.

His soft lips pressed on mine with hungry pressure, swallowing me whole. Where Jude was gentle and took his time, Kaden sucked on my lips and slid his hands all over my curves with a fierce intensity.

I turned into liquid right inside of his arms. My body melted into his. My panties moistened. Shame hit my heart, but lust burned the edges away until there was more desire than anything my conscience could touch me with. How many nights had I secretly imagined his lips on me like this? How many times had I touched my body with embarrassment about my dark crush on him? This was bad in every way, and even that very idea made each of his caresses on my behind feel so good.

"I have to have you," he murmured between kisses, gliding his hands up to my breasts, yanking the front of my dress down and exposing my bra.

My nipples perked his way. He found the points with his fingers and tugged on them until I let out a throaty moan.

"What's it going to be?" He pinched them harder, and the muscles between my thighs clenched. "Can I take you now, or do you want to wait for Jude?"

His mentioning Jude's name was all I needed to shove me back into reality.

I've got to get hold of myself.

I pushed him away, backed up, and flipped on the light. A white glow bathed the room.

"Come here, Rainbow." He undid his pants. His erection pressed against the material, pleading to get out.

I forced myself to not look any further as he opened them. But, God, I so wanted to see.

Don't do it. Jude would hate this. And even though the very thought of Kaden touching me makes me excited, nothing good is going to come from sleeping with him. Plus, I can't do this to Jude.

"That was a huge mistake. I'm sorry, Kaden. I can't." I rushed out of the room.

"Rainbow, what the fuck?" he yelled from behind me.

"I'm done with the painting too. This whole thing is too weird." I hurried past the canvas smothered in their urine and snatched up my bag. "Just lock up when you're done."

"Rain!"

After all this time, now he calls me Rain.

I did a quick scan of the room to make sure I left nothing else and then escaped. I couldn't trust myself inside and alone with Kaden anymore. I hadn't seen it before — maybe it was the fact that Kaden reminded me of the simple times when Dad was alive, before he'd gone crazy on drugs. I didn't see it then, but I couldn't visualize the real man that stood before me. He was a pathetic being, not worthy of mine or Jude's time. What did he expect from having sex with me? It would've just been sex and nothing more. And after we both came, what would be left but two shattered people more lost and confused than when they'd started off?

Jude sat on the pavement in front of my studio. The private road facing him remained bare, as was usual this time of day. He glanced off somewhere in the distant sky, his curls blowing in the wind. "You come out here to smoke with me?"

"No." Hoping Kaden wouldn't burst out of the door with his pants open, I nervously swung my purse back and forth. "I don't think the whole painting thing is a good idea."

He nodded his head and blew a smoky circle into the air. "Did he make a pass at you?"

I ignored the question. "Earlier, I said we could do whatever we wanted to do. I think I was just trying to be carefree. But in the end, we do need limits."

He continued to not look my way. "Okay. What are the limits?"

"I'm not ready for threesomes and orgies with you and anybody else, but most of all with your dad." I held up my hand to stop him from talking, just in case he tried. "And I don't care about how you're supposedly cool with it and how we're not together. I don't like the person I would be if I hooked up with both of you. You may not admit it to me or yourself, but you aren't happy about your dad and I having sex. So if I did it, I would be hurting you, and I can't do that."

He inhaled his joint and blew out more smoke. "So, you won't mess with him because of me?"

"And me. And because…I like you and what we have. A lot. It's not a commitment, but whatever this is, I enjoy it too much and love you as a friend too much to hook up with your dad."

Silence bridged between us for a few seconds.

His face was a stiff and unyielding mask that gave me no sign of his emotions. "Any other limits?"

"Yes. Family and friends are definite limits. Plus, people who we simply admit that we wouldn't like the other messing around with should be prohibited too." I tapped my foot and glanced at the door again. "I'm going back to the bus because this whole situation has left me feeling filthy and icky. I'm taking a shower."

I can't believe I kissed Kaden.

Finally, Jude directed his attention my way. "What happened between you two?"

"I'd rather not talk about it. It's embarrassing and...wrong."

"Did he kiss you?" He stood up and flicked the joint onto the street. Anger glazed over his eyes, yet he maintained a neutral expression on his face.

I figured it was best to leave the entire situation alone. I'd done enough damage, and I had no way of knowing what Jude's reaction would be. When it came to this new relationship between us, he was becoming harder and harder to predict.

"Did he touch you?"

I gripped my purse strap hard. "I don't think we should talk about it."

"I do."

"Too bad." I twisted around and headed to the bus. "I'm going to let the driver know that we can go. Are you coming, or are you going to say bye to your dad?"

"You're just going to avoid my question?"

"I don't want to argue."

"Then maybe Dad does."

I sighed. "I'll be on the bus."

CHAPTER 18

Whipped into Reality

After I cleaned off all the shame from my skin, I realized the bus was leaving Sarasota. According to T-Bone, Jude had ordered the driver to get us out of the city immediately, and that when his dad had told T-Bone goodbye, Kaden sported two black eyes.

Well, I doubt he will be texting me again.

Meanwhile, Jude had no marks on his face or skin as he stormed to the back of the bus and asked not to be disturbed.

Once an hour had passed, he approached T-Bone and I as we chatted in the front and declared that we should figure out where we were traveling. Although I was happy he still seemed excited about the road trip, he kept his distance between us on a physical and emotional level, not really answering any of my questions or wanting to sit next to me. I struggled to not give it too much thought and suggested the idea of taping a huge map on the wall and picking our destination from there.

We flung darts at the map to figure out where we would visit. Jude's dart stopped on Mesa, Arizona. Mine landed on Toronto, Canada. Everybody agreed Canada should be the overall destination.

Awkward silence remained between us after that. He barely looked my way as he played video games. After an hour of his moody behavior, I gave up and slept the rest of the day, thinking everything would be better eventually.

We just need time to pass. Kaden probably told Jude he kissed me. I can't expect him not to be mad at me a little.

Later at night, Jude woke me up, wearing red lipstick, purple shimmering makeup on his eyes, a big dog collar around his neck with a leash hanging from it, no shirt, and tight leather pants. "Rainy, baby. Get up. We're in Atlanta."

I yawned and stretched my arms. "Atlanta? Why are we in Atlanta?"

"It's kind of sad that you're questioning why we're in Atlanta first, instead of my clothes and makeup."

"I've learned to roll with the punches when it comes to you. However, since the elephant in the room has been slammed on his back, legs spread open, and pumped in its anus with no mercy, why don't you tell me why you're wearing makeup."

"Poor little elephant." He winked at me.

My spirits lifted as I realized he was in a better mood. "Why *are* you wearing lipstick and eye shadow?"

He shook his head, bent over, picked up a bag, and set it next to me. "I've been working on a new song while you've been asleep. I finished it, and all of a sudden it hit me that Maestro, that rapper you love, would be great for a feature on the song."

"Wow. Maestro is mega hot. Is the song sexy? You know he's all about hot and steamy lyrics."

"Yeah." A naughty expression covered his face, one with a succulent smile and lust-glazed eyes. "The song is really sensual. It's called 'Apple.'"

I formed my mouth into a frown. "'Apple?'"

He licked his lips. "Yes, and your moaning is all in the background."

I covered my face. "Please say you're joking."

"No, but it's sexy. Trust me. Think, 'Pleasure Slave' by Kings of Metal, but your moans replace the usual climb."

I sat up and crawled out of bed. "Okay, first of all, I've never heard and will never hear a song called 'Pleasure Slave.' Second, I have no idea what a 'climb' is or why my moans have to be in your song."

"A climb is the part of the song that differs from the regular verses and comes right before the chorus. It's the part of the song that gets the people listening and excited because they know the chorus is coming up." He dug his hands into the bag and pulled out a corset done in crimson pearls. "I bought this for you to wear to Maestro's party."

"You bought stuff. How long have I been asleep?"

"For close to eight hours."

I rubbed my eyes with both of my hands. "Wait a minute. My moans are a climb in your song which apparently is the signaling to people that the chorus is coming?"

"Oh yes." He winked at me again. "When people hear you coming, they know that the chorus is coming. Get it?"

Oh God.

"Jude, I want to hear the song before I give you my permission."

"I don't need your permission. I'm the reason why you're screaming my name."

"Oh my God." I covered my head with the blanket.

He wrenched it back down and tossed me a wicked grin. "It's true, but if you want royalties—"

"I don't care about royalties. I'm more embarrassed that millions of people will hear me moaning in a song."

"It's not like all of those millions of people will recognize you as the one doing it." He laughed and handed me the corset. "Okay, so we've been invited to Maestro's video shoot for his song 'Sex in the Dark.' It's being taped at a BDSM club, hence my get-up. I figured you would love to come since you read that stuff all the time."

"Not all the time, just a few books." I studied the corset. The entire thing was made with beads. I wasn't even sure if it could be considered a true corset.

"Maestro said everybody will be in fun costumes. I'll be doing a cameo on the video." Jude offered me a pair of fishnet stockings and tiny shorts next. "Well, you know how I love to dress up. I figure we should just go crazy and be master and slave."

I gestured to his doggy leash. "So, you're my slave?"

"For tonight."

"Hmm." I tried not to grin, but it spread across my face anyway. "Do I get to whip you?"

"Only if you say please."

"But if I was truly the master, I guess I wouldn't have to say please."

"You shouldn't have to ask either, which shows that I'm truly the master in this relationship." He took out a pair of ridiculously high-heeled leather boots and put them in front of me. "I went through your things for your clothing and shoe sizes. I didn't want to wake you up, so sorry if you feel like an invasion of privacy happened. You just looked so sweet snoring under the covers."

Rolling my eyes, I yanked off his shirt that I'd been sleeping in, and reached for the corset. "I'm cool with you going through my luggage. There wasn't anything valuable or naughty in there. And it's not like I'm adventurous with my panties and bras. They're just plain cuts, styles, and solid colors."

"That doesn't really matter to guys. The fact that they're panties makes most of us excited. Nevertheless, I didn't stick any of your panties or bras in my pockets."

"Funny."

"I try."

"Also —" he stood up and helped me with putting on my corset "—I was thinking we should probably discuss…us and this party. Due to the whole thing that happened earlier today."

I raised my eyebrows. "Okay? You sound weird. What are you talking about now?"

He got behind me, fitted the corset around my whole upper body, and placed all of the back hooks in their slots so the top gently squeezed me in place. "Maestro rented the club for the night. After the video, he and I are going to talk about him doing a rap on the song. I may have him come back here and check it out, whatever. But afterward, I was thinking we could party in the club."

"That's fine with me. It'll be as usual. You'll do your thing, and somehow my little college girl brain will manage on my own. I am an adult, you know." I tossed him one of his signature winks. "If you're worried about me, then don't be. I'll probably dance all night and have a few drinks."

A neutral mask spread over his face. Tension etched around his eyes. There was something still on his mind, something bothering him.

"What? I'm fine. I had no nightmares just now, and I'm not seeing any blood." I put the fishnet stockings on. "There's no need to hang around, nursing me."

"Are you sure?"

"Yes."

He still appeared uncomfortable.

"What now?"

"Well, you know how, generally, we go to a party together, dance, drink a little, and then after a while I do my own thing too, but in the end we always leave together?"

Do his own thing?

He rubbed his face and sighed. "Okay. You know how sometimes I—"

"Are you trying to say that you'll probably be hooking up with other people?" I battled to keep the annoyance off of my face.

He formed his lips into a straight line and nodded.

Can't he go a day or two without needing to sleep with other women? Well, who am I to judge. I was kissing his father earlier today.

My stomach bound into knots, but I didn't let my feeling of unease show on my face. Hadn't we just said earlier yesterday that we could do whatever we desired? If we wanted to have sex with each other, we could. If we yearned to make love to someone else, we could. We understood the limits now. It made so much sense and sounded so easy in that moment outside the studio. Now, I just felt like vomiting.

Jude is not mine. I am not his. We'll be fine as long as I remember those two sentences.

"Maybe we should add more limits," I offered.

"Okay."

I took my time, figuring out what would be the things that I absolutely couldn't deal with the most.

He crossed his arms over his chest.

"Are you going to have sex with people in this bed?" I pointed to it. "I'd feel icky about sleeping where other girls' juices and stuff were. It would be insensitive and disgusting. In fact, if you are going to do it, then I'll sleep in the front with T-Bone."

"Hell no." He looked me straight in the eyes. "The last thing I want to do is disrespect you. It's why I needed to make a clear line between us days ago and not have sex with you at all. But I can't, 'cause I love having sex with you."

"You're babbling. Just tell me. Sex with tramps in the same bed I'm sleeping in, or not?"

"Not. I'll never bring a female here or anywhere around you. If I sleep with anybody tonight or any other night, it will be out of your view. Okay?"

"Fine." I sucked my teeth and stepped into the tiny shorts. "And I feel the same way. I won't bring any guys on the bus or anywhere near you. If I do sleep with or make out with anybody, it will be out of your view too."

The muscle on his jaw twitched. "Sounds good. It'll be safer for everybody involved if I don't see another guy kissing you."

Well, at least I'm not the only person that's jealous in this situation.

"It may turn you on," I joked and held in my laughter. "You may be into voyeurism."

"I wouldn't put that to the test, Rainy. Just your talking about kissing someone else is making me want to cover you up in a jogging suit and lock you inside."

"That's not happening." I chewed the inside of my cheeks. A horrible thought slammed into my head. We'd had sex twice with no condom.

What the hell is wrong with me?

If anybody did a Google search for manwhore on their computer, articles about Jude's conquests would show up. "You and I have to use condoms. If we ever have sex again, we must use them."

He twisted his lips into an unusual expression. "How about I use condoms with other women like I'm already doing, but with you—"

"No."

He gritted his teeth. "Rainy, it feels so damn good when I'm inside you without a—"

"No way." I waved my hand. "I can just kick myself for not making sure we didn't use them already."

"I don't have anything. I get checked once a month."

"We're still using them. We don't need babies either. I might be on the pill, but that's not always a hundred percent effective. And just because you haven't caught anything yet doesn't mean you won't."

"I always use condoms when I have sex."

"You haven't with me."

"You're bloody different."

"We use condoms from now on." I stepped to the mirror and studied myself. My hair had transformed from silky curls to a fuzzy mess.

"Is that it?"

"Yes," I replied. "What about you? Do you have any more limits?"

"No. I'm good." His gaze washed over me. "You look captivating, as usual. Are you almost ready?"

"Just give me an hour to get my hair and face together."

He headed to the front of the bus and called back to me, "You've got thirty minutes at the most, then I'm returning here, picking you up, and carrying you into the club."

"Oh, spare me."

My makeup bag sat on the small dresser, not that the bag held a lot. My mom had bought most of the stuff, filled it herself, and provided instructions and "helpful" color suggestions. In the end, I'd ignored all of her suggestions and, to her horror, winged it. I'd smeared lipstick on my eyes if I didn't have the color in eye shadows.

I never wore foundation or eyeliner. Personally, I applauded women who could apply a black line directly on their eyelid and not poke themselves in the eye. They were simply on another level than me. I'd stabbed myself in the eye so many times that I decided I would just never wear the stuff again.

What Jude had said earlier rushed into my mind. He claimed he didn't want to disrespect me.

Good. I don't fancy you disrespecting me either.

Yet, the problem remained that it could happen. One of us could be hurt in the future if we didn't make sure to not cross any lines. Keeping his other females out of my view seemed to be the best solution for now. I hoped it would be enough.

This is just for the summer anyway. Then, when I go back to art school, things may change for the both of us. We'll probably figure out that we're not interested in sleeping with each other anymore.

I would try dating again if I met someone I liked. Jude, no doubt, would be touring all over the world, partying it up and sleeping with any women he could find.

This is just for the summer and then we'll figure out a way to only be friends.

I centered all of my attention on my reflection. "He's not mine and I'm not his."

It's such a simple concept. Let's see if we can put that to the test. The mind is the creator of everything around me. What I choose to see, is what occurs.

CHAPTER 19

Hotlanta

Georgia possessed a different feel than Miami. It could have been all the hilly roads in the state—which had made me wonder what was on the other side of the hill as we'd ridden up—whereas Miami was spread out pretty flat everywhere. I always knew what was in front of me from miles away.

Lots of people strolled Atlanta's streets, wearing clubwear. None of them had on flip-flops, miniskirts, or other things that were what I was used to seeing on South Beach.

Atlantans boasted a sleek style as they prowled around in leather and denim, dripping with exotic accessories and sporting hair styles that made me look twice and yearn to take a picture. The newness excited me. And a lot of the people I spotted were African American. I loved that part the most. Miami had a lot of Cubans, Jamaicans, Haitians, Bahamians, and tons of other people whose ancestors descended from the southern island countries under Florida. But a deeper African American culture existed in Atlanta. At times it didn't seem like a big difference to me, being half Jamaican. We all had different tints to our skin which gave us a kinship as black people. However, when heritage and culture entered the mix, a divide definitely formed. I enjoyed exploring that divide whenever I could, especially when it came to the different types of art that stemmed from various ethnic groups.

"What are you thinking about?" Jude helped me off of the bus.

"Black people." I giggled.

"Well, you're in the right city for that. I love Atlanta. Whenever I'm feening for a nice, lush…"

"What?" I leaned my head to the side. "What were you going to say?"

He cleared his throat. "Nothing. It's weird to say it to you now that we're…doing whatever we're doing."

T-Bone stepped off the bus. "He was going to say he likes to fly into Atlanta when he wants to hook up with women with big behinds. This white boy don't know how to act when he gets around the sisters. Boy looks like a rabid dog in heat."

I covered my mouth and laughed while I tried to conjure up the image of Jude on all fours with his foamy tongue wagging. My heels clicked on the sidewalk as we walked up to the club. A gold sign read: Grope and Munch.

"Anyway, let's have some fun!" Jude grabbed my hand.

I forced a smile.

T-Bone walked in front of us in baggy jeans and a huge leather vest. Somehow he'd found a pair of glasses covered in silver studs at the local mall. He glanced over his shoulder. "Rain, make sure you stay close to me."

"Why? Are you going to try and whip or paddle me?" I wagged my eyebrows at him.

"Just try to stay out of trouble, please. I don't want to have to run around after you too."

"Run, really?" Jude chuckled.

"Leave him alone." I laughed.

A short guy around my height crossed the street and waved his hand at Jude. "Yo, Jude? Is that you? Hell no! What are you doing in Atlanta?"

"What am I doing here?" Jude hugged the guy, which told me that he knew him well. He barely touched any other guy in a friendly way. "What are *you* doing here, Simon? How's your mom back in LA?"

"Great. She's keeping your mother busy. They're always clubbing, even at their age, and staying in everyone's business. I had to leave and take a break on the east."

Jude gestured to me. "This is my girl, Rain. I've had to talk to you about her before."

"Oh, yes." Simon rolled his eyes. "When we were growing up, and every time he came back during the summers to visit his mom, all he talked about was Rain can paint this and Rain already read that particular book. It's nice to finally meet you."

I shook his hand. "Thanks."

"So, you here for Maestro's video?"

We nodded.

Simon looked back at me. "Is this your first time in a fetish club?"

"Yeah," I said. "What about you?"

He raised two fingers. "My mom owns two in LA."

"Holy shit!" *No wonder his mom hung with Jude's mom. I think she did fetish films.* "So you're a pro at this."

He shrugged. "I guess."

"Then when Jude's off doing big rock star things, I hope you'll give me my own special fetish tour."

Grinning from ear to ear, Simon glanced at him, as if for his approval, and then after a few seconds said, "Sounds good. I can't wait."

We walked into the nightclub. I expected chains and whips, paddles and rope. Instead, the club gave off an elegant and sleek vibe. The whole space glowed ice blue. I scanned the area for where the color came from but couldn't find it. Crystal chandeliers hung from high ceilings. Leather couches lined the wall. Lush carpet covered the floors. A dance floor stood in the middle, and behind that was a stage. Throughout the whole place, energy pulsed from everybody and bounced off the walls. Adrenaline charged through me. I was pumped and ready to party.

"Oh, man. This is going to be a fun night." I released Jude's hand and clapped.

Although the place didn't fit my stereotypical idea of what a fetish club should be, the people represented everything that I assumed a fetish club would have. Still, I figured they were music video extras rather than the usual group that frequented the place.

Men dressed in tight vinyl bodysuits and high heels, higher than I would have ever worn. Striped black and white latex masks covered most of their faces, leaving holes where the eyes, nose, and mouth were.

"Stay together, everyone!" T-Bone guided us through a large crowd.

"Just focus on Jude." I adjusted my corset. "I'll be fine. I have my phone on me."

Everyone had dressed up for Maestro's fetish-themed video. Beautiful women of all races wore the tiniest skirts in so many different fabrics—from latex to crushed velvet minis that flared out at the bottom, see-through thin material to Catholic-school plaid. Tops varied as much as the skirts. Many only sported pasties on their nipples in the color that matched the bottom half of their outfit. Corsets abounded in the room—made of everything from leather to satin and transparent plastic. I didn't spot anyone who had on anything that resembled my beaded top. Either way, they all danced like it was the best night of their lives.

Big video cameras were spread out in the place. They zoomed around on mini railroad tracks nailed down throughout the club's floor. A few people sat in folded chairs with their names plastered on the back—the director, project manager, and others deemed significant. I spotted Maestro on the stage. I'd seen him so many times on television and had to admit that he was one of the most gorgeous hip-hop artists out now. He was blessed with a milk chocolate complexion, a thick muscular body, and a bald head. Tonight, the jacket he wore hung open and revealed his excellent six-pack decorated by a huge tattoo that read: Maestro.

His song "Sex in the Dark" blasted from the speakers.

"*Tonight, your body needs passion,*" he sang. "*Oh, baby. Individual satisfaction. Only the kind that I can provide. It's all on you tonight, boo.*"

Jude leaned toward my ear. "I had no idea he could actually sing. I thought all he did was rhyme."

"Me either. He does have a nice voice."

Five dancers surrounded him, wearing six-inch glass heels and bikinis made of white mink fur. They rocked their hips back and forth and then from side to side as the beat followed their rhythm.

"*Open your legs. Take off your clothes.*" Maestro opened his jacket a little more, taunting all of the females in the club with his body. "*Tonight, it's all about you. I'll take control.*"

Jude led me to the where the director sat. T-Bone and Simon stayed behind us. In that moment, Maestro stopped singing and made a cutting motion near his neck.

The music ceased its blasting. Dancers paused. The audience of extras quit dancing and took a break.

"Jude! Motherfucker, you actually showed up." Maestro jumped off the stage, headed to us, and gave Jude a half hug. "You're really serious about your album, aren't you?"

"Definitely. Especially this song. I want you on it."

"'Apple,' right?" His gaze shifted to me. "And is this the beautiful woman that inspired 'Apple'?"

"I'm just his best friend." I extended my hand to shake his and prepared to step to the side to let them talk.

Maestro captured me in a hug instead, filling my space with a come-hither cologne that teased my senses, and he whispered in my ear, "What's your name?"

It was crazy. His voice shuddered through me. I inched back when he let me go. "My name's Rain."

"Rain? I like that." Dimples emerged on each of his cheeks as he smiled and turned back to Jude with a questioning look in his eyes. "So, just best friends?"

Jude shook his head. "No. She's definitely more than that. She's mine."

Mine? What is this, a vampire romance?

"I'm not yours." I giggled.

"Word?" Maestro raised one eyebrow and dipped his head.

I tossed Jude a puzzled expression and mouthed, *"yours?"*

He avoided my look. Annoyance seemed to creep around his eyes and cause the muscles in his jaw to twitch. "Rain has been my friend for as long as I've been alive. We just recently took our relationship to the next level."

All righty. Will we be showing him pictures of us having sex too? What the hell is all this confessing about?

"Well, I'm glad you said something." Maestro inched away from me. "I definitely was going to make shorty mine for as long as she would allow it. You better keep her close tonight."

"I'll remember that." Jude set his hand around my waist and drew me hard into him, until our bodies molded against each other.

My breath lodged in my throat for a second before releasing out of my parted lips.

He tilted my way enough to kiss me on my cheek. "And yes, she's the inspiration to 'Apple.'"

I cleared my throat. "But I would like to keep that a secret."

"Why?" Maestro widened his lips into a large smile. "Jude, you told me moaning was on the track. Don't tell me this sweet thing is the one who made those moans."

My face heated as I blushed. I climbed out of Jude's arms. "I'll be right back. I'm going to grab a drink. Nice meeting you."

I walked off and did a quick glance over my shoulder. Both of them studied my behind. I blushed again and disappeared through a line of body guards and the crowd of dancers.

Simon ran up to my side. "Jude asked me to tag along with you."

"Sure. Let's get a drink." I slipped through couples and groups of chatting women. The bar was on my right. I squeezed through another group.

"Is that Jude Everett?" A blonde with long hair and massive breasts nudged her blond friend. "Kim told me he had a big one."

"Are you going to see if the rumors are true?" Her friend giggled.

"I can try, but look, there's already a line around him."

I twisted toward Jude's direction and realized the blonde hadn't lied. I'd been gone for less than a minute, and women of different sizes and shapes swarmed him. Jude didn't seem out of sorts with the situation at all. In fact, he appeared incredibly pleased. One whispered in his ear and he laughed. Another tugged on his leather collar, and his hand wrapped around her waist just like he'd done with mine seconds ago.

So much for his declaration of how I was his and that our relationship had gone to the next level. Some things never change.

Meanwhile, Maestro returned to the stage, and his dancers followed. The beginning of his song came on with just the music and none of the words. I assumed the starting of the song was a signal to go back to work since everyone raced out to the dance floor and jumped back into their respective positions, leaving Simon and me at the bar. Somewhere in the haze, I lost my view of Jude and two of the girls that had hung on him. I scanned the club left to right, front to back. I couldn't find him anywhere.

"He went to the bathroom," Simon offered.

"Jude?"

"Yes."

"Alone?"

Simon hit the bar and laughed. "Jude? Of course not. I've personally never seen him go to the bathroom alone when the place is full of women."

I put on a weak smile. "Yeah. Of course not." I checked my watch. We'd barely been in the club for five minutes before Jude had jetted to go mess with other women. I knew he was probably going to hook up with someone tonight, but not as soon as I'd left his side.

Jude is not mine and I'm not his. Remember it. Just have fun. Don't over-think this.

I blew out a long breath and hit the bar's damp surface. "Fuck it. Let's have some drinks."

What the hell else am I going to do, sit in the club and wait patiently for him to finish and then trot after him like a little puppy, wagging my tail to get his attention? Never.

I clapped my hands. "Let's party like rock stars, Simon. No worries. No regrets. No long thoughts about the past or the future. Let's just focus on the present."

He scrunched his face in confusion. "O-kay. What do you like to drink?"

I stared at the area where Jude had been standing. "Strong and fruity, but heavy on the strong."

He signaled for the bartender and then leaned my way. "And are you only drinking?"

"What do you mean?"

"Do you need an extra kick? I'm good at finding things. What's your poison — pill or powder?"

"Neither. I'm a natural girl. You get me some green, and I'll be happy all night."

"Oh, that's easy." He slipped his hands into his jacket and pulled out a thick blunt. "You want to drink first and smoke later?"

"Hell no. Smoke first, and if we remember, then we'll drink later." I hopped off of the bar stool. "Where do you want to smoke? On Jude's bus?"

"Naw. Let's do it in the girls' bathroom."

"Girls' bathroom?" I looked him up and down. "You can't go in there."

"Fuck. You can't tell, huh?" Simon seized my hand and dragged it into his pants. I cringed as he yanked my fingers against a vagina. "I'm a girl. I haven't gotten the operation yet. I mean, I still like to be referred to as a guy, but I can go into the girls' bathroom."

I tensed as he took my hand out. I lost the ability to talk.

What does one say to that?

"You look blown out of your mind." He seemed a bit upset.

"I am." I stared at my hand. "You know, I think I would have appreciated it more if you had simply told me that you had a vagina versus having me touch it."

"Oh, yeah. I guess that could have been strange."

"Bizarre."

"A bit." He shrugged.

"No. Really, really bizarre."

"I've already smoked a few joints today. I'll blame it on that."

I extended my hand to him. "Okay. Let's try this again. Hello, my name is Rain."

Simon shook my hand. "Hi. I'm Simone, but everyone calls me Simon. Ignore my vagina and embrace my metaphorical penis."

I beamed. "Glad to meet you and your metaphorical penis. Additionally, do not have me touch your vagina again, and I promise to not have you touch mine."

He chuckled and saluted. "Now, let's go smoke this jumbo blunt. I packed it tight with good stuff."

Okay. I'm in a fetish club while a hip-hop video is being taped. I'm hanging with a guy who is really a girl, and we're heading off to the bathroom to do illegal drugs so I can cloud my mind about Jude having a threesome in the men's bathroom. Interesting evening so far.

I'd craved an escape from my past, and that was what I got.

CHAPTER 20

Legalize It

Marijuana smoke obscured my view of the bathroom. I sat on the counter by one of the sinks. Two dancers, one African American with braids and the other Hispanic with long wavy hair, lounged next to me, passing Simon's blunt. At first, they'd been shocked that he was in there. I'd explained that Simon was a she before he seized their hands and rubbed them around his secret area. He'd cracked the window open, but still, a sweet fog drifted around us. I had no idea how long we'd been in there. It must've been close to half an hour. My body had gone numb and calm, almost soothing. I found myself laughing at my earlier thoughts of Jude.

Why would I even care what he's doing? What am I, a lion tamer? Some sort of special forces unit for manwhores of the world? Jude is not mine and I am not his.

I'd been saying the statement like a mantra every time my mind coasted toward thoughts of what Jude was doing with those other girls.

What is he doing? Well, Rain, he's sticking his cock into them, that's what.

"What are you thinking about over there, girl?" Simon handed the little bit of blunt left to me.

I waved it away. I was so blown. A hum sounded in my head, and I couldn't tell if it was real or something my brain was playing out for my sanity. My shoulders slumped forward, and I comfortably lounged on the sink.

"Rain?" Simon waved his hand in front of my face. "You with me?"

"I'm here. I'm just chilling." My words streamed out in lazy slurs. My tongue weighed heavy in my mouth. My body tingled with ease and relaxation. "I'm just really high right now."

Everyone burst out laughing, and I joined them.

"Well, at least you're laughing." He approached the stall in front of me, dropped the tiny bit of his blunt in the toilet, and flushed. "You looked sad earlier."

"Yeah?" I exhaled. "I was just trying to adjust."

"To what?"

"My new life."

The dancers began talking about some other rapper that groped them whenever they shot a video with him. Apparently, he took them all to the side and explained that whoever gave him a blow job would be promoted to the feature dancer in the video. Both claimed they'd never done it.

"Do things like this happen a lot?" I interrupted their conversation.

"It's the music business, girl." The one closest to me tucked long braids behind her ear. "Women get no respect in this business. We're treated like sex toys, especially in hip-hop. That's straight-up male dominated. Females have to fight for everything more than ever. These guys don't respect our personal space. These ugly-ass rappers think we're their personal porn stars, here to pleasure them at their own convenience, when we're all working and trying to get ahead like them."

The Hispanic dancer high-fived her. "That's why I only work for certain ones, like Maestro. He's mad cool. He's not cray cray like the other ones. Plus, he don't do hard drugs and be on the set throwing up or wilding out."

"Oh, yeah. He's mad respectful," the other one agreed. "No touching. I think he even has a policy of not messing with any video chicks, dancers, or whatever he thinks is a groupie."

"Good policy," I agreed.

Groupies were all just hanging around these guys because they had money. That was it. Did Jude get that? I hit my head. *Does it matter? And seriously, as hot as Jude is, women would be in his face regardless.*

I blew out a long breath. "New topic, please. No more discussing talented men that drip with so much pussy they forget their manners and just treat women like playthings, toys, and blow up dolls."

"Your girl is hilarious." The dancer with braids pointed to Simon. "She's off the hook, for real."

A boom sounded at the door. "Ladies? What's taking so long? We need you on the stage. You both are close to losing the gig."

Both dancers quickly gathered their things, cursing under their breaths. They'd taken their shoes off and now rushed to put them on.

He banged at the door. "Hurry your asses up!"

"We're coming," one yelled. "Sorry."

He banged at the door again.

I didn't know what it was. It could have been all the discussion of what the dancers had said about how badly they'd been treated. Perhaps I was pissed with the whole situation with Jude. Either way, I scooted off of the counter, stomped toward the door, and pushed it open. "Are you fucking kidding me?"

The director stepped back with a shocked expression. "Who are you?"

"It doesn't matter. They've been wearing fucking glass shoes and dancing in them for hours." I poked his chest. "Then rappers are expecting blow jobs."

He raised his hands. "Hold up. No one said anything about blow jobs. This is a sexual harassment-free video shoot."

"Sure it is." I showed him my middle finger. "I bet you're the main one begging for head."

"Miss Apple?" Maestro stepped out of the men's bathroom, looked at me, and then glared at the director. "Is there a problem, Roger?"

"No." The guy held his hands out. "She started yelling at me. I don't even know who she is."

Maestro faced me. "What's going on?"

"Hey. Maybe I overacted." I held my hands up in defeat. "I was just annoyed that he was banging on the door and yelling at them to hurry up."

"Who? The dancers?" Maestro asked.

"Yes."

He leaned his head to the side. "Rain, right?"

"Yes."

"Do the dancers need some more time?" He smiled.

Both of the women ambled out in their heels with smiles plastered on their faces. "Oh, no. We're ready," one of them said.

They were behind me, so I couldn't see who was talking, but it was in that moment that I realized I must've appeared like the crazy person who almost got them fired from a gig.

"So, can we shoot the scenes I need now?" The director's voice had lowered since Maestro had entered the hallway, but he still appeared displeased.

"We're ready," the dancers said in unison.

"Do you need me now?" Maestro asked the director. "I need a few minutes."

"Your scenes are done," he replied and marched off.

"Good." Maestro sniffed my way and leaned closer than he should. "Do you have any more bud?"

I blinked a few times. His gorgeous face, sensual scent, and nice body triggered an interesting reaction to mine. Hormones jumped inside me. I cleared my throat and managed a screechy, "No."

"I have some in my trailer. Do you want to come and smoke with me?" His gaze traveled over my body. I considered what the dancers had said, that he didn't go after groupies. I guess now the problem that came to my mind was whether he considered me a groupie or not.

I bit my lip. "I'm not giving you a blow job or anything else."

He jerked back as if he'd been slapped. "I didn't expect you to give me one or anything else."

I covered my mouth with one hand. "Sorry. I'm already pretty blown right now. I'm not going to go with you. My friend is in the bathroom. I'm going to go back with him and calm myself down."

He peered at the girls' bathroom and then back at me. "He's in the women's bathroom?"

"Yes. He's a guy." I shook my head, realizing how crazy I looked. "I mean—"

"Who are you with, Simon?"

"Oh. You know him?"

"Yeah." He placed his hand at the center of my back. "Simon will sit in the bathroom and smoke and snort all night. Come on. I just want to hang with you."

I edged away. "Why?"

"Because you're beautiful."

Okay. So at least he didn't make up an elaborate reason.

"And if I was ugly?" I raised my eyebrows.

"No one has ever asked me that. They usually accept the compliment and come with me." He smirked.

"But what's your answer?" I crossed my arms over my chest.

"If you were ugly, I probably wouldn't say anything to you." A wrinkle materialized on his forehead, as if he was worried.

"That sucks."

"That's life." He rubbed his hands together. "Will you come with me?"

"And what is your plan when we go to your trailer?"

"Damn, you don't play around." He wiped the sweat off of his forehead. "I plan to talk to you for a while, show you how witty I am, hopefully get your number, and if I'm really lucky, a kiss."

"What about Jude? He said I was with him."

"What about him?" He gestured to the men's bathroom. "Currently, he's getting a blow job, so I believe I'm in my rights to intervene. From what I heard in the next stall, he was really enjoying it."

Everything crushed inside of me — my heart, my soul, my insides. It all crumbled into balls of nothing. I knew Jude had been in there with the two girls. I was aware, but for some reason, confirming the fact only brought pain. Before, I'd assumed. Before, I hadn't been sure. I'd had hope. Jude had disappeared, yes, but maybe not with other women. Perhaps he'd gone with some guys to check out a song or something else. But now I knew for sure that wasn't the case, and it hurt. I hated to admit it to myself, but I was jealous.

Jude is not mine and I'm not his.

Saying that in my head didn't push away my disappointment as it mingled with heartbreak.

"Okay. Let's go." I hooked my arm around Maestro's.

CHAPTER 21

Tempting Distraction

Maestro's trailer looked bare, but it had the essentials — a long milky white couch in the center, solid black carpet on the floor, and a flat-screen TV propped on the wall. A chair with his name lounged in front. He placed the joint between his lips.

His music filled the room. He'd been playing all the songs on his album the whole time. I found it odd and a bit pretentious, but for some strange reason I enjoyed his company. Granted, earlier I'd been sitting in a bathroom smoking, so maybe this would seem like a step up in entertainment.

"Do you have any music on your iPod besides yours?" I asked.

His eyes widened. "Sure. It's just that most girls make this big deal about how they like hearing my music and want me to play it for them, so I usually get that part out of the way."

I snorted. "So you have a method."

He laughed. "I'm not that bad, but I do tend to play my songs for all of the women I date."

"Or have sex with?"

His gaze journeyed up and down my body. "If I'm lucky."

"What is your real name?"

"Tyrone. I hate it. I'd rather you stick with Maestro. It's the only one I answer to."

"All righty." I shrugged.

Why did I come to his trailer? To get Jude out of my head and maybe show him that I can mess around too. But how far am I going to go with this?

Maestro rested on the other side of the couch. One hand rubbed the bottom of my foot. The other hand held a tiny joint. We'd been in his trailer for an hour, talking mainly about his life. He'd explained that his friend had recorded him rapping lyrics and then loaded the video up on YouTube. Just like Jude, his video had received a record number of hits, and a music company had signed him.

"Are you sure you don't want to smoke this with me?" he asked.

"I'm good."

My phone beeped. A text message from Jude flashed on the screen. Unease, anger, and desire pulsed in my chest. I hated that just seeing his text triggered something inside of me.

Where are you? I'm done with what I was doing. ~ J

So now that he's done, I'm supposed to rush to him and make myself available? I don't think so.

I'm busy. I'll see you later tonight. ~ R

Busy doing what? Where are you? ~ J

I'll see you later. ~ R

I shut off my phone and dropped it in my purse.

There. How does that feel, Jude?

I used to flinch whenever I would overhear conversations between women about how they played mind games with their boyfriends to get the guys to respect them. I used to wonder if the games ever worked or if the women ended up playing themselves in the end. As I lounged on the couch, I promised myself that I wouldn't make this a game, that I'd make the effort to actually get to know Maestro. Even though I immaturely longed to make Jude feel how I'd felt earlier tonight, I didn't want the entire situation with Maestro to be about Jude.

But what were Maestro's plans for me tonight? If he figured we'd be having sex, he was wrong.

"Okay. So where was I at?" He put the joint out on an ashtray in the shape of a rose. "Japanese?"

"No. Neither one of my parents are Japanese."

He'd listed off many races as he tried to guess my ethnicity. But, shockingly, he never even considered African descent, which was surprising being that he was African American himself. "Italian and Dominican?"

"Nope. It's so obvious at this point that I think you're just going to feel like a moron if it takes you longer." I winked.

"Ouch. Are you always this brutally honest?"

"Only when I'm really high and can't hide my true feelings."

"Interesting." He focused both hands on my foot, kneading swirls near the area under my toes.

Delight soared through me. For one, he had serious skill in foot massaging. Additionally, he was the top hip-hop artist out nowadays and one of the hottest. Being that he was spoiling me with a foot massage, I couldn't help but feel special.

Now who's turning into a groupie?

"So, what are you mixed with?" he asked.

"My mom is Jamaican. She's Alana Stein."

"That name sounds familiar. What does she do?"

"She was Miss Jamaica and later became a talk show host." I offered a weak smile. "My dad is white. His name was Jack Kenner."

He slapped his forehead. "That's why you look so familiar. I saw the big news about Depraved Minds doing a huge concert for Jack Kenner's daughter's birthday."

"Yeah. They may have shown my face."

"That's how you know Jude, right? Since his father was the lead singer?"

"Yep." I bobbed my head. "We kind of grew up together."

"Now everything is making sense, but hold up — was your dad the one who went all crazy and killed…I mean…Fuck. Never mind."

"No. It's okay. Yes. That was my dad."

"I'm sorry."

"Don't be."

"Damn." He frowned. "I think we really should change the subject."

"Me too."

He crept his fingers along my ankle. "You said that you're brutally honest when you're high, so that means whatever I ask, I'll get a truthful answer?"

"Maybe."

"What's going on with you and Jude?"

"Your guess is as good as mine. However, we're not in a relationship, if that's what you're getting at."

"So, he wouldn't mind my hands on your feet like this?"

Would Jude? Knowing him, he'd be annoyed but pretend like it didn't matter.

"I don't know and don't care if he minds."

He tiptoed his fingers further up my leg, his fingertips stepping through the holes in my fishnet stockings. Shivers of anticipation ran through me. He continued until he reached the bottom of my tiny shorts. "So, I guess the questions should be focused on you. Do you mind me touching you?"

I swallowed. "No. I don't mind."

"Yet, you're shaking." He dipped his fingers under my shorts, didn't go farther, and massaged the skin.

"I'm not that experienced."

"I don't believe that."

"It's true." I shrugged. "Jude was my first. It happened just recently."

"No way."

"Yes. I have no reason to lie to you."

"You would never know around here. Women lie to me about who they are all the time." He squinted his eyes at me. "Maybe you're trying to make yourself sound more attractive to me."

"You would've had sex with me regardless, and I'm not looking to be your girlfriend or wife or even try and get your money. I have my own so there's no need to lie." I tucked my hair behind my ear. "Jude is really the first guy I've ever been with, so excuse me if I seem nervous."

"Will I be your second?" He grinned.

"I-I…what? No."

"Now that you're telling me this, it makes sense that Jude called you *his*."

I rolled my eyes. "I'm not his."

"Well, I see that." He pierced me with a heated gaze. "I was just shocked. He and I have partied before. Girls are always with him. We've even shared a few. Once or twice, he passed them on to me right after he'd had sex with them."

I held my hands up. "I really don't want to hear about it."

"Oh, of course. I'm just saying that he treated you different. He was holding your hand and claiming that you were his. I didn't get the feeling that he would like to share you. He treated you like you were special to him."

So much for the special treatment. As soon as we were apart, he grabbed two groupies and took them in the bathroom.

"Do you both have an understanding?" he asked. "Maybe you can hook up with other guys, and he can mess with females as long as you both come back to each other?"

"It's something like that." I shifted in my seat, feeling uncomfortable. "Either way, I don't have a boyfriend, and I'd rather not discuss Jude anymore."

"I would like to be something special in your life."

Why? Because you saw me in a corset and tiny shorts? Or is "something" special code for "fuck me"?

"Granted, that's not a major statement," he continued. "Most of the guys that spotted you tonight desired you. I'm just the only one that was lucky enough to catch you at a vulnerable moment."

"Which is me being deliriously high and standing outside as the guy I'm in love with gets his dick sucked?"

"Wow. I didn't realize you were in love with him."

Wait a minute. Am I? I love him, but am I in love with him? Is there even a freaking difference?

I chewed on the inside of my cheek. "Well, not love—"

"Too late. You already said it." He gripped my thigh and drew me to him so that I sat on his lap.

I liked feeling his body near me but wasn't sure if it was too soon to be this up close and personal with him. The best part was that I didn't experience the usual sensation of needing to vomit, though I was sure I would soon enough.

He took his hand from under my shorts. "I guess what I should be wondering now is if it's too late for me to step in and try to be in your life in some way."

I laughed. Could his line have sounded any more fake?

"What?" he asked. "Did I say something funny?"

"Just because I haven't slept with tons of guys doesn't mean I'm stupid or need to be told some silly, romantic stuff." I climbed off of him and stood up. His hands had felt wonderful on me, waking my body up and causing a yearning between my thighs. But, did I revel in his touch due to being high, because I was hoping to get back at Jude, or was it that I really enjoyed it?

Or am I just over-thinking this? Why am I even in here? Oh, yeah. I'm trying to get my mind off of Jude.

"Are you leaving?" He rose with me and raised his eyebrows. "I didn't mean to insult you."

"You didn't." I smoothed my shorts down. "No. I'm not leaving. I'm just giving us space."

He walked up to me and trapped my waist between his strong hands. "I kind of like having no space between us. Can I kiss you?"

I opened my mouth in shock. "Um…"

"Is it Jude, or are you nervous about kissing a guy you don't know?"

"Both."

He licked his lips. "You're fucking amazing. You must be the only woman in this scene that is this innocent and tender-hearted at the same time. Jude's messing up by taking you for granted."

I cringed. "Seriously, I would rather not discuss him right now."

"Then what would you rather do?" He brushed his lips against mine at first and then leaned in for a full kiss.

It was nice. He tasted like tea and sugar. But, more shocking was that I could kiss him without vomiting or having my father's blood flash in my mind.

So far so good.

His tongue circled mine with skillful finesse. This was a big moment.

Has Jude really broken the spell?

"What can I do to have you in my world?"

"I'm here right now."

"Hmm." He sucked on my lips and cupped my behind. "I don't live here. I have a house out in Los Angeles. Have you been there?"

"A few times."

"I'm flying back tonight. Come with me."

I edged back and giggled. "I can't just gather all my stuff up, jump on a plane with you, and go off to your house in LA. For one, I don't know you, and two, that's crazy."

Three, I'm not sure I like you enough to spend several days with you. And four, there's no way I want to end up turning into your Icky Vicky.

He squeezed my behind and whined a little, displaying those cute dimples. "I would really like you to reconsider."

"That's not happening. I'm sorry." I shook my head. "Do women usually just go with the flow and fly back with you?"

"All the time." He pressed his body against mine. "But you're definitely worth changing up my style and being more patient. How long are you in Atlanta? Where are you staying?"

I twisted my lips to the side and leaned away from him. "I'm on a huge bus. Jude's, actually. We're doing a big road trip to Canada."

"Why? For a music tour or something?"

"No." *Because I had a mental breakdown, and Jude is trying to help me get my head straight.* "Maybe we can see each other again after summer. I go to school in Sarasota, Florida."

"I'm not waiting until the end of summer to see you."

"Maybe I can tell you the next stops —"

"Convince Jude to stay here for a few days. I'll get a hotel room and we can explore Atlanta together. Have you been here before?"

"A few times." I grinned. "My mom's always dragged me around. But I really don't feel comfortable trying to get Jude to change our traveling plans just so I can date another guy. You do see that it's a bit trifling?"

"You say that after he has a threesome in the bathroom?"

I gritted my teeth in embarrassment. "Nevertheless, you and I can figure something out later."

He rubbed his hands over the curve of my behind. "Damn. I really need to spend some time with you. I don't like to wait for what I want."

An exasperated breath left my lips. "And what do you want?"

"You. All of you." He returned to savoring my mouth. And I enjoyed it. He may have just been trying to get into my pants or been a bit too spoiled when dealing with other women, but his lips contained magic. "Come back on the couch with me, beautiful."

Lust glittered in his eyes. I swallowed down my fear, followed him to the couch, and sat down next to him. Before my behind rested on the seat, Maestro seized my breasts with both hands. The crimson beads pressed against his fondling fingers. My nipples reacted and hardened.

"Where are the buttons or snaps to this top?" He gazed at me with pleading eyes. "I have to see those titties. They've been teasing me since the first time I spotted them."

This is all going so fast. But what did I expect?

I cleared my throat. "I'm not interested in doing anything more than kissing tonight."

Oh goodness. I must sound like I'm in high school.

I had to give him credit. His face didn't look shocked or disappointed. He simply bobbed his head and licked his lips. "Cool. I can do just kissing tonight, but one day I would like to do more."

"I would need to get to know you if we ever went that far." I scooted off the couch and rose. "In fact, I'm ready to go."

"Stay for just a little bit longer." He tried to grab my hands.

I stepped away. "I'm sorry, but no."

He formed his lips into a frown. "Will I see you again?"

I smiled. "Yes. I'll give you my number."

"And another kiss?"

I moved to him and pressed my lips on his. After several delicious seconds, I stopped.

"A few more kisses?" He licked his own lip, like dots of honey coated it.

"I have to go."

"To a guy that doesn't care about you."

"No. To a guy who is my friend."

Jude was a really shitty man to date or get involved with. But overall, he was my friend, and a good one. Maybe that was the problem all along. Originally, I figured we could just have sex with each other and do the same with other people, and no problems would arise. But tonight we'd tried, and for whatever reason, I felt betrayed.

We needed to return back to normal — stop the sex and the taking of our friendship to another level.

I'd given his lifestyle a chance and tried to fit into it as Rain, his best friend and sexual partner, but in order to do it successfully, I think I would've had to change my way of thinking and my reactions to him continuing to sleep with lots of women. I didn't think I could do that. We were too close, and he was too important to me. Jude would never change. I would have to be the one to do so, and that wouldn't be fair to me.

"You look like you just zoned out. Are you with me, beautiful?" Maestro asked.

"Yes."

"Tonight, you came back to my trailer and only blessed me with a few kisses, but that's cool. I like your style. I like that I know where those lips have been and who's been touching that body instead of wondering how many other rappers and celebrities you've been making out with." He pulled out his phone. "Will you call me if I give you my number?"

"Definitely."

CHAPTER 22

Tainted Apple

The moonlight shined on all the vehicles in the parking lot as Maestro and I traveled through it. Crowds of tired people scattered out of the club.

They must be done shooting all the scenes for the video.

Maestro and I darted through many of them with his guard trailing several feet behind us. I'd been with him in his trailer for an hour and now was in a hurry to get back to Jude, figuring he would be worried. I planned on sitting down with him and letting him know that I may have over-done it with thinking that we could casually have sex and be friends. In the end, I just couldn't keep my heart out of it. I couldn't just not over-think our situation or not care when he hooked up with other people. My heart and mind were too deeply involved with him. Someone had to be the mature person and stop us before we ended up hurting each other.

"You didn't have to walk me back." I spotted the bus up ahead. Only twenty feet remained between the coach and us as I held Maestro's hand.

"Are you crazy? You're hot and sexy in this sweet little outfit you're wearing." He studied the tops of my breasts as they jiggled while I walked. "There's no way I'm letting you return alone."

I sighed. "Okay, but when we get close, I'd rather go there by myself."

"You're scared to let Jude see us together?" He gently squeezed my hand.

"No, but I'd rather he not see us."

"Too late for that, huh?" Jude stepped out of the shadow of a nearby van, holding a bottle of gin.

Why was he over there?

He took a swig and wiped his mouth with the back of his hand. "Don't be scared, Rainy. I don't mind you hanging with Maestro. He's a good friend of mine. Isn't that right, Maestro?"

"Yeah." Maestro appeared as startled as me.

"I wasn't scared. I just thought it would be weird." I tucked a few curls behind my ear.

"No. Don't worry about that." Jude gazed at Maestro's and my hand linked together. "We're free to do whatever we want, right?"

I nodded but wasn't relieved.

He gulped some more of the gin and gestured for us to follow him. "Maestro, you never got to hear my song. It seems we both had a busy night tonight."

"Yeah. I saw those two chicks you had with you in the bathroom, man." Maestro guided me forward, or more like dragged. "They were definitely dime chicks, sexy and beautiful."

I was reluctant to move on. I didn't like the edge in Jude's voice or the insinuations in Maestro's words. Both guys smiled, but their eyes spoke of annoyance and anger. Tension thickened in the air around us. With each step I made toward the bus, goose bumps rose on my flesh, and a cold fear crept up my spine. I thanked God that Maestro's bodyguard was with him and Jude had brought his along, even though I didn't see him.

"The girls were all right," Jude muttered.

Maestro let out a chilly laugh. "They had to be more than all right. You were real busy with those two."

"Yeah, I was. They did what I needed them to, but clearly you snatched up the biggest bounty tonight." He didn't even look at me.

"Snatched, huh?" Maestro laughed. "More like saved, I think."

Jude glanced over his shoulder. His face shifted to serious. "You needed saving, Rainy?"

My throat went dry. "I got pretty high with Simon and ended up yelling at the director. I made a little embarrassing show of myself. Maestro came in and stopped me from being more foolish."

"Hmm." His gaze dropped to mine and Maestro's hands again. "Maybe I shouldn't have left you alone tonight."

"It was no big deal." I averted my eyes.

"Clearly it was since you left and wouldn't tell me where you were at."

"I texted you that I was fine."

"That's not enough for me. I want to know where you're at, and who you're with," he said through clenched teeth.

I ceased with walking. "You know, guys, maybe tonight isn't a good time to listen to the song."

"Why not?" Jude turned around.

Maestro remained quiet as he glanced from me to Jude.

Because there's bad negativity flowing from all of us.

"You can't be worried that Maestro over here is going to hear you moaning on a song." Jude pierced me with a furious glare. "I'm sure he's heard you moan enough tonight. You've been gone for a while."

"We didn't have sex," I blurted it out fast and felt like a kid in front of a reprimanding parent.

"Well, too bad for him. Sex with you is better than breathing. It damn sure is worth dying for." He placed the bottle to his lips and swallowed some more of the gin. "What do you think, Maestro? Is fucking my Rain worth dying for?"

My Rain?

Maestro shrugged. "You know my background, Jude. I've never been scared of death."

His guard moved to his left.

Jude let out an evil chuckle as he studied the guard.

"Maybe you should let me hold that bottle," I offered.

Jude centered those angry eyes on me. "I'd prefer it if you held my dick instead."

My breath caught in my throat. Maestro stiffened at my side. I lost all possibility of talking. I'd seen Jude be an asshole to people at parties and in night clubs before, but he'd never been harsh or crass with me.

"I guess that's a no then." Jude turned back around and stumbled off to the bus.

Maestro leaned my way. "I don't feel comfortable with you staying with him tonight. Come back with me. I'll get you a hotel room to yourself. No strings attached."

"I'll be fine." I pulled away from him and took my hand out of his.

"So, what are we going to do, man?" Jude glanced over his shoulder at Maestro. "You want to hear the song, or not?"

"I think we should all call it a night," I said.

"Like I said before, not much scares me. No way. Let me check out this song." Maestro pushed ahead of me and walked side by side with Jude. "Plus, I want to make sure Rain gets on the bus and to bed safely."

This is so stupid and insane.

"Don't worry about tucking in Rain. I'll be doing that tonight." Jude slung the bottle at a car in front of him. Thankfully, the bottle missed the vehicle and smashed onto the pavement. Bits of glass spread all around us. I didn't even waste any words to tell him how stupid that was or to explain to both of them how ridiculous everyone was being.

Enough is enough. When we get on, I'm going straight to the back. I won't be around this craziness anymore.

With no further male posturing or bottle smashing, we approached the bus. T-Bone stood outside with a worried look. He glanced at me, Maestro, and then finally at Maestro's guard, probably sensing that tonight might not be a drama-free one.

He held his hand out. "Everybody can't get on."

Maestro's guard waved him away. "You know better than anybody that I stay with my person."

"Then he doesn't get on." A dangerous mask plastered on T-Bone's face. "It's hard for me to guard Jude and Rain when a bunch of people are on there. Tight quarters and all."

The guy looked at Maestro for an answer.

"You scared to get on this bus without your security, man?" Jude climbed the stairs and chuckled.

"Are you?"

He scoffed. "I'm not afraid of anything." He nodded to T-Bone. "Why don't you enjoy the stars."

"But, sir—"

"Enjoy. The. Stars. Got it?"

T-Bone gritted his teeth and crossed his bulky arms over his chest.

"So, are you scared?" he asked Maestro again.

"Never." Maestro motioned for his man to wait outside.

The guards stayed but didn't look happy about it all. My fingers shook. I didn't like how Jude was acting and the things he'd already said. He had to be drunker than he'd ever been around me. And being familiar with how Jude loved to party, I figured he'd done some coke or popped an ecstasy pill too.

"My studio is close to the back." He stood next to the empty bus driver's seat, let Maestro walk by, and studied me as I climbed the stairs. "You need any help?"

"No, but I do need you to not do this tonight." I arrived at the top, inches from him.

He leaned his head to the side. "What are you talking about? We're just going to listen to 'Apple' and maybe decide if we're going to work on it together or not."

"That's it?" I headed to the back too.

He caught me by my arm before I could take another step. "What did you do with him tonight?"

"Nothing."

"He doesn't look like nothing happened." His grip on my arm began to hurt. "He looks pretty fucking happy, if you ask me."

"We didn't do anything. Now let go of me." I shoved him away.

He released his hold but stepped so near that I had no space from his presence. "What did you both do?"

"You have a lot of nerve being such a dick tonight after you had a freaking orgy in a public restroom." I shoved at his chest, but of course he remained there, only an inch or so away from me.

"That's why you ran off with Maestro, to prove a point?"

"No."

"I'm not stupid, Rainy. You don't have to whore yourself out with another guy to show me that you're fucking valuable. I know how much you're worth."

"I didn't whore myself!" I marched away from him and hurried through the bus. The white door was open. I could see Maestro standing outside of the studio, waiting for Jude and me to arrive. I wondered if he'd heard the conversation as both of us approached him.

"Nice place, Jude." Maestro backed up. "Good idea to travel with a studio."

Jude didn't say anything and opened the glass door. Lights came on. The stools from earlier were no longer there. He pressed buttons and pulled back levers so quickly I couldn't tell what he was doing.

Maestro stepped in and held out his hand for me to come. The studio barely looked like it could fit all of us.

I shook my head. "I'm going to sleep, guys. You both have fun."

"I want you to hear it." Jude's lips transformed into a straight line.

"I'm tired."

"No, you're not. You just think I'm going to keep being an asshole."

"Are you?" I asked.

"Not if you stay and listen to the song."

I rolled my eyes. "Fine."

I entered the studio. It was a tight fit but doable. We all had a few inches of space between us. I stood in the middle. Maestro hung in the back. Jude continued to play with buttons in the front.

After another minute, he faced me. "Here we go."

"Oh! Oh!" My moans filled the air. They flowed out of the speakers and vibrated through me.

My body responded, remembering what had brought on those sounds of ecstasy. My nipples stiffened, a scorching hot sensation warmed my center, and my heartbeat increased. I stirred, ready to get out of the studio where I lingered between these two gorgeous men that I'd both kissed.

"Oh! Please."

My own groans turned me on. I stared at the ground with hormones bouncing around inside of my core.

"Damn." Maestro rubbed his face.

Jude moved to my side and leaned back on one of the glass walls. "She sounds like heaven, doesn't she?"

"Hell yes," Maestro murmured.

I twisted the bottom of my shorts in my hand.

"I had to put that in a song." Jude closed his eyes and exhaled. "Her orgasm is a beautiful instrument, probably the best one on earth."

My moans lowered, stopped for a second, started, and then ceased again, only to return with more strength. Soon, my moaning poured out of the speakers in a pattern that served as the beat. From my peripheral, I noticed Maestro bopping his head. I turned Jude's way and caught him with his eyes open as he longingly stared at my breasts.

An electronic piano note came in next. Just one note. Each time the beating of my moans stopped, the piano note chimed in and added to the cadence. It was almost like the piano stroked my sounds of pleasure. Another instrument let out a smooth, taunting tune that triggered thoughts of sex to dance in my mind—Jude's mouth enveloping my nipple and his fingers between my thighs, teasing. There was no doubt in my mind that he had a gift with music and merging sounds together that no one would ever consider trying.

"This style kind of reminds me of Radiohead." Maestro appeared amazed.

"I'm a big fan of their work. I love the way they test out various noises and make it theirs." The whole time Jude spoke, he centered his attention on me.

And then his singing started, and all the conversation ended.

"She changed the game when she came to me one night." His voice rode the waves of my moaning. *"She smelled like a ripe apple and offered me a chance for one bite."*

I bit my lip and squeezed my thighs together, trying to calm down the pulsing of my clit.

"That fruit made me hunger and teased me down to my soul," he sang. *"So lush, so plump, I yearned for her. She was warmth from the cold."*

I ran my shivering fingers through my hair. "I'll be right back."

"I should've never tasted her, never taken a bite." His singing became more intense. *"It all changed when her fruit hit my tongue, when she came all over me that night."*

Jude licked his lips. "Don't leave."

"I just need to catch my breath." I opened the door and rushed to the bedroom. My moaning drifted out of the studio and followed me, as well as Jude's seductive voice.

"And she's surrounding me. She's ripping me apart." His voice shifted to a scream of insanity. *"Oh, baby! She's encasing me with her love. She's seeped into my heart."*

Moonlight poured in through the bus's window. I kept the lights off and paced back and forth in the small bedroom with no escape. The song sounded louder. My moaning increased as Jude's singing died out to only the sounds of my orgasm and the piano's note.

His singing returned. *"And she's surrounding me. She's ripping me apart. Oh, baby! She's encasing me with her love. She's seeped into my heart."*

And then this explosion of guitars began. Hard-hitting riffs accompanied by a heart-pounding bass. Just like Jude's song "Downpour," I got this immediate rush to my head like I was under the influence of some heavy stuff. Prickles of need spread all over my flesh. My arousal saturated my panties.

I paced until the song finished and then, as if to torture me some more, it came back on, louder than before.

How can he do this to me? How can his freaking music take control of my body like this?

"Did you leave because you hated the song?"

I paused from pacing and turned to see Jude standing in the doorway. Shadows hid his face.

"It's incredible." I placed my shaking hands behind my back. "You're more talented than our fathers ever were."

Step by step, he prowled my way. "Then why did you leave the studio?"

"It was uncomfortable being in there and having the reaction I had from your song."

"It turned you on?"

"Yes."

He moved around me in a circle. The moonlight hit his face a few times and then light flickered back to darkness. His woodsy cologne looped around my senses. My nipples ached, and my flesh yearned to be free for him to touch and taste, bite and devour.

He stopped in front of me and towered over my hungry body. "You only kissed Maestro? Nothing else?"

I lifted my head and looked into his eyes. "Yes."

"I don't like that. I'm not happy that anybody else had their mouth on your lips."

I inched back. "I didn't like the idea of you making love to two women tonight either."

"You think I made love to them?" He closed the distance between us and trapped me into his arms. "One gave me a blow job. Then, I fucked the other from behind while the first one watched. At no point was I ever making love to them."

"You're disgusting." I smelled the scent of gin on his breath.

"This is who I am. Women are in my face every moment of my life. Some I fuck. Some I don't. But regardless, no one matters but you."

"That's not enough."

"I never thought it would be. I knew I was running on borrowed time with you from the very beginning. We live different lives."

"And I'm not enough for you, basically?"

He let out an evil laugh. "Rainy, you're more than I can even handle in one life. I love you more than I love myself."

"Don't say that." I looked away.

"Can I make love to you right now?"

I thought about Maestro being on the bus and Jude just confessing what he had done with those girls. "No."

He stepped close to me. "Can I taste you?"

I bit my lip. "No."

"Hmm. I asked to be nice, but we both know I don't have to ask with you, don't we? Your body craves me, doesn't it?"

"No."

"You're lying. I'm going to take off your clothes and lick you until you're dry and exhausted."

He unsnapped the back of my corset, one tortuous snap at a time. His hands were wet. My corset dropped to the ground. My breasts fell heavy in front of me as my stiff nipples pointed his way. He cupped my breast, and I almost died right there as my pussy clenched. He smeared whatever liquid was on his fingers into my breasts, massaging them.

"Why are your hands so wet?" I groaned.

He buried his face into my neck and sucked. "They're probably bloody."

"What?"

"I didn't like him kissing you." He fondled my nipples, delivering hot sparks through me.

I moved his hands away. "What does that mean? What did you do?"

"You have every right to do things with other men." He didn't touch me anymore and just studied me with a weary gaze. "Just never let me know who touched you."

"Why not? What happened?"

He didn't say anything else.

My pulse sped up. I covered my breasts with my arms and hurried out of the bedroom. Jude didn't try to stop me as I pushed through the curtains.

The song blasted louder. He must've put it on repeat. A peculiar odor hit me first. Blood drops sprayed the studio's glass walls.

Dear, God. Please say these are delusions. Please say the blood isn't real.

The door was half open. Maestro lay face down, unmoving.

"No, Jude. What did you do?" I asked as I stepped over Maestro's legs.

A groan sounded beneath me, and I jumped back, startled.

Maestro slowly turned over, revealing two swollen eyes. Blood leaked out of his busted lips and flowed from his nose. He sat on the floor like a drunk man who'd fought three guys at once "That motherfucker caught me by surprise," he screeched. "Sucker punch."

"T-Bone!" I ran out of the studio with no time to grab a shirt to cover my upper body. "T-Bone!"

The bus rocked as T-Bone's massive body stormed onto the bus.

"What happened, Rain?" He spotted the blood smeared around my neck from Jude touching me. "Did he hurt you!?"

"No. He beat up Maestro."

"Motherfucker!" He wrenched his phone out and dialed some numbers.

I tried to hurry back to Maestro and make sure he was okay.

"Hell no, Rain. Get over here!" T-Bone quickly pulled off his shirt and handed it to me. "Please get outside. Jude's mind is gone right now. Let me make sure he's okay before he does something else stupid."

I rushed to put the shirt on. It hung down close to my knees. "But—"

"There's no fucking 'but' about it. Earlier tonight, as soon as he realized you were off with someone else, he started getting himself as messed up as he could." He led me away and hauled me down the stairs. "I have no idea half of the things he's even on right now."

Maestro's guard waited for us to get off before running on the bus. T-Bone explained what had happened in between the commotion.

"Do you want me to call an ambulance?" I asked. Every once in a while, I would let my gaze linger to the bedroom window where I knew Jude stood.

"No way. Neither of them will want any authorities involved. It's just a guess, but I bet I'm right."

"Okay," I whispered. I hadn't stopped shaking since I'd spotted the blood.

How could Jude do this? He just beat the crap out of him, as if that was the most natural reaction to have.

I hugged myself, feeling cold even though it was a summer night.

This is too much. Jude is too much like Dad. I can't deal with this.

And still the song played as Maestro's guard carried him off the coach, and T-Bone yelled into the phone. Jude's lyrics penetrated the bus's walls and floated out to me while I stood outside in T-Bone's huge shirt.

"And she's surrounding me. She's ripping me apart. Oh, baby! She's encasing me with her love. She's seeped into my heart."

CHAPTER 23

Out, Damned Spot. Out, I Say!

"**M**a'am, we've already sent a bottle of cleaner up to you." The hotel front desk receptionist sounded accusing, like she was insinuating that something was wrong with me. "Miss Kenner, if you believe the room is dirty, then we can send up a maid to —"

"I didn't ask for a maid," I said. "I would just like some more cleaning supplies."

"To clean what?"

"Really? I pay three hundred dollars a night for this room, and I can't ask for a two dollar bottle of bleach to be delivered to me?"

"Ma'am, we're just concerned that —"

"I'm not destroying the room. You know what? Never mind. Forget I asked." I slammed the phone down and paced. The shower curtain trailed behind me. I tugged it up over my breasts and tried to tighten the belt over the make-shift curtain dress I'd made so it wouldn't fall down.

I bet the maid is why they're acting all strange now.

When she'd brought me the cleaner, I'd heard her muttering in Spanish as she set the bottle down. Little did she know, I was from Miami, where Spanish was the first freaking language of the city. I knew enough to gather that she'd found my shower curtain dress a bit crazy and figured I was high as a kite on a tornado-stricken day.

I could ask T-Bone to get another bottle, but he'll just curse me out, scream that there isn't any blood, and preach about how Jude and I need help. I don't need help. I need cleaning supplies!

Blood leaked down my hotel suite's walls as well as coated the desk, phone, chairs, couch, and bed. That crimson liquid shifted the blue carpet to a sticky purple. Everywhere was red. My footprints trailed through it. The room reeked with it, clogging my nose and making me choke every few seconds. I'd opened all the windows. Every surface seemed hot and sticky, closing in on me and suffocating me. Cleaning helped. The blood would go for a while, at least an hour or so, but it always came back. I picked up the bottle and shook it. Only a little liquid remained.

Knocking sounded at the door.

"Thank God!" Perhaps the hotel had decided to give me a break and just send up the cleaner anyway. I grasped at the ends of the plastic on my dress and ran to the front door, avoiding the river of blood that streamed out of the open closet door. I'd handle that first, as soon as I got the supplies. I opened the door.

Jude stood on the other side in a black hooded jacket with sunglasses wrapped around his face. Drops of blue rain bordered the shades. He kept his hands in his pockets. "Can I come in?"

I hadn't seen him since the moment before I'd found Maestro beat up. T-Bone had made Jude stay away from me until he sobered up and came down from whatever high he was on. Plus, I wasn't sure what to do about him anymore.

"I don't want to argue, so if you're coming in here to yell or fight, it's not going to happen." I moved out of the way to let him in. The door slammed behind me.

"I won't be arguing either. I just missed you and needed to be near you."

"We've only been away from each other for barely six hours."

"That's too fucking long for me." He grabbed one of the towels and gestured to the walls. "Where's the blood?"

I tensed. "Everywhere."

"T-Bone said you made him get a bottle of bleach."

I leaned back on the closed door and watched him as he poured some cleaner into the towel and wiped the blood off of the desk.

"He got it for me," I said, "and bitched about it the whole time."

Jude wiped the wall in front of him. "You think I should raise his salary?"

"Definitely. He damn sure deserves it. Who else would deal with us?"

"No one." He tossed another towel to me. "Are you going to help me clean this or just stand there and watch?"

I caught it and worked on that river of blood that flowed out of the closet. The good thing was that it began lowering right as I touched it. The white towel turned to pink right before my eyes and became so heavy that I dropped it.

"There's a lot over there, huh?" He balanced his weight on the desk. "You may need to take off that shower curtain and bend over to get it all up."

"Really? Is this strictly an honest opinion from cleaner to cleaner, or are you trying to get me naked?"

"Both."

I gathered up more of the blood, using towel after towel and slinging them in the corner with all the other wet and bloody ones. The metallic-scented odor transformed to bleach. It was a strong smell, but I would take that over blood any day. Every now and then, I'd check on Jude and spot him mopping up drops or washing off crimson lines. He moved fast. It must've only taken us an hour. Surprisingly, the last bit of cleaner I had was enough. Jude added water to the bottles, explaining that I only ever need a few drops in a large tub of water to make the blood go away.

He was right.

"Is there any more left?" His voice came from behind me.

I scanned the room, walking in a big circle. "It's clean."

"Good." He dropped the bottle and took off his jacket. "When's the last time you ate?"

"I don't know."

"You didn't eat on the bus or at the club. Did you eat with… Maestro?"

"No."

"So, you probably haven't eaten in over twenty-four hours." He raised the right side of his lip up and sneered a little, before catching himself and forming his mouth back to a straight line. "I'm going to order us something to eat. Is that okay?"

"Yes."

"Do me a favor." He headed to the phone.

"What?"

"Take off the shower curtain, start up a nice bath for us, and get inside. I'd like to talk to you."

I shook my head. "No. The last time we talked in the bath tub, you decided you didn't want to have sex with me and needed space. If you have something deep to say, just say it now."

"I don't want space from you. I'm hoping for the opposite. Now, fill up the tub with bubbles and get in there so we can talk, please."

"Fine." I stalked off down the suite.

It took him a while to finally get in the bath tub. He'd gone back and forth with the front desk receptionist about why the cleaner delivery was none of their damn business. Next, he'd explained who he was and how he'd tweet and post on Facebook that the hotel sucked. They had changed up their tone in seconds. Our food was now free.

By the time he finished on the phone and arrived in the bathroom, hot water surrounded my body, and peach-scented bubbles tickled my chin.

"It smells good in here." He kicked off his shoes and undressed. "How did you get the fruity smelling shampoo? My room's bathroom doesn't have it."

"I asked T-Bone to get me some bubble stuff too."

"Hmm." He unbuckled his jeans and let them drop to the floor. His cock flipped out and dangled between his thighs.

"Why don't you wear underwear?"

"It gets in the way of quickies. I just like to open my jeans, stick it in, pull out when I'm done, and be on my way."

I groaned and leaned my head back on the edge of the tub. "I can't believe I'm even in love with you. Out of all the things that are wrong with me, that has to be the worst."

"You're in love with me?"

"You're a manwhore."

The water wavered as he stepped in. "Don't say that so many things are wrong with you."

"Why not?"

"There's nothing wrong with you that a good therapist can't fix. And loving me is one of the best parts of you."

"A good therapist?"

"Which brings us to why we're in this bathtub."

Not this again.

It had been a while since Jude had preached to me about getting some help. I groaned again and sank all the way down into the tub, until the hot water rose over my head and enveloped me. Tiny bubbles skittered past my skin as pressure filled my chest. I rose and sat up while water streamed down my face, and my hair stuck to my cheeks and back. I sniffed the air. Marijuana smoke drifted around me.

He must have lit a joint.

"You shouldn't be smoking." I wiped my face and opened my eyes right as he inhaled some of the tiny joint.

"Well, I'm enjoying my last day before I become a sober, boring Jude."

"Sober? You're thinking about quitting?" I pulled my hand out of the water and dried it off on the towel hanging next to me. "Let me have some."

He handed the joint to me. "Yep. I'm considering a no drug future. I've been thinking for a while that I should probably change parts of my lifestyle. Last night was a wake-up call."

"Why now, all of a sudden?" I inhaled some of it.

"You mean, besides the fact that I beat up someone who was a decent associate of mine for two years, and I did it simply because he kissed you? Or maybe it's because I've been high since I was fourteen?"

"Fourteen? I guessed sixteen."

"Nope. Dad couldn't wait to teach me about drugs." He coughed and took the joint back. "And speaking of Dad…after you ran off the bus, I called him. I just needed someone to talk to about the whole situation."

"What did he say?"

"He thought what I did was funny. That he was proud of me."

I blew out smoke.

"It hit me as he was congratulating me that I was going to end up being just like him." He grabbed the joint back from me. "I don't think he's happy. I don't want that."

"Me either."

"I don't want to be an old man in my forties, sharing girls with my kid and being in the newspapers for disorderly behavior and shit."

"You won't."

"I know I won't, because I'm going to do every damn thing I can to avoid it. I've been researching rehab clinics. There's a few that have regular psychiatric wards there too. Not the crazy stuff, but the ones for rich people, with suites, room service—"

"You think you need a psych ward?"

"No." His face transformed from relaxed to serious. "I would like you to come with me and stay at the psych ward."

"No."

"Rainy—"

"You're the one that beat up somebody, and you're the one that's running around sticking your dick in everybody like the world is going to end the next day." I jumped up, rushed out of the tub, and almost slipped as I stomped away. "Get out of my room."

"Just listen to me." He hurried after me. I had no idea where he'd thrown the joint, probably in the bathtub.

"I'm not listening to you." I searched for a clean towel among the bloody ones and was relieved to see that every towel on the floor was clean.

Thank God.

I grabbed the closest one and wrapped it around my body. "I was going to pretend like we could move on from last night, but now I don't think so."

He seized my arm and pulled me to him. "So, what are you thinking?"

"I don't think we should have sex or be friends or anything—"

Jude tossed me a wicked smile. "Well, you don't get to make that decision for us anymore. You lost that right last night."

"How?"

"By walking by me and holding another's man hand and causing me to realize I didn't like seeing that shit. By making me realize that two fucking hot women in a stall couldn't drown out the feel of your skin, or hide your bloody peach scent, or get the sound of your moans out of my head. That's how!"

"Don't yell at me." I shoved at him.

He drew me in tighter. "I'm sorry about messing with those groupies. I wish I could take it back. I wish I could've not taken them in the bathroom. I wasn't even horny. I did it because I could, like a fat kid with his mouth smeared in chocolate, grabbing for that last donut. I did it because they were there, and every damn man in the club was staring at you like they were hungry, and I didn't know how to deal with it—"

"Don't make this about me." I poked my finger at his chest.

"But it is about you." He lifted me up and carried me to the bed.

I didn't even fight him. I'd learned by now that he would just ignore it and take me wherever he wanted.

He laid me down and hovered over me. His face was a foot from mine. "Why did you try to correct me when I told Maestro you were mine?"

"This isn't about that. Don't try to blame me for you having an orgy."

"Why did you correct him?"

"Because I wasn't yours."

"That changes right now." He tore away the towel. "We're together, Rainy. No more friends that fuck, or friends that hang around each other wishing they could fuck, or friends with stupid limits that get blurred or stepped on. We're together like normal people."

"Do we even know what normal is?"

"That's what we're going to these clinics to find out."

Air brushed against my bare body. I covered my breasts with my arms. He moved them away and kissed the nipple on the right and then the left. They woke up under his lips' touch and hardened. I struggled to hold in the moan that lodged in my throat.

He traced his tongue along one stiff nipple and sucked. "What's on your mind?"

"Why ask, when you're going to make all the decisions for us anyway?"

He leaned his head to the side. "You don't like me being your man?"

"No. I have a feeling you'll be a shitty one."

"Too bad. We're together." He returned to sucking on my breasts and lapping at my nipples with his tongue.

This time I couldn't keep in my whimpers.

He grunted and slipped his hand between my thighs. "This is only the beginning for us, Rainy. We were just so fucked up in the head that we never realized how great we were together until that night in the Bahamas."

"We're not—"

All words left when his finger entered me.

"We're not what?" He growled, slipping his finger in and out of me while his thumb rubbed sensual circles on my swollen clit. "We're everything. Every possible good thing about this world you can imagine is what we are. You can't walk away from that or me, because I'll follow you, and when I trap you, there's no getting free."

I whined as he pulled his finger out and licked it, as if my arousal was the sweetest thing he'd ever sampled.

"Put it back. Please," I begged.

"Are we together?"

I sighed. "Can we talk about this later?"

"Later?" His gaze traveled down my squirming body. "What do you want to do in the meantime?"

"Fuck."

He chuckled. "God, you're so naughty, but I'm not starting anything until we're on the same page."

I spread my legs out and placed my hands between my wet folds. "Please."

His cock grew stiff next to my thigh.

I yearned to touch the head and outline it with my hungry fingers. "You're getting hard."

"I never said I didn't want you too. I said we need to agree."

I groaned and stopped touching myself. "Agree on what?"

"The first thing we need to agree on is that we're together."

"Fine. If you think you can keep your dick out of another female for a whole week, I just might consider giving you my heart."

"I already have your heart. And I'll be faithful. The clinics I found have sexual addiction counselors too. I figure why not get the whole buffet of psych shit in one big swoop of time."

I rubbed my face with shaking fingers, not liking where this conversation was going. "You think you're addicted to sex and drugs?"

"Maybe." He shrugged. "I just don't care for being someone that hurts you. I see how my dad's treated women all my life. Now he's sitting around at forty-one, all alone and hanging with women that are in love with his music and not him. I deserve more. I doubt I deserve you, but I can try to earn your love."

My eyes watered, and I didn't understand why I felt like crying. I turned my face away. "There's nothing wrong with you."

"Yes. There is. You just don't want to admit it."

"Not true."

"True."

"Get off of me." I formed my fingers into fists and hit his shoulders. "Move."

"No." He kissed my cheek. "And you know why you can't deal with me being fucked up?"

"Leave me alone."

"Because then you'll have to face the fact that you have problems too."

"I'm seeing a therapist at school."

"That's not good enough."

"How do you know?"

"Because I just cleaned a room full of invisible blood for a whole hour with you. And because just a few days ago, we were talking about your mom." He buried his face into my neck and nibbled the skin. "I love you."

Tears spilled out of my eyes. I didn't have anything else to say. I just knew I didn't want to go to a psychiatric ward or any place where crazy people went. "Can't we just stay here? We could Google-search our symptoms, figure out the ways to fix it, and just do that."

"No." He planted a trail of kisses from the curve of my neck to the divide of my cleavage and cupped my breasts with his hands. "If the roof on your house was destroyed and water leaked in, would you search the Internet and try to fix it yourself?"

"No."

"If you broke your leg, would you check online for ways to fix it instead of going to a doctor?"

I rolled my eyes. "No, asshole."

"Then why would we let our minds continue to need repair and not get help from some geeky-ass guy that has degrees in head shit?"

"I had no idea that *head shit* was a degree."

He tenderly bit my breasts. "We're going. We can visit them all when we fly to Toronto, and I'll even let you pick which facility we'll stay at."

I slumped in defeat. Of course I possessed the ability of free will and to do whatever the hell I desired, but in the end, the path to the solution always led right back to Jude. All the moments in my life, he had come to the rescue. Even the darkest ones.

That terrible night, when Dad had woken me up with the gun pressed against my forehead, blood covered his face and hands as well as dripped on my blanket. The scent assaulted my senses. He'd asked me about being a duppy, and I'd passed the test for not being one.

"What do we do now, Daddy?" I sat in my bed, trying my best to not appear afraid.

"This is going to be the hardest thing you'll have to do in your life, Rainbow." He walked over to the bed, handed the gun to me, and sat on the floor next to his guitar. The cool metal stuck to my hand. It felt so heavy.

I moved my hand away and saw more blood. "Whose blood is this, Daddy?"

"Your mother's." He tuned his guitar and hummed. "I couldn't let her live."

"But you said you couldn't kill her." I shut my eyes up tight and squeaked out, "Is she…is she dead?"

"Yes, Rainbow. I had to kill her."

My fingers shook. I wrapped both of my hands around the gun, scared he'd charge for me and get me next. As far as my mom's death, I didn't even allow myself one second to think about it, not even half of a second. It would've drowned me in too much pain and stopped me from escaping him.

"Wait. Just let me sing to my baby girl, please," Dad pleaded with the shadows in the corner. "Okay. Just one song."

"Song?" I didn't wipe away my tears.

"I'm a duppy too, sweetheart. I don't have much time now. It just couldn't be helped—"

"You're not a duppy."

"I am." He strummed the melody of "Ribbons of Rainbow."

"If you don't kill me now, I'll just try to kill you later, and I won't stop. I think about it every day. For years, your mom tried to say it was all in my mind, but it wasn't. Kill me."

"N-No."

"Do it, Rainbow. Don't let me live without your mother by my side. Don't let me live with this guilt from her death. Do it. Pull the trigger. Remember when I showed you at the gun range?"

"Yes," I choked out.

"Do it." The guitar notes filled the room.

"Daddy?"

"Do it while I sing your song to you. That's how I want to die. I want to see your face and hear the song I wrote for you. Please, Rainbow."

"D-Daddy—"

"Come close so they'll think it was a suicide."

"I-I don't—"

"Do it!" Rage blazed over his face. In that moment, he did appear like a demon. I jumped off the bed and stumbled his way. His face didn't relax. His eyes seemed enraged. "Come close so the gun is next to my lips."

With a shivering body, I got right next to him.

"Shoot me."

"N-No."

"Now!"

I pulled the trigger.

The bullet boomed out and pierced his chest. His body jerked back a little. Blood gurgled out of the hole the bullet had made.

"Good girl, Rainbow. Good girl. I wrote a letter to the police, explaining everything. You won't be in trouble. They'll know it's a suicide." He blinked a few times. "At the end of the song, aim for my mouth. Okay?"

I couldn't even speak.

"Ribbons of rainbows don't compare to you," Daddy sang as crimson drops fell on his guitar. *"Swollen rain clouds envy the shades that shine from you."*

I stood there, frozen. My legs wobbled under me. My childhood flashed before my eyes, as if I was the one that was going to die. My vision clouded with tears.

A noise came from within the room. I didn't even turn around, too scared of my singing dad in front of me.

"At the end of a storm, it's not the clearing of clouds or the sun that brightens the skies. It's your love, your existence, the hope and happiness in your eyes."

Another bump sounded behind me. It had to be my window or the bathroom door being opened. I wasn't sure and didn't care as I fell to my knees, sobbing, unprepared to take my daddy's life.

"You're my escape when I am falling. You're my salvation," he cried, barely able to hold up his guitar. *"You lift me up and wipe the tears away. You're my salvation."*

I heard footsteps approach. A hand landed on my shoulder. I glanced back to see Jude standing there with a scared look on his face. "Rain?"

I couldn't find any words on my tongue and turned back to Daddy. He never noticed Jude in the room. He just sang and played his guitar.

Jude got down on his knees with me and wrapped his arms around my waist from behind. His body pressed into my back. Later, whenever I would think back on this moment, that's the biggest thing I'd remember: Jude holding me.

When Dad finished, he still didn't say anything about Jude. I doubted he realized he was even there.

"Go ahead, Rainbow. Put the gun to my mouth and pull the trigger."

"I don't want to, Daddy. Please don't make me do this. It's wrong."

"If you don't kill me, I will kill you." He frowned. "It may not be tonight, but it will be soon. One day when you're sleeping in your bed, I'll come and hurt you. I think about it when I close my eyes. I dream about peeling your skin just to hear the sounds you would make."

I gasped.

Jude's body trembled against me. He slipped his hands to where my fingers wrapped around the gun and helped me raise it to my dad's mouth. We held the gun together, both of us shaking.

"Don't cry, my Rainbow. It's going to be okay. You'll be better."

"I love you." It felt like he was already gone.

My chest caved in with pain. Both of my parents would be dead in one night, and I had never seen it coming. The week had been normal. The morning had seemed fine. But by the end of the night, they would both be dead.

"Daddy, please. I don't want to," I cried until snot dripped from my nose and spit dribbled out of the corners of my mouth. "Please, Daddy."

"Sometimes it's okay to kill, if you're saving someone else in the process, Rainbow." Dad wiped my tears from my face with bloody hands. "Go ahead, sweetheart. Do it for Daddy. Pull the trigger."

And I did.

With Jude's help.

I shoved the gun inside my dad's open mouth and pulled the trigger. The back of his head and all the contents sprayed to the wall behind him.

Jude wrenched the gun from my hand, set it down, and carried me away. Not one time did he ever ask me what happened that night. Not one time. He took me downstairs, searched for the phones, put one in, and called the police.

No one asked me questions. Apparently, Dad had footage of what he'd done to Mom and maintained a video diary of how he dreamed of killing me too. I never saw it. I could barely watch them load the discs into the boxes.

I just slept in Jude's arms that night and for days afterward in his bedroom. I never knew how I became clean or ate. In one moment, the cops had been carting my dead mother's body up from the basement. In the next moment, I'd woken up in Jude's bedroom with his arms having been around me for weeks, until my grandmother flew in from Jamaica and began taking care of me.

She never took me to Dad's funeral. I wasn't allowed to say his name or keep pictures of him around.

Jude was always there to help me. He'll be there again.

CHAPTER 24

Just Jude and Rain

always wondered what Jude had thought about that night. We never discussed it. Back in the hotel suite, he moved off of me and lay in the space on my right.

"What's going through your mind?"

"The night my parents died." I rolled over and faced him.

"Why are you thinking about that?" He ran his fingers through my curls.

"Why did you help me kill Dad?"

"Because he said he would hurt you one day."

I scooted over, buried my face in his chest, and let him wrap his arms around me. "I don't think most people would have helped me like that."

"We're not most people. We're just Jude and Rain. Don't you like the sound of our names together?"

"Jude and Rain," I whispered. "Yes. I like that."

"I can see us having a good life one day, if we can clean up all of the blood from the past."

I squeezed my eyes shut. "Let's not mention blood. Let's save all of that for the doctors in Toronto. I'm done cleaning that stuff up."

His body tensed under me. "So, you're saying that you'll come with me, to get help together?"

"Definitely. If we're going to be together, the last place I want you hanging out by yourself is at a clinic full of female sex addicts."

"Hmm." He laughed. "I didn't think of it that way. There would be lots of females there. Better yet, why don't you stay here?"

I punched his thigh.

"Rainy, that was too close to my happy stick."

"Just make sure your happy stick stays in your pants while we're there before I snap it into two happy twigs."

He shuddered. "You're a cheeky little wench aren't you?"

"Oy, don't give me any rubbish. Just be making sure your willy stays in your pants. I'll not have you wanking about."

"Please stop. This bad British accent is degrading to me, my mom, and every person that has connections there. No one even says 'oy.' What the fuck is that?"

"They do too say 'oy.'"

"Just for that, I'm going to make you pay." He whipped me around so that his cock pressed into my behind. "I'm going to make you say 'oy' right now."

"Oh, really?" My breath caught in my throat. "How are you going to do that?"

He rubbed the head near my opening. "I love how any time I touch your pussy, it's just dripping. I'd lick it all up right now if I didn't crave feeling that pink, moist flesh tight around my dick."

"There you go, Rainy," he said, thrusting into me, and I screamed.

"Oh, Jude."

He moved in and out of my slick tunnel. "Fuck. Lift up a little. I have to touch those big breasts of yours. I was thinking of them the whole time I sat in my room."

I raised my head. He slipped his hand around and grabbed my breast. Sparks of desire lit everywhere he touched. I rested my head on his arm, and he stroked me with those succulent fingers.

God, this feels so good.

He slid his other hand around my hip and captured my hungry clit. "You'll never know another man's cock in you, will you?"

"No." I drowned in wet, heated passion.

"I'll earn your love, Rainy. I promise."

"You already have it." I gasped.

So many pleasures hit me at once: my nipple ached as he squeezed and gently twisted it; my wet clit glided through his fingers as he massaged the bud over and over; his cock pounded into me, stretching me wide open as his body slapped against my ass.

Dear God, how can he concentrate on so many things at once?

Pleasure, so pure and hot, sliced me open bit by fucking bit. I couldn't breathe or see, couldn't think or speak coherent words. My whole body was an instrument that he strummed and played to his own tune. I couldn't even move. Rapturous sensations surrounded me as I screamed in delight.

"Someone touches this, and I'll hurt them." He groaned and rocked his hard cock into me. "No clinic will cure me of that. Ever."

He tenderly bit my shoulder and grunted. An orgasm spun around in my gut, spread out to my pussy, rolling and tumbling, heating up my flesh and bursting out of me. Slapping noises shifted to sloshing as I soaked his cock and came so hard my body spasmed.

"Oh, Jude!"

"Yes, baby. Whose dick is in you?"

"Yours."

"Will there ever be anyone else?" He pushed into me hard.

"Never!"

"Damn it. There's never any control when I'm with you." He released my breast, quickly put both hands on my hips, and pounded into me like a madman. "Fuck, Rainy. Take. This. Dick."

"Yes!" I cried. Tears streamed down my face. The best tears. The ones I had always wanted to experience. The ones that screamed that life wasn't all that bad, wasn't all dark, that there was good if I just took the time to feel it.

"I love you, Rain." Jude stayed inside of me and shuddered against my back. "Let's make sure we make this work."

"Can we?"

"We're not our parents."

"No?"

"Never." He pulled out, gently rolled me on my back, and seized my lips. "Never. We're so much more, baby."

"How do you know?"

"I don't know." He shrugged. "But I do know that sometimes when you love someone, it's okay to change and try to make yourself better."

And I agreed.

EPILOGUE

Jude's Birth Weekend

"Why do you think you pretended that your mother was alive?" Dr. Johnson crossed her legs and peered at me from under her glasses.

"I think I liked imagining that I had saved her, instead of the truth."

"What's the truth?"

I shut my eyes. "I let her die."

"Did you?"

"It feels like that sometimes." I opened my eyes and picked at the red sequins on the front of my shirt. They were formed into a huge apple that had been bitten. Everyone wore a shirt like this now that "Apple" topped the music charts.

Even though Jude had beaten him up, Maestro, being a true insane musician, had begged to be featured on the song. Jude had allowed it, although he couldn't leave the clinic to go to the studio while Maestro laid down the lyrics. Either way, their remix of "Apple" was number two on the charts, right under the original.

"Why do you feel like you let your mother die?" Dr. Johnson never gave me a break. She just attacked me with questions that made me think, and never provided any real answers.

Isn't the point of this counseling crap to come into her office, sit down, open my skull, let her rummage around in it, and poof, I'm all fixed?

"I had seen the signs that Dad was crazy, abusive, and a drug addict. I knew that he would never get better. I guess I just hoped he would."

"You were a teenager. Don't you think your mother spotted the same signs and realized the same things? She was more experienced in life than you. Don't you think she saw the signs too?"

"Yes."

"Do you think she could have taken you both away from your father?"

I kept my mouth closed and hated this line of questioning. "I know what you're doing. You're blaming her for dying."

"No, I'm not. But I do want you to consider this question: did your mom have a role in her own death?"

I sighed. It must've taken me five minutes to come up with the answer, but in the end, I admitted, "Yes."

Dr. Johnson smiled that annoying, knowing smile. "I see you're not wearing the blue contacts today."

"I threw them away. I thought wearing them was stupid."

"Why?"

Everything is a question with this woman.

"I've tried to remember if Mom ever told me to wear them or ever said she hated the color of my eyes. I'm still trying to figure out what are actual memories and what was the stuff I put in my head. I knew she hated her skin and eye color. Maybe I just thought she hated mine too."

Dr. Johnson knitted her fingers together. "I think we're done for today."

Booming sounded at the door. "Rainy, come on, baby. It's our first weekend of freedom."

God, I've missed my Jude.

I grinned and stood up, ready to finally see him after three months. The doctors had believed we were too emotionally dependent on each other and that we needed to learn how to heal separately first. We could only write to each other. I had boxes of poetry and letters from him. After three months, all of our counselors and doctors approved us for a weekend together away from the facility.

Dr. Johnson's smile left her face. "I would like you to call me if you start seeing visions again. Continue to take your pills, and no drugs."

"Never."

"Even marijuana."

I gritted my teeth. "It was planted on earth by God. I'm just saying."

"Nevertheless, let's stay away from God's earthly gifts this weekend."

Wow. Did she make a little joke? I may be able to save her sense of humor after all.

"Okay. I'll see you on Monday." I rushed out of there and opened the door.

Before I could take one step, Jude enveloped me in huge, muscular arms. He was so much bigger. He'd written in his letters to me that he'd been working out, but I had no idea he'd been training as if he was trying to be a body builder.

"I missed you so much." He rubbed his face against mine. His short beard scratched my cheek. "You look so fucking good. I might take you on the helicopter."

"Helicopter?" Dr. Johnson came out into the hallway. "Mr. Everett, we said nothing about flying away from the city."

"It's my birth weekend." Jude kissed me.

I leaned away and battled to catch my breath. I forgot how much he could consume me in seconds. "I'm sorry. Jude's right. It's his birth weekend. I've planned twenty-three surprises for him. We'll need the helicopter for a few of them."

Dr. Johnson shook her head. "I don't remember approving this. I'm going to need to know what these surprises involve and what—"

"Don't worry, ma'am." T-Bone strolled down the hallway, taking up most of the space and dressed in a priest's outfit. I'd told him to look responsible, not come as a goddamn holy servant of God. "I've been designated as their chaperone for the evening. Here's the papers. Everything was authorized by both of their lawyers months ago."

She looked him up and down. "Are you a priest?"

T-Bone placed white glasses with gold crosses on his face. "No. Of course not. It's Halloween weekend, baby. What are you doing later tonight?"

I covered my face in embarrassment. "Okay. Let's go before you both just get us in trouble. Don't worry, doc. We'll be fine. We've survived a whole lot of shit. We can survive forty-eight hours in South Beach."

"South Beach?" Her shocked face reddened. "I only approved a fifty mile radius."

I hit my head. "Yes. I meant Toronto."

She tossed me a skeptical look.

Jude winked at her and dragged me off before I could say any more. "Let's go."

We rushed down the hallways. Everything glowed white and clean. I think that's what I loved about the place the most. It shined so clean. No blood anywhere. I hadn't seen any since that day in the hotel. I hoped to never see any again.

"You have no idea how many times I masturbated to you moaning on 'Apple.' My iPod is disgusted with me." He lifted me up and carried me through the doors.

"You think that's bad? I sculpted your penis and then tried to put it inside of me. It got stuck. After an hour, I was forced to call a nurse to help me get it out."

T-Bone's face scrunched up in horror. "Lord knows you both really needed to be in here."

I laughed, faced Jude, and tensed. His gaze bore into me, causing me to shiver.

"I love you," he said. "I could never have been saved without you."

"I agree. I love you too."

And so we left Toronto, against the wishes of our facility, to party at South Beach. But, not the usual way we used to storm through the city. No drugs or groupies. No hysteria or guilt. We made love in the sand, among lit candles, listening to a blindfolded orchestra, and with chocolate covered fruits dripping in our fingers. We made love until the sun set and then rose again. I licked places I'd never thought existed, and he devoured me whole.

We learned a new way to consume each other, without the need for any drug or conflict. We smothered each other in kisses and dreams of our future and poetic wishes that ended in moans. Our addictions shifted to our obsession with *us*.

And on the next day, we trick-or-treated as Bonnie and Clyde.

ACKNOWLEDGMENTS

To my huge group of Beta Readers: Jacqulene Sheats, Megan Martin, D.T.Dyllin, Tiffany Patterson, Kirtrina Baxter, Tamara Porche.

Lots of love to my agent Jewelann Cone who helped put together the great deal with Elizabeth Harper of Omnific Publishing.

ABOUT THE AUTHOR

Kenya Wright always knew she would be famous since the ripe old age of six when she sang Michael Jackson's "Thriller" in her bathroom mirror. She's tried her hand at many things from enlisting in the Navy for six years as a Persian-Farsi linguist to being a nude model at an art university.

However, writing has been the only constant love in her life. Will she succeed? Of course.

For she has been coined The Urban Fantasy Queen, the Super Iconic Writer of this Age, The Lyrical Genius of Our Generation. Granted, these are all terms coined by her, within the private walls of her bathroom as she still sings "Thriller."

Kenya Wright currently resides in Miami with her three amazing, overactive children, a supportive, gorgeous husband, and three cool black cats that refuse to stop sleeping on Kenya's head at night.

Erotic Romance

The Keyhole Series: *Becoming sage (book one)* by Kasi Alexander
The Keyhole Series: *Saving sunni (book two)* by Kasi & Reggie Alexander
The Winemaker's Dinner: *Appetizers* & *Entrée* by Dr. Ivan Rusilko &
Everly Drummond
The Winemaker's Dinner: *Dessert* by Dr. Ivan Rusilko

Paranormal Romance

The Light Series: *Seers of Light, Whisper of Light,* and *Circle of Light*
by Jennifer DeLucy
The Hanaford Park Series: *Eve of Samhain* & *Pleasures Untold* by Lisa Sanchez
Immortal Awakening by KC Randall
Crushed Seraphim & *Bittersweet Seraphim* by Debra Anastasia
The Guardian's Wild Child by Feather Stone
Grave Refrain by Sarah M. Glover
Divinity by Patricia Leever
Blood Vine & *Blood Entangled* by Amber Belldene
Divine Temptation by Nicki Elson
Love in the Time of the Dead by Tera Shanley

Historical Romance

Cat O' Nine Tails by Patricia Leever
Burning Embers by Hannah Fielding
Good Ground by Tracy Winegar

Romantic Suspense

Whirlwind by Robin DeJarnett
The CONduct Series: *With Good Behavior,*
Bad Behavior, and *On Best Behavior* by Jennifer Lane
Indivisible by Jessica McQuinn
Between the Lies by Alison Oburia

Anthologies

A Valentine Anthology including short stories by Alice Clayton,
Jennifer DeLucy, Nicki Elson, Jessica McQuinn, Victoria Michaels,
and Alison Oburia

←---→Singles and Novellas←---→

It's Only Kinky the First Time by Kasi Alexander
Learning the Ropes by Kasi & Reggie Alexander
The Winemaker's Dinner: RSVP by Dr. Ivan Rusilko
The Winemaker's Dinner: No Reservations by Everly Drummond
Big Guns by Jessica McQuinn
Concessions by Robin DeJarnett
Starstruck by Lisa Sanchez
New Flame by BJ Thornton
Shackled by Debra Anastasia
Swim Recruit by Jennifer Lane
Sway by Nicki Elson
Full Speed Ahead by Susan Kaye Quinn
The Second Sunrise by Hannah Downing
The Summer Prince by Carol Oates
Whatever it Takes by Sarah M. Glover
Clarity by Patricia Leever
A Christmas Wish by Autumn Markus
Late Night with Andres by Debra Anastasia

coming soon from
OMNIFIC PUBLISHING

The Weight of Words by Georgina Guthrie

Theatricks by Eleanor Gwyn Jones

The Sacrificial Lamb by Laura Pintus

The Art of Appreciation by Autumn Markus

Return to Poughkeepsie by Debra Anastasia